SPARE PARTS

a rollicking ride through the late 60s and 70s

DIANA B. ROBERTS

Spare Parts
Copyright © 2022 by Diana B. Roberts

ISBN
978-1-958690-18-5 (Paperback)
978-1-958690-19-2 (eBook)

Table of Contents

PROLOGUE

Lacey sat at the kitchen table looking down at the pieces of silver wandering which ones no longer represented parts of her life. Maybe she could let them go now to the pawn broker at Glory Daze.

She reviewed each item carefully before beginning to wipe away years of tarnish with a fine silver polish purchased by sending away for it. The set of silver had been in the basement a long time, way in the back where Lacey made sure she could not reach it easily. Once, a few years ago, she asked her house cleaner to polish a few of the pieces. When she discovered the woman had used Brillo instead of a soft cloth she became so enraged that she put the pieces back in the cellar even further out of reach. But now it was time to sell. It was like selling her life in stages, the remnants left after a lifetime of use.

Lacey was not a meticulous person by nature. She did not aim to scrutinize every piece of metal in front of her for its potential resale value. Rather she was gathering information in a review of the times in her life when she was given certain gifts by well-meaning people with good wishes. She was taking it all in, deciding what parts to keep and what to discard. She was a firm believer that everyone should reinvent themselves every decade and she was about to do it again her seventh.

As she looked down, she saw that none of pieces had been broken. Each one was tarnished, made dull over time, but still whole. It occurred to her that these relics of the past were like her, tarnished but resilient. She picked up the three sterling shells that had once been a hair brush, a comb and a mirror designed to rest on a dressing table, edged all round by a pink patterned muslin skirt that matched the curtains in the room where she grew up. She could almost see the room looking at the backs of the silver pieces, each clearly engraved in swirling script with her three initials LBP, Lawrence Babcock Pierce. Could she give these up?

To the left of the brush and comb set was a complete set of silver cutlery left to her by her grandmother. It sat solid and closed in a faded brown leather box with zippers on both sides protecting inside the knives, forks and spoons and other pieces made in the "Fairfield" pattern. Lacey had wanted to have a real wooden chest to house the silver but never got around to ordering one because more important home improvements got in the way. Now, thinking about selling the silver because, as a widow she needed the money, she was glad she had not bothered to buy such a silly, showcase. Lacey was a practical woman.

The silver was still and always a reminder of the fading glory of life at the turn of the last century now so irrelevant in an era of fast food eaten without knife or fork, sushi with its chopsticks and pizza eaten right out of the box. No one was sitting down to Sunday lunch anymore, so what did it matter? Except that the stuff was still beautiful.

The sterling silver set included a lunch place setting for twelve and the same number for dinner. Each piece of the cutlery was engraved with GEP, Lacey's grandmother's initials, for Grace Elizabeth Pierce. The set had been given to her in a bequest. There were short knives with rounded blade tips for the midday meal to be used with the smaller forks. There were also grapefruit spoons shaped so that one could gouge out the pink fruit most easily from its peel without a fuss. And there were fish knives with pointy blades that could most effectively lift out tiny flecks of bones that might lurk in any single serving from the sea. There were butter knives and serving spoons and soup spoons and dessert spoons. All the pieces had participated in festive occasions through the years when Lacey invited family for holidays or merely to celebrate with Granny's silver.

She never knew why her grandmother gave her the silver. Perhaps it was because, of the sixteen grandchildren, Lacey was the only to be separated from her mother at an early age. When it came time to take it out of the lock box at the bank and to give it to Lacey, the Pierce family decided to withhold it from her while she was living a precarious "hippy" lifestyle because they feared she might sell it.

To the right of the hair brush set was the one piece of jewelry she had worn to the wedding ceremony in Iowa. It was an Arab wedding bracelet she had bought on her last day in the Peace Corps in Tunisia. Now the six inches of silver engraved with Arabic script looked more like gray pewter than genuine silver. The one silver wedding gift she had received was a pair of silver candle sticks engraved with her own initials from the mother of her maid of honor, Molly Bradley, her best friend in high school. Her

Iowa in-laws found the gift odd, embarrassing and not useful. That day was now long gone and far way. Yet the remaining symbols of her life were all right there in front of her.

The silver tea service stared at Lacey from its place in the middle of the table. The platter was silver plate with a copper base showing through in the middle after years of use. There was the large coffee pot with the handle on one side and spout on the other, accompanied by the tea pot, a smaller version of the coffee urn. The sugar and creamer pots stood idly by but still with some luster. Each piece was engraved with the initials LMB, Lillian Mark Byron, Lacey's mother. For decades Lacey had polished these symbols of finery and social prestige to keep alive the memory of a family that never really existed.

The "silent butler," brought back memories of her Dad, for its slightly puckish tip to the upper middle class life her father tried to live but had no means to do so. GBP was engraved on the lid which could be flipped open by the butler or George Pierce himself to capture his cigarette butts and ashes during the cocktail hour or dinner. Though it was useless now in an age of smoke free drawing rooms, Lacey could imagine it being inserted at her father's bridge games or at "smokers" with port following Sunday lunch in the big dining room. From the beginning she knew and understood the pains and perils of privilege.

There were sterling vegetable dishes, giant serving spoons with scalloped edges and a large sterling wire basket for serving rolls. The best part of this trove was a very large platter in the shape of a sea shell for serving chilled shrimp. At one end a silver cup was embedded in the platter to hold the cocktail sauce. The dish came with its own set of silver tooth picks and an indented place to put them after you had nibbled on peeled shell fish. There were two silver martini shakers that had been in her father's family long before he began his love affair with drink during his college days at Harvard.

The silver flask lay tipped over on the table with her father's initials, GBP and 1934, the year he attended his first Harvard/ Yale football game as a freshman on the team. Lacey had gathered trophies from all over the house. Many from tennis and squash games played by her father over the years. The tall deep silver vase that dated back to before 1900 when her great grandfather she never knew played tennis on the green grass at a famous club in Boston. Small plates, picture frames, ice buckets, wine coolers had dotted the house in every room.

Lacey surveyed the symbols of her past and wondered if the sum of one's life parts could amount to so little, or at times, mean so much. At this point she didn't care. She was interested in revisiting her past in search of a more permanent and palpable perspective. She was realizing perhaps, too late, that her life was made of spare parts without a defining whole. Lacey turned away from the silver and moved to the TV to watch her favorite game on the Tennis Channel.

PART I: IOWA

"Is it true," the man asked, "that you women who join that Peace Corps thing are lesbians? Where were you stationed, anyway?"

Lacey had an instinctive, negative reaction to the man in the booth next to her. She had been recruiting volunteers on campuses since September. By now she was growing bored with telling her story about building a daycare center in Africa, repeating the tale to starry-eyed students ready to sign up for a two-year stint. The man's voice made her tense and she shot back. "Yes, it's true, I'm a dyke, and I was sent to the North Pole to help make toys for Santa's annual run."

"It seems like all you lonely single women are looking to find a husband in some foreign country before you're too old to have children. Find yourself a prince over there?"

Lacey lit up a Marlboro and thought about her next words. "No, I found a prince at the North Pole and went around the world with him on a one night stand."

"Are you making fun of me? Or are you some kind of queer? You don't look like a lesbian but I could be wrong. I suppose you wouldn't say if you were. They don't usually. I can just tell."

"And I don't look like Santa's toymaker either. Let's get even and call it quits."

Annoyed by the pelting questions, she turned her attention to the wide-eyed student waiting to speak with her.

Lacey's booth looked like all the others, a cardboard set up at the job fair in the student union. Hers was the exception because she was not there to find recruits for a corporation or the military. She was at Kent State to sign up students to volunteer to serve their country for two years in a developing country. She felt sure her cubicle had been placed at the very back of the student union to give preference up front to the military recruiters and the team from the National Guard. Still this recruiter had somehow been placed next to her.

Not many seniors were coming to hear about the Peace Corps that day. But the one coming toward her looked promising. He had seen the poster in the booth next to where Lacey was sitting: IS THE GLASS HALF FULL OR HALF EMPTY?

"Hi, my name's Willy. I am from Lincoln, Nebraska. I came here a year early after high school but I am a sophomore now, about to turn eighteen, and I think I am going to get drafted. My family is on the farm back home. I'm trying to figure out what to do. Is there any way I can help—I mean be a farmer in the Peace Corps in some country?" Willy was tall, red headed with freckles, clean shaven and wearing khakis that hung loosely off his hips held together by a string that passed for a belt.

"You've come to the right place," said Lacey, this time without irony. She did think he looked like he was still in high school. "Yes, there are a number of people like you who are teaching farmers how to rotate their crops to create better soil for better yields. Or you could do community development in Latin America or possibly India."

"That all sounds good. But I just don't know. I want to be in school but I want to serve my country. My dad was in World War II and he won't talk about it but he says I have a duty. I kinda wonder if there's another way." Just then came the interception.

"Son, my name's Sargent Roy Silver, U.S. Marines, and don't you listen to her. I've been told those Peace Corps types are really just imperialists disguised as hippies sent overseas by J.F.K. himself before he died to conquer them foreigners for the U.S Government."

The student looked at Lacey and then at Sargent Silver as a glaze began to fill the young man's eyes. He was listening to the machismo in the recruiter's voice she despised. She knew instantly that Willy was going to become a Marine.

It was the end of the day and she was tired of interferences. She folded the cardboard stand and hauled it to the gray Government-issue sedan where Wayne Wagner was waiting for her. He had been pitching the Peace Corps all day in campus classes, talking about his two years in Bolivia. Exhausted, they rode in silence for six hours back to the regional Peace Crops office in Chicago.

Lacey could hear the soft sound of rain on the car windows. She dozed in and out of thoughts about her recent return to the States from Africa: people had told her there would be some culture shock, but she hadn't expected what awaited her in Chicago that first morning she reported for work. The Democratic National Convention had come to town. She spent the night before in a hotel and in the lobby the next morning introduced herself to a new recruiter, Dan Perini. He was short and square and looked little like Brando with better hair. Somehow he seemed out of sorts in his gray suit having spent the last year in Ethiopia. She invited him to walk with her across town to the Peace Corps office.

"I don't know," Dan began as they walked toward Michigan Avenue, "Hasn't this been a terrible year? It's a good thing you and I were out of the country for most of it. We missed the violence in a lot of cities. But now, with the Democratic Convention here in Chicago, I think we're in for more."

"Did you see the paper today?" She started right in. "That guy, Jerry Rubin, singer Phil Ochs and other activists are putting up their own mock presidential candidate, a pig they call Pigasus."

"Yeah, and we missed the death of Martin Luther King," Dan went on ignoring her.   "No we didn't. The world watched him die. Even the people in Tunisia were grieving. The *yellelas*, the girls who worked in my kindergarten, brought flowers and food and kept asking me if I knew "Mr. Martin." They cried in Arabic and I cried with them and then I cried myself to sleep in English.

Lacey and Dan could feel the city on edge as they moved from one street to another. "Do you think we can make it across town through the crowds and the cops?" Michigan Avenue was jammed. Finally they reached the Peace Corps office, where the rest of the crew had gathered for the first of several training sessions. But no one was talking about work.

"Do you think they'll nominate Humphrey and Muskie?" Ed Langley from New Orleans, spoke in a slow drawl asked, then answered his own question.

"I'm not sure who's going to nominate whom," he said indignantly," but I can feel a dark (pronouncing it daahk) cloud gathering, and I bet there are going to be a hell of a lot of arrests today. Those Yippies didn't do us any favors."

Jim Slate, the New Yorker with the slick tongue and the goatee took umbrage. "Au contraire, mon amie, ma cherie" he replied, showing off the French accent he had acquired in Morocco. "We're lucky we live in a country where people like those Yippies can protest freely. I bet Pigasus will be a hit on the news tonight. "And I'm not sorry they did their bit."

Lacey returned his silly French accent with a full blast of "oui, monsieur, mais il faut que vous avez de bonne raison quand vous parlez ses mots. What the hell do we really know anyway?"

While the assembled office group pondered the situation, out on the streets a series of riots were brewing between demonstrators and the Chicago police backed up by the National Guard.

Luckily that same day Lacey and Wayne got an assignment together away from the media and mayhem in Chicago. They would be partners on the road as they travelled around to colleges and universities the Midwest. Now in the car she felt safe next to Wayne who often joked with her to pass the time.

"I'm out and I'm proud, baby," was his mantra. Lacey adored him for his openness and flamboyant sense of theater in everything he did. But she worried about him, too. Gays were society's outcasts, treated like scum and forced to stay underground in relationships. Sometimes Wayne would go off for a one-night-stand while she stayed in the hotel, watching TV until she heard the key turn next door in the early morning. The next day he would appear at breakfast haggard and miserable, cursing himself for roaming before.

She was glad that he was with her, in part so she could look after him and also because he liked to drive and she didn't. She hated driving and still wasn't sure how she'd passed the license test back home in Boston. Probably it was because she complimented the police officer on his uniform not because she passed the parallel parking test. As it was, Wayne would drive and for her part she would sing Broadway songs to keep him awake during the long haul.

In the silence of the car, with time on her hands in the front seat, she pulled out the maps she had picked up at the last gas stop. She took the flashlight from the glove compartment and looked to see her future for the next few weeks after the layover in the Windy City. *Hello, Rapid City, South Dakota, and Des Moines, Iowa, here we come!*

Slow Dance

Doug Rogers caught the ready smile and the bounce in her step as she came across the field. He found the rhythm amusing, like watching a linebacker trying to walk in a skirt. She looked vaguely annoyed, and he kind of liked that, too. *Probably a straight shooter, doesn't hide her feelings,* he thought. The man with her was Doug's roommate whenever he could get home to Des Moines. He and Lacsy had come to relax for the weekend, starting with a football game on the local campus at Drake University. They had agreed to meet Doug just outside the entrance to the stadium.

"Doug, this is Lacey," said Wayne, "I don't think I've told you about her. She's from Boston. We travel together on the road."

"Nice to see foreigners from the East Coast invade the Midwest territory from time to time," Doug said with mild sarcasm as he reached to shake her hand.

Well, at least he's got a sense of humor, she thought. But she didn't want to be there. She didn't want to put on a fake smile to meet yet another stranger. She wanted to be on her own in Chicago, to stay in her hotel room or see a movie or go for a walk down Michigan Avenue. The Christmas lights were already up there, even though Thanksgiving was a week away, and she wanted to walk by the store displays, look at all the skinny mannequins dressed in rich winter plaid and simply have coffee somewhere—alone. She was still mourning her father's death on Christmas Day the year before.

After the introductions the three walked in silence through the entrance to the field and luckily found three empty seats high up in the stadium. Lacey sat between the two men, mostly silent since she knew nothing about the football.

At the start of the second quarter Drake was in the lead and Lacey could no longer stand the game. "You know, I have always considered this game kind of like training for war. Practice butting heads on the field so you can shoot people in the jungle." She didn't care if they didn't like what she said.

"Hey, Lace, you're just saying that because you are an ignoramus when it comes to this game. All you care about is tennis. So East Coast of you!"

She threw Wayne a look like "shut up" and hugged her knees to keep warm. Without a word Doug took off his jacket and placed it around Lacey's shoulders.

Grudgingly, she had shaken Doug's hand earlier. Now she remembered it as warmer than she expected. She glanced at the man sitting next to her. The soft, gray-blue eyes seemed full of understanding, maybe even pain. He looked like a man who could forgive much, though she didn't know why. In spite of herself, she smiled a real smile as she gazed out on the field. Drake 13, Miami of Ohio 10.

"Thanks. Nice of you to keep a fellow human being warm, she said." Immediately she regretted her comment. *Damn, Lacey, you can do better than that.*

"I mean, thanks. So did you play on this team or do you find this a form of pugilism, too?"

"You do seem to have a heavy hand with words. Pugilism? No. Everybody where I come from loves football. Me, I played in college, not because I was good but because I could warm the bench for the rest of the Simpson College team. The team I played on was the college newspaper. I was lucky enough to become the editor. That got me into law school."

Lacey could tell Doug was at least a little interested in her. She wondered if he shared this much about himself so quickly with every woman he met. And she was warming up to him, huddled together as they looked out at the action on the field. But she was afraid to ask what it meant to make a first down for fear of sounding stupid. From time to time when she could do so without Doug noticing, she glanced at his sandy, curly hair and the neatly trimmed mustache that complemented the square jaw and the chin with the Kirk Douglas dimple. The sideburns were trendy, perfectly trimmed on either side of his face. The tan corduroy jacket and the cowboy boots Lacey thought were just plain cool.

"That's pretty impressive, to be the editor of your college paper," she said. What do you do now, now that you are a lawyer?

"I am hoping to practice, but right now I am facing possible jail time."

Oh my God, he's dangerous. For an instant Lacey was stunned, then intrigued.

"It's kind of a long story I'd like to have the chance to bore you with later when the game is over, if that's okay with you."

Is he kidding? Lacey wanted to hear right then what Doug could have done to be facing a possible jail sentence. Did he kill somebody? Did he commit fraud? In the short time sitting with him she couldn't imagine he could hurt anyone.

As the game proceeded Lacey began to feel very not cool. She was wearing the same plaid kilt she had worn every day that week. She was tired of that skirt and of the road trips. The green and red pleats clung to her knees, held the skirt together by a large round silver pin, at the lower right edge. Her family's kilt pin was a fashion piece back East, but not here in Iowa.

While Doug and Wayne cheered, Lacey contemplated the profile of the man next to her. She saw a certain reserve in Doug's body and guessed he wouldn't ask her for a date even if he were interested. It would be up to her to ask him. She knew she was a high speed freight train, moving too fast down the track into conversation with new people. She could meet and greet all day on the road. But not here, not now. *Slow the train, girl. Just stand here and look at the guy.* He was definitely as good-looking as her father. She eyed the wide shoulders and narrow waist, built to play football, or maybe, in his case, haul pigs (Lacey assumed that was what most farmers did in Iowa). Her father had been just about six feet tall, too. She had no idea that, even on a superficial level, she was looking for him in every man she met.

"Wayne tells me the Peace Corps gave you a medal for being a great volunteer," Doug said framing his words almost like a question.

"No medal, just a recognition that I had done a good job." She didn't want to upstage him, whom Wayne had told her had been forced to leave the Peace Corps in Bolivia before his time was up.

Once or twice Doug turned to look at Lacey. He liked the healthy ruddy face with no make-up and the natural curl of her long brown hair that fell loosely around her shoulders. She was attractive but that's not what caught his attention. *She seems earnest and direct,* he thought. *More so than the few women I have known. There's a no-nonsense air about her.* His limited experience had taught him good looks and common sense were a rare combination.

After Drake won the game, the three headed to Wayne's and Doug's apartment. Lacey had come straight from the plane to the Drake field and still had her small, pale-green carry-on bag, with the pink initials LBP embroidered on the side. When they reached the top of the stairs, Wayne opened the apartment door with a swift kick of his boot. She marveled at Wayne's trademark Frye's with the thick heels and lifts inside, disguising his short stature and skinny frame. She often admitted to Wayne that she could never manage her own heels as easily as he did those cowboy boots.

"Sorry about the mess in here," he said. 'We're still building the bathroom. Guess we should have done something about it before now." He winked at Lacey.

The front door opened into a kitchen with a toilet and a tub in one corner next to a doorway leading to a living room. The bathroom was a work in progress.

The other tenants in the building were mostly single guys like Wayne and Doug but there were a couple of girl renters. The neighbors on the first floor were a rock band called Naked Eulogies and were trying to get gigs in Chicago. Mostly the group made loud noises late at night that annoyed the rest of the neighborhood made up of Drake students and old people living on fixed incomes. That area of town was safe and clean for the most part.

Wayne caught the look of dismay in Lacey's eyes. She was remembering the hole in the ground that passed for a toilet back in Tunisia. That one seemed preferable because there were no grown men on hand to watch her. "We'll think about finishing that later," Wayne said, "but let's go have pizza and beer now and scare up some dancing."

The local tavern looked like all the other college dens Lacey had frequented in the last two months: very little light, orange flames coming from an open oven sunk into the wall behind the bar. A sullen pizza-maker was sliding slabs of sauce-covered dough into and out of the fire on a big flat wooden board, bringing an occasional rhythmic wave of heat to the room. In the back of the room a juke box stood ready to play popular songs of the day for twenty-five cents. Th.e room was dotted with tables for four, covered with red–and white-checkered plastic table cloths.

Lacey moved to the bar swinging her legs over a stool in front of the oven so that she could get some heat. Doug slid onto the stool next to her. Half playing hard to get and half full of jitters, Lacey jumped up and moved across the room. She lit a cigarette and dropped a quarter in the in slot on the side of the juke box.

"This is the dawning of the Age of Aquarius...." She knew the lyrics by heart. She had seen *Hair* and loved the hippies on stage, singing about change and free love. She sang along softly with the Fifth Dimension, tapping her fingers on the top of the big, colorful machine. She looked down through the glass at the selections listed, each song title printed in its own little white rectangle. She gave up on picking another selection because she couldn't decide between *Delilah* by Tom Jones or *Mrs. Robinson* by Simon and Garfunkel. Wayne had gone off to talk to some friends about an idea he had shared with her on the road. It was something about a community or a commune, Lacey wasn't sure. When she returned to her stool, Doug was still there, waiting for her, just as she hoped he would be.

"Want to dance?" He stood up and pulled her toward him. She felt her palms warming to his touch.

"I love to dance, especially with your roommate, in those cowboy boots. He swings me around the dance floor in a way that makes me feel groovy. Many nights when we're bored in little college towns in Michigan or Wisconsin, we go dancing in the town's lone bar. That time we went to False Notes, I was sure it was a gay bar but Wayne swore it wasn't. I never worry when I am with Wayne. He never wants anything more than to dance and be my friend."

"He's my friend, too, but I have never tried to dance with him," Doug said with a smile.

"Very funny, maybe you'd like to try one day," Lacey replied, smiling at Doug and at her own little joke.

Doug led her to the small square that passed for a dance floor. She could tell he wasn't much of a dancer. His feet didn't move to the beat of the music. The jukebox was playing Smoke Gets in Your Eyes, the old Platters version.

She wished now she hadn't said Wayne was such a greater dancer. Had she hurt Doug's feelings with talk of Wayne? Early on in dancing school with all the other eighth graders she had been taught never to lead the boy who was your partner, let him lead you. That wasn't going to work here.

She remembered the time her dad led her onto the ballroom floor to be presented at the Cotillion with the rest of the Boston debutantes. She was surprised that he didn't feel the same rhythm she did. She loved the fast beat of the swing bands at coming-out parties, the party favors and those beanies the band handed out with "Lester Lanin" Stitched across the top. She could forgive her father his two left feet because she loved him so. She wondered if she could do the same with Doug.

They danced for a long time, barely moving, holding each other closer and closer. Doug brushed her right ear with his nose, lowering his head to kiss her cheek, folding her hand gently into his chest. "Do you always smell this sweet?" He whispered, wrapping his arms gently around her until there was no space between them.

She could feel the warmth rising in her body. *They asked me how I knew, my true love was true, I of course replied, something here inside cannot be denied.* She felt the words inside her skin. She liked the feel of this new man, the smell of Old Spice on his cheeks, the way his chin rested on her cheek. She didn't care anymore that he couldn't dance. "I don't think I've never been around a girl like you," he said softly. He kissed her hair, cupping her fingers in his hand as they came to a standstill on the dance floor.

"Does that mean I am a freak or a friend?" she said trying to be sexy but thinking she had missed the mark.

"I'll have to decide that later, won't I?" Doug said, giving nothing of himself away.

They were still kissing when they heard a tired bark from the owner: "midnight, kiddies, heads up, lights out, time to go home."

"I'm sorry this is over," Doug whispered. Lacey didn't know if he meant *over* because he didn't want to see her again or because the evening had come to an end. They lingered on the floor until it was empty and were the last to leave to go in search of Wayne's truck.

On the ride back to the apartment, she nestled between the wo men. All she could think about was how to handle the bathroom. Or was it a kitchen?

"Look, if you want, you can go first. I am sure you have had a long day. Doug and I can wait in the living room until you are done." Wayne was trying to be polite.

"No. Wait. We'll go first and then you can have as much time as you want." Doug wasn't sure how much time a woman needed. "Forgive us for not having had many female overnighters. We'll try to do better in the future, right Wayne?" Doug said with a small chuckle under his breath.

When she was done with the toilet and the sink, Lacey came into the living room fully clothed, not knowing if she would be sleeping on the floor or if one of the roommates would give up his mattress. Doug had already made a palette for her on the living-room floor, with a sleeping bag, pillows and extra blankets. He must have known earlier in the day he wanted someone near him that night. *Good sign!*

"Come over here, on the couch," he said. "Let's get warm and talk for a while. You know very little about me and I'd like to know lots more about you."

She sat down uncertainly in the middle of the couch, not knowing what would be next. She knew about the too many one night stands between recruiters on the road and this was not going to be one of them. Slowly Doug reached out, put his arm around her and gently pulled her closer to him. The scent of his skin came back to her and she relaxed as she began to talk.

"While I was in Tunisia," she began, "I had a man in my life, Alan. He was a Peace Corps volunteer, an architect, stationed with me in the same town. We lived together against all Peace Corps rules, until he was sent to another part of the country. Later, back in the States, we saw each other one last time in New York, and then the relationship was over. I spent one night beating myself up for losing him and then let him go. I don't look back. At this point, I feel the occasional diversion is a better bet."

"Me, I grew up in Scranton, a tiny town of about five hundred people, an hour and a half from Des Moines. Our biggest claim to fame is that we have the ninth oldest water tower still in use in the United States! No kidding. This is a really big deal, especially for my dad." She chuckled. "I guess, in truth, not that much happens in little towns in Iowa," he admitted with a small smile.

"After law school I joined the Peace Corps. At the time my draft status was 1A, dangerously high in such a small town. It meant I had to be ready for military service at any time." Lacey thought about her brothers, glad that one had flat feet to keep him out of the service, and that the other was only fifteen years old.

"My dad didn't really need me on the farm and I wasn't interested in raising pigs. I was done with all those years of doing chores."

She slid down a little, brushing Doug's chest, to lay her head in his lap. She was sleepy but she wanted to hear more.

"I went off to Bolivia after three months of training, knowing I was draftable. The notice was sent to my home in Scranton but didn't reach me in Bolivia for quite some time." She was watching him talk, looking up at him, her head nestled in his lap. She wondered if anyone this good looking could really be a nice guy. Would he judge her as too aggressive or just the good listener lying in his lap? It was growing hard to concentrate.

"When I returned to Iowa from Bolivia, I filed a suit declaring my draft notice illegal."

The words shook her into focus. She hadn't caught why his draft notice was illegal. "The case will be coming up in court this spring. I'm nervous but hopeful," he said. "This case is important for others, not just me." It seemed important to Lacey, too, even if she didn't yet understand. She wondered if a person was born with the courage gene or was it a choice one made.

Doug looked down at her, pulled her up into his arms and kissed her gently on the forehead. Then he laughed, tickling her neck and arms, letting her know in his way he was happy she was there in that moment listening to him.

"Now get some sleep, friend," he whispered. On the wall overhead were Joan Baez and her two sisters staring down at her from a giant poster bearing a popular phrase in bold letters: "Girls say yes to guys who say no." It had been created to raise money and awareness for those men who resisted the draft and to assure them that there would be certain rewards if they continued to say no. Yes, she thought, as she drifted off to sleep, I want to say "yes" to this man who has said "no" to the army and to me tonight. Would this weekend be all there was or would there be more?

The Brotherhood

It was late on a Friday night when Wayne got to the apartment. The roommates clapped each other on the back, their usual greeting, and settled in for the weekend. Doug took the pony-express-mail satchel that was Wayne's backpack and put in the living room closet. Wayne offered Doug a rolled joint which he declined and Doug handed Wayne a beer. The TV had been on with the late night news and weather but Doug turned it off as soon as Wayne came through the front door. He was home for the Thanksgiving weekend.

"Doesn't it look great?" Doug said. "See what I did? The bathroom is for real now. I put up a wall around the tub. What do you think? Am I a good carpenter or what? Had to haul the boards up here myself and put up the plaster."

"What do I think? I think you were thinking of Lacey the whole time you were sawing wood!" Wayne couldn't resist the jab.

"Not really. It was just something that had to be done if we are going to make something out of this place."

"Bull shit! Tell me, what you really think of her?"

"You know, I have to be careful these days. I am under oath and anything I say might come back to bite me."

"C'mon, man, this isn't a courtroom. This is about a girl. One who is my damn good friend. I love that lady and she loves me if that's possible. I would do anything for her. And you can't even say if you like her? Give me a break!"

"I'll admit I'd see Lacey again, but, like her, I have insecurities that kept me quiet. I haven't been around many girls for a long time. The volunteers in my group that trained for Bolivia were all men. I am in pretty unfamiliar territory when it comes to dating"

"The truth is you're afraid to think about the new woman you've just met. You are twenty-eight, facing a possible prison sentence. She is twenty-five, bopping around the country with countless opportunities to meet guys whose futures look a lot brighter than yours."

"Thanks for that bit of analysis. If I needed a psychologist I could get one. I try to think about her objectively. But I can't. She is intelligent, seemingly adventurous, even sympathetic to my cause, and full of energy. I keep seeing her coming across the field with that look on her face that read "don't mess with me." She was full of expression and passion, emotions I was brought up not to feel. I liked that about her.

"You are so full of shit, Doug, your eyes are turning brown. Man, you got to get out of your head and get out of your own way before her train passes you by."

"Wait, Wayne, don't make fun of me. She is different from any girl I have ever met."

What he didn't want to admit was that he missed the taste of her kiss, the fresh smell of her hair, the turned up nose and the moment he first felt her touch on the dance floor. That he missed the sound of her voice, low, clear and saucy.

"She did seem genuinely interested in my effort to resist the draft. Most of the girls I've dated couldn't care less about Vietnam. Sorority girls, mainly, who'll to go to nursing school after college until they get married and move to their husband's farm." Then he thought about her good legs. He told himself that such things were unimportant in a relationship.

"Don't you think she's pretty, Doug?" Wayne said. "I am warning you, looks mean a lot to Lacey. Call her shallow, but she has a real eye for beauty. The great thing about her is that she has a taste for both the refined and for the renegade. That's in your favor, buddy."

"She's pretty sophisticated for my standards," Doug said. "I bet my grandmother would say she's a little too worldly for the folks in Iowa." He chuckled as he pictured his grandmother meeting the girl from Boston.

"We didn't talk much. At first I thought she was kind of stuck up, probably had a big ego. She ran away from me to the jukebox just to see if I'd be interested in her when she came back to the bar. I thought she was just a flirt. But as the night went on I sort of felt she was a sensitive person used to hiding her feelings."

"I think she got pretty used to doing that as a child," Wayne said. "Her mom was nuts, put away for most of her childhood having shock treatments. Her father died while she was in Tunisia."

"I'm sorry to hear that," Doug said, surprised he felt genuine sadness for a woman he hardly knew. He wanted to know more about her and about his feelings for her.

"She's pretty smart, Doug, Even you might have a hard time keeping up with her. She's the type who wants a guy smarter than she, to keep her guessing. When I first met her, like you, I thought she was some kind of social butterfly, so chatty she could talk to a stone. All that stuff about Boston and coming-out parties. The only coming-out party I ever went to was my own." Wayne laughed.

"Travelling with her, though, I learned that she has a real ability to lift people's spirits, including mine. I counted on her more than once when we were on the road and I was asked to leave our hotel because of my predilection."

He clapped Doug on the back. "You could do a lot worse than to have someone like her pulling for you. You're very smart, too, but a little too cerebral. Lacey's a quick study, up for almost anything. You don't drink, you don't smoke and you don't seem to have much fun these days. Lacey has a zest for life, a little of that could rub off on you, buddy."

"Are you calling me a prick or a prude, my friend? Either way you could be right," John laughed. It's just that I am not always a good judge of my feelings that's why I seem wary or cautious."

"Lacey operates on instinct. You pride yourself on being reasonable in all things, with logic, not emotion. At heart you are a cogitator who agonizes the same way over a debate or a debacle. I know you feel things acutely sometimes but rarely your feelings, preferring to play them out in actions instead. You didn't talk much about this draft situation, you just resisted from the start."

"Jesus, now you are becoming my shrink. Thanks, but no thanks. I don't need your diagnosis. Listen, practically speaking, I know this is not a good time for me to have a girlfriend-- when I might be going to jail. On the other hand, it would be good to have something in my life other than this court case. I know I am becoming a loner and ought to spend more time with people other than you and the lawyer defending my case. I rarely even go home to Scranton now, because I don't want to embarrass my father and brothers any further: already they are being shunned in the town because of my actions.

"Hey, I have an idea," Wayne said, sending a wink Doug's way to change the subject. "Let's finish off that bathroom with a can of paint so we have some visitors in the future." They both knew who that would be.

City Child

Lacey Pierce's real name was Lawrence Babcock Pierce. Her parents loved Gertrude Lawrence, whom they saw perform in Gershwin's *Lady in the Dark* when they were first dating in New York in 1941. They loved the actress but not her first name. The G was too harsh and the only Gertrude they knew was a 92-year-old spinster. They were young and living in the Village, the war was still on, and theater provided George and Lillian a great escape. Lawrence was a thoughtfully chosen, if somewhat quirky, selection.

So Lacey got stuck with Lawrence. In truth, when she was old enough to consider her name, she did not mind, because she liked sounding a bit masculine, more tough than tender, not like a Julie or Jane. After all, her own mother was always called "Markie," never Lillian, from Mark, her middle name, after some distant male relative.

Early on, while other children wondered why Peter Rabbit's ears were long or what happened to Old Mr. Toad or Christopher Robin, Lacey was living in a world of Greek myths which her mother insisted on reading to her from the time she was barely two years old. "Read me the one where he kills the Medusa with all those snakes on top of her head," Lacey would plead. Even when she was reading, Markie's attention would wander off the page and she'd start talking to herself. "He failed me, that Perseus. He should have acted sooner to save me. I am stuck here on Athos."

"No, Mom, not Athos. We are here, here in my rom. Read to me. Daddy will be coming home soon." She was anxious for her dad to come at the end of every day to let her know all was right at home.

When her father came home from the war they rented a small apartment in the Village. It was narrow with a tiny railroad kitchen on the second floor of an ancient. Markie called it the "caboose" because she thought it looked like the back a railroad car. Sometimes she would call out "all aboard" imitating the porter of some train she had once ridden.

The walls in each room were pale green. "They're the same color as my doctor's office," Lacey commented more than once, meaning she didn't like it. Her parents slept in a Murphy bed in the living room that doubled as a couch by day. She often cuddled between them on cold nights. There was only one bedroom which was Lacey's. Her dad decided to paint it yellow because he thought it was a color for kids. "You know, sweetheart, I hope you will have a little brother soon, so I didn't want to paint the room pink or blue, didn't want to show any favoritism." He winked as he said it, and Lacey was glad because she liked yellow a lot more than pink, though she wouldn't have minded the blue.

"There were three Gorgons, of whom Medusa was one,' " Markie went on, "each with wings and snaky hair, most horrible, to mortals, whom no man could behold and draw again a breath in life. When Pallas Athena stood beside Perseus, she took off the polished shield that covered her chest and held it out to him. 'Look into this when you attack the Medusa. You will be able to see her in it as in a mirror, and so avoid her deadly power." Markie closed the book. "And that's how he killed her, Lacey, and with the help of Hermes, the messenger of Zeus, he flew home, met Andromeda, and married her. End of story for tonight."

"Come talk to me while I take a bath." Her mother was off again, not there. "You must always be clean like your mother. When you grow up be sure to shave your arms, your eyebrows, all the parts that could carry filth." Lacey nodded dutifully, not asking why and not wanting to know.

Her mother's odd regimens and admonitions filled her early life. "No pillows, darling, because they will ruin you posture. You must wear those Buster Browns, boys' Oxfords for arch support."

The daily diet was hamburgers for protein and a can of Franco-American gravy for flavor. And mashed potatoes. Once the Lone Ranger was over, no radio after 7:00 pm. No white sugar, only brown. Every day a spoonful of cod liver oil. No white bread. Socks were two sizes too big, so her feet could "breathe."

When Lacey's brother George was born, Markie became more and more distracted. Her hair was disheveled. She sat in the tub in the hot water with a cream shaving the hair off her arms, her legs, and her eyebrows. She covered her face in some strange white powder and she talked to someone Lacey didn't know. Was it to herself or someone not there? Was she, her mother, acting like Medusa, or was that just in Lacey's imagination?

"Daddy, why does Mommy act like the Medusa? I know the story. She doesn't have snakes coming out of her head but seems wild and when you are not here she is in the tub. Why does she shave everything?"

"Don't you worry, sweetheart. Everything will turn out okay. Besides you will soon have a little brother or sister. Maybe that's why Mommy is acting strange." When George Pierce, Junior was born it was time to send his sister to school.

"Lacey must have an alternative education," Markie insisted. Lacey didn't know what "alternative" meant. Her mother sent her in a cab every day from the Village to school on the Upper East Side. The woman was called a "proxy" by her mother, whatever that meant. Markie never came to the school like other mothers and never seemed to leave the apartment. She wore blue shorts winter and summer, a white tee shirt every day and big clunky leather green shoes that came from a catalogue. It was becoming clear to Lacey just how different her mother was.

"That's Prometheus up there," said Lacey's dad, all tutelage and cheerful. He didn't know just how many Prometheus stories his wife had read to their daughter. There was the great gold god hanging recumbent above the rink, watching the skaters gliding round and round. Lacey knew all about Prometheus. She knew it was his job to bring fire to mankind in ancient Greece. She guessed he was up there to keep watch over all those flags from around the world flying high above Rockefeller Center.

George Pierce laced up his hockey skates. The laces were wearing thin from the many nights he laced them up to play semi-pro hockey after work. He had been a star athlete in prep school and Harvard. Football, hockey, baseball and tennis, he loved all sports and played them all with great joy. He had gone to medical school briefly, only to realize he didn't have the intellectual stamina to continue. Now he was selling insurance in New York and feeling little satisfaction in his work. And he was beginning to feel uncomfortable at home. There was no real joy in his life now, except those hockey games and his daughter, who was the one bright spot in his every day.

"Hey, let me help you, sweetheart," he kneeled down in front of Lacey's feet, loving the ritual of putting on his daughter's skates. His big hands wove the white laces back and forth across her shins, looping the laces into the right metal hook, pulling them just tight enough to give her ankles the right support as he readied her to stride onto the freshly made ice. Skating with Lacey meant everything to him. And for Lacey, her dad was her Prometheus.

She loved the smooth ice when it was new like glass and without "scratches." Unlike Markie, George went places with Lacey. He left the house with her, holding her hand always. He took her to Howard Johnson's, and that museum with the big paintings, and the place with all the dancing girls kicking their legs out straight at Christmas time.

On the ice, she teased him, skating away into the crowd so he couldn't see her. She loved seeing her own breath flow out in front of her in the cold air as she sped half way around the rink. When she looked at George Pierce from the other side she thought he was the handsomest of all the dads on the ice. She knew how much he loved skating and hockey by the way he always talked about the game with his friends, who greeted him around the neighborhood. Even as a six year old she could tell he preferred skating to selling life insurance, whatever that was. And she knew her mom didn't like that. Maybe mom and dad weren't living together because of that. Is that why the woman they called "the proxy" was with there every day at home now?

"Hey, precious, my little athlete, show me how fast you can skate," Lacey's dad shouted through little groups of skaters blocking his sight though he knew exactly where she was. As Markie's health deteriorated, he had become even better, taking on the role of both father and mother at just thirty years of age for both Lacey and her brother.

"What a little darling you have there," came from a man who stopped dead on his skates in front of George ad Lacey. "Those brown eyes are gorgeous and huge. How's the family doing? I've stopped a few times in the morning on my way to the studio but no one's home."

"Thanks, Skitch, your orchestra sounded great the other night on the radio," George commented to the band leader. Skitch Henderson lived on the third floor in the apartment above the Pierces.

Lacey took in every word of the exchange. She knew her mother was there when the man came by. Why didn't she answer her neighbor's knock at the door?

"C'mon, Daddy, let's go around once more," Lacey begged, not wanting to hear the rest of the man's comments. She pulled at George's knees trying to get him to move his big hockey skates. "Please, let's go."

George did not budge. He leaned from side to side shifting his weight on his skates to steady himself as Lacey continued to pull at his pants. "Thanks for asking, Skitch," George began. Then leaning into Skitch's ear he whispered, "My mother and I are thinking of sending Markie away for a while for a rest."

Lacey caught the whisper. Looking down at the man's skates, she noticed they were figure skates like hers, only black. She thought men only wore skates to play hockey. She didn't like Skitch or his skates or what he said to her dad. She was glad when he glided off to the other side of the rink.

George and Lacey skated a few more times around the rink before it was time to stop. Lacey didn't say anything while George carefully removed Lacey's skates, put her shoes on her feet and tied the laces of her skates so she could carry them over her shoulder. He even put the rubber tips on the blades so the skates would stay sharp and also not hurt her. All the while Lacey said nothing.

"Daddy, I didn't like that man. What kind of name is Stitch?"

"Not Stitch. He's Skitch, Skitch Henderson, the band leader. He was only concerned about your mother, that's all."

On the ride home in the subway between stops, when there was less noise, but still noise in the underground, Lacey could not hold herself back. "Why," she screamed, "are you and granny sending Markie away for a rest?" Several passengers looked up briefly, then looked down into their laps or newspapers. "She isn't tired and doesn't need a rest. She's there every day, all day long resting" Lacey gathered what "away" really meant but she didn't know to where or why. And just how long was "a while" going to be?

<hr>

For a number of years, while Doug was milking cows as a teenager in Iowa and attending 4H meetings with other kids, Lacey and her brother ricocheted between divorced parents, living first with one and then the other in out of the way places around the country. They moved to Texas where George had a job with a company that made arms for the Korean War. The next year Markie came and took them to live with her father in Maryland. George must have visited his ex-wife at some point because along came a second brother, Bret in the summer of 1953. Once again, as with the birth of each of her children, she needed a "time away."

George left the job in Texas and took the children to live in in his hometown of Middleford, Massachusetts with his mother and widowed sister and her daughter.

At the time, in the 1950's, legal custody was almost always awarded to the mother, even to one who was not fully fit to raise children. So technically, George was harboring Lacey. George and Bret illegally. Though she did not know this, Lacey sensed the daily tension in her dad and it made her uneasy. "Put a smile on your face, Lacey," her father would say. I can't stand it when you don't smile," as he sank into his pitcher of martinis. Smiling only made her feel sorry for her dad.

When Lacey was eleven she entered Middleford Academy from which her father had graduated many years before. She was determined to lift her dad's spirits by making him proud of her. She put her heart and soul into the sixth grade. From the start she loved the new school. It introduced her to theater and Latin and soccer and all kinds of new friends she never would have been able to make moving around so much. She was cast as the father in the spring musical production of *Hansel and Gretel.* Lacey loved the nights when her dad would cue her for the lines she had to learn.

"Okay, the mother says there's no food in the house and they must do something," began George. Lacey giggled as her dad spoke in a high pitched voice, signaling that he was the mother and looking ridiculous in the large scarf on his head he had tied under his chin to play the part. He read directly from the script:

> *"Listen, husband, early tomorrow take the two children, give each of them a little piece of bread, then lead them into the middle of thickest part of the woods, make a fire for them, and leave them there, for we can no longer feed them."*
>
> *"No, woman,"* said the man (Lacey in a deep, gruff, voice), *"I cannot bring myself to abandon my own children to wild animals that would quickly tear them to pieces."*
>
> *"If you don't do it,"* said the mother, *"all of us will starve together,"* and I'll give you no peace until you say yes."

And that was how they rehearsed. He would wiggle his ears, which were large, as a way to signal Lacey's line was coming up. Actually, he genuinely loved using them to cue Lacey. And he came to every single performance, leaving work to do so against the advice of his colleagues.

That same year he introduced her to a new game. Learning to hit a tennis ball back and forth, back and forth, to and fro, Lacey was in perfect rhythm with her dad until one of them would get out of step, drop the ball in the net and they would begin all over again. For Lacey the game was love at first sight and forever after. Those moments were the essence of her dad that would come back to her again and again, keep her steady and in peace whenever she recalled him alive and then gone. When she grew up she would seek it and test it in every man she knew.

When Lacey began high school, or what Middlefod referred to in the English manner, as Class IV, she developed another interest almost as strong as tennis: BOYS. Not that she wanted to date them. She wanted to know what made them tick.

On many days there were long walks in the cemetery a few blocks from the school's main building, Wexford Hall. She would go there with one or another boy to pass the time after school or on Saturdays. When there were no benches they would sit on the ground, often leaning their backs against a gravestone. Mostly they just talked and passed the time together. Lacey had never really kissed anyone except members of her family.

And then there was Billy Rider. He was the star pitcher on the varsity baseball team. He was six feet two, skinny and blind as a bat without his glasses. He wasn't exactly good looking. There was the crooked smile, very sexy, if Lacey even really knew what that meant. His tawny thatch of hair gave her the impression he might go bald prematurely. Best of all he smelled good. She had played a lot of tennis with at the local club the past summer and the camaraderie between them had definitely caught fire.

"Come on, Lace, you know you're not going to let me beat you because you're supposed to let me win."

"I am not supposed to let you do anything. Get lost."

"You get lost. Get real. You can hit the shit out of the ball when you want to."

"Thanks for the sweet talk."

"Now show me."

That's the way it went between them – a kind of mutual challenge.

One Wednesday, game day at the Academy, they left the school after the last class bell rang at 3:00 and sneaked off to the cemetery. Spring had already made its mark on the town. It was warm and breezy with sun and no clouds. A perfect time for a peaceful walk on hallowed grounds.

"Man, I'd rather be here with you any day than on the mound with that jerk of a coach standing over me," Billy said, delighted that he we was openly disobeying the baseball coach and missing the afternoon practice.

"Are you sure you'd rather be here? I mean what if they kick you off the team?" Lacey asked. She always tried to play by the rules and wondered if this little tryst might come back to haunt one or both of them.

Billy leaned over and kissed her, at first haltingly, gently, as both were new to and tentative about this. Lacey wondered vaguely whether seventeen was the right age to take up the business of necking. But she wanted to learn so she kissed back, until gradually they began exploring each other's tongues, "Frenching" it out for what seemed like hours, stopping only to breathe here and there.

Finally Billy sat back to relax before he reached the point where he might go too far. He didn't know any more than Lacey about how to pet but he was a gentleman and knew when to stop.

"Is your family buried here?" he asked out of the blue, breaking the spell of Lacey's clear enjoyment of the afternoon session.

"Yes, they are here. All of them go way back." Lacey spoke with pride, knowing the Pierces were one of those families.

"How about you, Billy, do you have a family plot?" Lacey inquired thinking it must be so.

"Are you kidding? My dad came to Boston from Alabama," Billy chuckled, "I don't even think he knows where his father was buried, let alone where he came from."

Realizing the haughtiness with which she had just spoken about her family she was quick to say, "Aunt Matty says that, more probably than not, our ancestors were heretics from England, criminals not wanted in their country and just plain riffraff." "But there are a few famous people buried here."

Lacey took Billy to the gravesite of Howard Johnson (1897 – 1972) of the twenty-eight flavors of ice cream to impress him with her sense of history, and then moved on to the Pierce Family plot on the other side of the cemetery. She quite liked teasing Billy, making him think she was so smart here in this place where her family historically rested. She had no idea her father would come to join the plot so soon.

A Bond with Doug

Back in Chicago, despite being busy with work, Lacey thought about Doug often. What did he mean when he said, "Sorry this is over"? Did he mean just that night or forever? Should she write to him? Call him? She heard nothing from Doug and was too proud to ask Wayne about him. Whenever she thought about Doug, she heard parents' voices: a girl should never make the first call. Was he thinking about her but afraid to call? It had been nearly two months since that first night with him. By now, maybe he had a girlfriend.

She missed his way of speaking slowly, choosing his words carefully, looking to see their effect on her, the self-assurance she felt in his presence. She missed his little sarcasms about power and government that were making her more aware about the world at large. Physically she missed his touch. From afar she could almost feel his soft brown mustache, the chiseled chin, the long slow sweep of his torso. And she missed the way he stroked her hair when she was cuddled beside him.

Over Christmas break, home in Boston for a week, she distracted herself by ice skating with her younger brothers and visiting her best friend from high school.

Molly Bradlee was better at almost anything than Lacey. Most school mornings Lacey would walk from house to the Bradlee's, wake Molly and have breakfast with her family. Molly was skinny and blond, sweet and practical. She could play the piano and the violin. Lacey loved her and was envious of her at the same time. Molly had great parents and lots of talent.

"You know, Molly, I've met this guy. So different from the Harvard preppies. I think this one is for real. He comes from the Heartland, a farm in Iowa. He says he's committed to ending this war, even if it means his own sacrifice."

"Oh, Lacey, I know you. You're probably hot for his bod. You always liked a pretty face!"

"No, Mo, this is different. I can't figure it out. Is he a committed activist or am I just a fool? Is he a patriot or an imposter looking for glory? I don't mean "imposter," that's too harsh, I mean is he just "some guy." I want to give him the credit I hope he deserves, but I don't know. And look at me, I have only seen him once, haven't heard from him and I can't get him out of my mind! Hopeless."

"You know, Lacey, the way you are talking about this guy reminds me of what your dad used to say about confusing moments. Remember what your dad used to say? Why is a mouse when it spins? His answer every time was the same: "the higher the fewer." He meant sometimes there is no rhyme or reason to what we think or do. And there's none here. All I can say is I hope you can figure this man out soon or move on to a new playmate."

The day after New Year's, Lacey returned to Chicago. She was anxious to see if Doug had written her or called the office while she was away. She had never given him her phone number.

"Hey, Lacey, look at this!" Wayne handed her a telegram he received from Doug. Happy New Year. Stop. PLEASE COME. BOTH OF YOU. Stop. The message brought back all the thrill and excitement of the first time they met.

"Thank you, thank you, Wayne! It's what I've been waiting for—I mean hoping for. Thank you."

"Don't thank me. It's Doug who wants to see you. Not I. I get to see all too much of you week after week," Wayne said jokingly, visibly pleased that Lacey was so happy to hear from Doug.

✦⸺✦⸺✦

The following Saturday night, Lacey and Doug lingered over pizza in the Des Moines apartment.

"Hope you like pepperoni. I wasn't sure when you'd get here so I just ordered ahead. I am really glad you could come. I am sorry I never wrote or called. Honestly, I wasn't sure how to find you...or what you would think of me. I admit, I could have done better."

Lacey didn't care. She wasn't listening to his words. She was reading his face. She watched his shadow on the wall in the candlelight as he began to talk. She could feel how much he wanted her to know him.

"Me and my younger brothers, George and Walter, attended a one-room school house for all of the elementary grades."

She could tell, by the way he spoke about helping his siblings, that he was quiet by nature, not exactly shy, but used to commanding the front at home or in the classroom. He looked so good to her in the light.

"My mom died when I was in high school and I had to be there for everyone, to keep the farm running while my father and grandmother grieved. It was hard on Dad. My mother was very social, always away from home, at church suppers or visiting sick friends. I didn't know her well. And then she was gone. I'm not all that used to women." His words came faintly, almost as a warning or an apology. She wasn't sure which.

"The ride through college was pretty smooth for me. Simpson College wasn't far from home, so I could check up on Dad. I fell into some leadership roles. You know, big fish, small pond."

"I don't believe people 'fall' into leadership roles," Lacey said earnestly. "They're born to lead others. You're being too modest. I think you seem very confident. People would want you to lead them."

"Maybe so." He smiled at her. "Not on the field though. I wasn't athletic, I have a stigmatism in my right eye but they let me play on the football team. I didn't mind spending most of my time on the bench. I was just happy to be on the team."

"I've heard from Wayne things have really changed for you since those days." Lacey said not wanting to push Doug further than he wanted to go.

"Well, I'm not so much of a joiner anymore. I'd like to be more active in protesting this war, and the injustice of punishing demonstrators like the ones in Chicago, but my hands are tied until this trial is over, or never over."

She could feel the sadness in his words. Sensing perhaps her uncertainty, Doug took her hand and led her to the couch, shoving the newspapers to the floor. He sat down pulling her beside him. He stroked her face gently and began to kiss her neck. She welcomed his touch on her breast. After a few moments he abruptly stopped and asked a question he had obviously pondered for a while:

"Look, I could be really interested in you. But I worry I might not be good for you. Do you know what you want for your life? The security of a banker or a risk taker-wanderer like me for a mate?"

"You know, I thought about that over Christmas with my best friend. I told her I had met a man unlike any I had known in school or the guys in the Peace Corps. I wouldn't call you so much a risk-taker as an *altruist*. And that suits me fine." Lacey was glad she responded in that way, not compounding his worry about the trial.

Doug moved to the closet, pulled out the sleeping bag and pulled it up next to his bed. He pulled the cover back on the bed he had made earlier in the day. He motioned Lacey to lie down on it. As she lay back he unbuttoned and took off her shirt. He slid her skirt down off her hips, then pulled off her boots and socks. He was gentle, tender, as if he were taking of the clothes off a child. Lacey felt completely calm in his presence.

Doug knelt down on his knees next to where Lacey's head lay on a pillow. He brushed her lips with a soft kiss, then opened her mouth with his tongue, going deep, licking her teeth, caressing her breasts and ready for much more. But he wasn't sure she was ready.

"Sleep now. I will be right here beside you all night."

The seriousness of their conversation filled the air. Somehow it wasn't the right time to make love. But as she fell asleep beside him she knew that he had already flooded her life with a meaning she did not fully grasp.

The next morning Doug kissed Lacey awake and handed her a cup of coffee. "Come on, slug- a- bed, no more shut eye. I don't want to waste minute of time away from you."

It was January 20. Nixon was being inaugurated in Washington that morning. Lacey and Doug sipped coffee for most of the morning and read the Des Moines Register's coverage of the event. Doug noticed the black activist Julian Bond would be speaking that day at his alma mater Simpson College.

"Come on. Let's go. I want to show you the campus before you go there officially on Monday. We'll hear someone I admire speak on campus today. Julian Bond. There's some kind of fall speaker series and I really want to hear this one. Besides, this way you'll get a personal tour from a member of the class of 1963!"

"I wish I had a motorcycle instead of this old rattle trap," Doug said as he tucked Lacey into the passenger seat of the truck. "Wayne and I share this rattle trap. He calls her Bets. He likes to call her his only girlfriend! Good thing for us he went to see his sister today"

Barely half an hour later they arrived in Indianola, home of Simpson College. Most of he students weren't visible on campus on Saturday morning as they parked at the edge of the campus and started the long walk to the student center.

"Hope you don't mind hoofing it. I really like to walk. It calms me down when I'm anxious."

"Me, too," she said, content simply to walk quietly beside him across the campus quad.

"It seems funny now, but I actually invited my cousin Bernadette to the Simpson senior prom because I was too scared to take a chance with any of the girls on campus. I'd never really dated and I didn't want anyone to know how little I knew about girls."

From the little time she had spent with him, she felt he might be more comfortable in the company of men. She hoped to change that.

As they reached the student center the student government president, a clean shaven, clean cut, senior in khaki pants and a madras jacket, announced the day's speaker. "That was me at one time," Doug said. "It sure wouldn't be me today.

"This Bond guy is amazing," Doug said, starting to recite Bond's biography. "He's led protests against segregation in the Atlanta parks, restaurants and movie theaters. In Raleigh, he helped form the Student Nonviolent Coordinating Committee in 1960. The next year, he left College to serve as its communications director. Now, he's back in school finishing a degree in English. Man, does he ever get my respect."

"I think he was in Chicago the day I was there during the Democratic National Convention. Wasn't he nominated as a vice-presidential candidate-- the first African American ever? But then I think he withdrew his name because he was too young to hold the office."

"I figured you'd know who he was," Doug said as they moved into the auditorium in the student center.

The auditorium looked more like a small church. Lacey figured it was about the size of a tennis court without the lines. There were single wooden folding chairs stretching twenty rows back and ten seats wide on both sides of the auditorium separated by a wide isle down the middle. The room was all beige pine wood and the walls covered the space with an off white light. Tall stained windows lined both side of the auditorium and plaques decorated the walls with names of college donors. A perfect place for an intimate talk by a young and passionate activist.

The place wasn't full, but filled enough to be welcoming for the speaker. Julian Bond's message to the students was clear that day, impassioned and to the point. "Many of you are attracted to social service." He began. "The rewards are immediate, the gratification quick, but if we aim to have social justice, we won't need social service. Social justice, economic justice for all, not just a few, is where it's at."

"Damn, he's right about that," Doug said squirming in his seat "And to think just four years ago, I was volunteering to help get Barry Goldwater elected President! Promise me, you'll never tell anyone I did that."

Lacey wondered how he could have made such a mental switch but she didn't want to break the mood of their time together. Maybe later, she would ask. Doug was still a new element in her life.

Lacey could feel how deeply this gentle, Southern apostle for civil rights had affected Doug. Like Julian Bond, Doug wanted to make a difference with his life, not just to toe the mark of being a do-gooder.

Doug nudged Lacey in her seat. "Service work just puts a Band-Aid on cancer," he said in her ear half way through the speech.

"I think Bond helped you find the moral imperative you were looking for."

John didn't respond to Lacey's off- hand comment and changed the subject.

"I promised you a tour of the campus and we kind of got side tracked by the big event," he said apologetically.

"See that hall over there? That's where I tried out for the glee club my freshman year. I even tried to join the Simpsontones. I showed up to sing tenor in a quartet. When we finished, the glee club director pointed at me. "Can you tell me precisely why you came here today?" I was mortified and knew I was terrible!" The laugh he let out let her know he had long since abandoned any thoughts of being a singer.

Just before they reached the truck, Doug slowly broke into song: "And He walks with me and He talks with me…." The Methodist hymn was the only song he knew.

"And he tells me I am his own…." Lacey stifled a giggle she knew would hurt Doug's feelings. *Thank you, glee club director, for saving me from having to tell him he is tone deaf.*

The ride back relaxed them both. The autumn sun was warm on the windshield as they passed farms where field hands and farm owners busily gathered the last of their crops before the frost.

As they wound upward around a curve in the road which was slippery and wet from an earlier rain, a truck with a load of hay came around the outside edge of the oncoming lane going too fast on the slick decline. The truck couldn't stop and slid full force into the pickup. The impact was so sudden and swift the pickup rolled over off the road tumbling down an embankment into the plump grass above a group of cows grazing in the valley below. The passenger door swung open and Lacey fell out onto the ground with Doug tumbling after her. It was a classic Steve Mc Queen escape, shaken, maybe bruised, but essentially uninjured.

The driver of the truck, an aging white-haired man, never broke speed and never stopped. He just disappeared on the horizon in the distance.

They lay still in the grass not too far from each other. Each checked their own body parts and put a hand out to make sure the other was okay.

"I am okay, but how about you? I'm not dizzy, but I think we may be in shock.

They rolled into each other in the grass, giddy and grateful to be unharmed. They held each other close in silence for a longtime. Doug stroked Lacey's hair, then touched her face, her fingers, and arms, to make sure all of her was there, unbroken, beside him. The afternoon sun was fading before they fully realized what had happened.

"Can you believe that farmer just kept on going?" John said angrily banging his fist to the ground. "He's a criminal for leaving the scene of an accident. I would have practically strangled the guy if he were still here. Damn. Too bad I didn't get his license plate."

Slowly Doug got up and started toward the pickup above them. Luckily, it had flipped entirely over and was standing upright on the slant of the hill. The doors on the downside of the truck gaped open. Doug got into the cab, struggling to keep his balance in the now tipped truck and turned the key. The car wouldn't start.

"Damn, we'll have to get a tow truck from the nearest gas station, wherever that is" Doug shouted down the hill to Lacey, still angry about the farmer and thinking about the expense. "I'll have to hitch a ride in town to get someone out here.

He walked back to where Lacey was resting. He knelt beside her and began to kiss her, gently at first, flicking bits of grass off her shirt. "I want you now," Doug whispered, and Lacey knew this was the right time and place for them. Doug kicked off his pants, shoes and socks and threw them aside. The ground felt soft and safe, cushioning them from the small bumps and bruises of the day and inviting them to make love on the blanket of grass for the first time.

"Guess this was meant to be." She said looking up into his eyes, sounding far away and a little hazy. Maybe there's a reason we're still here." Lacey nestled close to Doug, sliding off her skirt and panties and sneakers. Doug rolled on top of her, gently inching her legs apart, covering her body gently with kisses. Lacey pushed her body upward off the ground, in spite of still a little pain from the accident, for Doug to enter her. She welcomed his thrusts and caught his rhythm, moving with him in and out for what seemed like a long time. Then suddenly they were spent, almost at the same time.

The moon was just beginning to hang its head over them in the sky. Doug rolled over and lay on the ground beside Lacey. They began laughing, slowly, and then fully, in happy release. They had survived the crash.

That was the first time they made love overlooking a chorus of cows, oblivious to the mooing accompaniment to their pleasure. The repairs would have to wait. Soon it would be too dark to leave Lacey with the pickup. She was glad they would go together in search of a gas station.

Kitchen Convocation

"I can see the place now, tie-died curtains and Indonesian batiks. All the colors of the rainbow!" Wayne was holding court for the motley group standing in front of him in the kitchen. One person was sitting on the toilet, on another in the tub, others were cross-legged on the floor. It was January, time for a new beginning.

"So what do we all want to get out of this besides colorful curtains?!" Doug deadpanned, aiming his sarcasm good naturedly back at Wayne. He had taken up his post against the wall beside the front door.

"Well, we're all a part of an unusual and excellent sense of commitment to end this war. Amen." Richie piped up.

"And we are all committed to a life of service each in our own way," he added quietly.

"And each of us has some unusual and excellent personal talent to bring to the group as we live together," Wayne chimed in.

"We are all committed activists, the best and the brightest, as Halberstam says," Doug intoned with hyperbole, upstaging Wayne, appointing himself spokesman for the group.

Lacey raced up the stairs soaking wet, doused by a sudden shower as she got out of the cab and burst through the door, her heart bounding in anticipation of seeing Doug. She looked around the room but didn't see him. Everyone still had their coats on because it was February and because the heating needed repair.

Doug was leaning against the wall behind the opened door. When Lacey shut the door, the two nodded at each other, nothing more.

Doug did not know that Lacey had already made up her mind. She was prepared to join in the experiment she had come to learn about if she liked what she was about to hear. She had decided her relationship with Doug would not be a factor. They had talked on the phone a few times, they had written a few letters to each other but there was no real commitment. They could be together in this or not.

"Well, hey, Lacey, glad you could finally make it! Sorry about the rain and ice. We've been talking about you behind your back. Just kidding! I think you're familiar with some of this motley crew."

Not really. Lacey looked around the room at those she had met once or twice before but hardly knew. The smiles were casual not familiar. She sat down on the floor near the door and waited for the meeting to start. Doug looked down at Lacey from time to time, her back to him so she couldn't see. Doug liked looking at her from above. He wasn't sure she would come but he was glad she was there.

The kitchen looked a little better than she remembered it from that first time. Plaster board now framed the toilet on both sides and there was a door that was open. A woman was sitting on the toilet listening to Wayne and Doug. The kitchen walls were now white instead of gray and though there were no windows, a Columbian poncho had been tacked up on the wall overlooking the tub. In the middle a dart board covered the space for a head with a few darts sticking to it in the center. Someone had been practicing.

She recognized Richie whom she had met back in the fall when he had recently arrived in Des Moines as a VISTA volunteer for an irrigation project. He told her didn't like the assignment. She remembered their conversation.

"Do you get that line from people out here, that I get, who say you must be smarter because you are from the East Coast?"

"Makes no sense, but I do hear that one. But I like most of the people I've met out here. And how about the names of these towns?" They laughed, shouting out What Cheer, Pee-ru, Resume Speed and Montezuma which reminded them both of a stomach bug.

Richie had graduated from Marist College in upstate New York where education by the priests had turned him into an atheist.

"Hi, Richie, how's it going?" said Lacey by way of hello. "How are you doing with the Vista thing and the water project? Glad you want to be a part of this, whatever THIS is."

"Still trying to lose all my teeth so I can get them fixed for free at the hands of a student dentist," Richie laughed and showed her the missing front ones. He had lost almost all of his teeth and he was only twenty-seven.

"Come on, let's get this show on the road. No sense pussy footing around, except around a pussy!" His joke fell flat and the others ignored him. Velta rolled her eyes and stared into the bottom of the tub.

Denny was fidgeting with the silver peace symbol dangling from the chain around his neck. He seemed unable to sit still. He had obviously tie-dyed the cotton shirt he was wearing because the red sunburst in the middle of it was lopsided and off center like a runny fried egg.

Tom Loesser, a Peace Corps Volunteer just back from teaching farmers to rotate crops in the Philippines, came bounding up the stairs and took his place quietly on the floor next to Lacey. "I am really up for this and ready to hear how we get started." Tom wore khakis and a simple plaid shirt. He had a pack of Marlboros in his shirt pocket. That appealed to, Lacey, a fellow smoker. He had soft gray eyes, a high forehead underneath a wave of wiry blond curls and a shy, intelligent looking smile. He had a long face like the snout of a beagle.

Lacey looked up at Wayne who was standing up in the middle of the room. She was familiar with the paisley bandana that covered his balding pate to hold those long, blond locks to his head above the bushy, red sideburns. From time to time she had teased him about the color. "For Christ sake, you look like Emmet Kelly. All you need is a little grease paint and a three ring circus to make you happy."

Lacey knew Wayne came from a large Iowa farm family, from a much bigger farm than Doug's, in the much bigger town of Davenport. He talked to her about his parents, how they had raised corn and soy beans successfully for decades. She knew the Wagners, like other Iowa farmers, were generally more knowledgeable about the statistics of agribusiness and weather predictions than the average farmer on the East Coast. When it came to the politics of war and gender issues, they were purposely uninformed and conservative.

She remembered the day Wayne told her. "When I received my draft notice, I immediately stepped forward without fear to speak to the draft board. "I am a homosexual, or gay, or whatever you want to call it, and have always been. I was immediately let go. Hearing the news for the first time, my parents were at first stunned, then horrified, and ultimately banned me from the house. That's why I want to start this commune. So I can have a real home."

"Okay, everybody. I think we are all here for the same reason. We want to live together intelligently, communally and in peace with our neighbors and the world. So we need to find a place here in Des Moines to do that.

People are beginning to do this in other parts of the country. Lacey and I have seen some of these pop up in our travels recently."

"It is kind of a far out idea for this hick town" said Denny. Don't we need to "advertise" (he made quotes with his fingers in the air) who we think we are with a motto or a mission statement or something?" No one jumped in right away.

Then Doug said "we haven't even found a place to live yet. When we do, how about something a bit more traditional? We could hang out a sign at our place that says 'Our Home in the City.'"

"Come on, Doug, that's too staid. You're the big risk taker around here. Don't you want a name that makes clear who we are?"

The verbal combat continued until Velta who had been sitting quietly in the tub, entered the fray.

"Frankly, I don't give damn what we're called since I don't know how long I'll stay. So call it whatever you want," she said, her level of commitment sounding shaky.

Finally, Tom Loesser burst forth "I think bold is beautiful so why not go with H.O.U.S.E, House Of Unusual Sense and Excellence?"

Richie concluded the meeting with, "I think Doug and Lacey should find us a nice big house, close in town and cheap so we can all fit into it safely with a big common room where we can all eat together."

That night, following the meeting, the future commune converts sealed the deal with pizza, beer and brownies that Wayne had made after trading his homemade leather jewelry for some vintage Mexican weed. Everyone got sleepy after dinner except for Doug and Lacey who didn't want dessert. The others left one by one. Wayne fell asleep in the tub after Lacey threw a blanket over him.

Lacey and Doug were hungry for something else. They moved from the living room to a corner in Wayne's bedroom. They could hear Wayne snoring and chuckled knowing he would sleep long past dawn.

It was 2:30 in the morning. A chorus was snoring in the other room. They were in Wayne's sleeping bag. Doug began gently stroking Lacey's shoulders, moving down her back with a soft, firm hand. Though she was half asleep she could feel him rising firmly against her back side. It was delicious and new again and worth the wait if this was for real.

H.O.U.S.E Plans

"The place has got to be big enough for people to come and go easily and for room to grow our numbers if that happens," Doug said as they finished looking at a house on the outskirts of Des Moines that looked more like a Quonset hut than a home. "And we need a sense of style, a place where we can be creative," Lacey said.

The group had written a kind of collective manifesto on the requirements of the living arrangement they were about to undertake. On a single sheet of paper Doug had typed out the rules of engagement with carbon copies for everyone:

- Get a house with multiple bedrooms and a garage.
- Gather a group of people with complimentary skills, goals and life-philosophies.
- Have a sign-up sheet for chores week to week and month to month.
- Maintain a rule of egalitarianism.
- Believe in the benefits of "intentional communities".

At first glance the words seemed a little lofty to Lacey but she stood by her man's printed edict. She had learned a lot about Iowa in her short and recent time in Des Moines, not just about her comrades and the new way they were going to live collectively, but about life in the Midwest in general.

The houses were so different from the houses back home, many of them built long before Iowa became a state in 1848, some in the 1700's. Back home she lived with her father in her grandmother's mansion. It had three floors, maids' quarters and a dumb waiter from the second floor the basement. It had high boys and a chaise lounge right out of a French Impressionist painting. There were three garages and her father had made a putting green outside in the turn-around gravel driveway. He put a flag in the hole in the middle of the grass.

In Iowa, the homes were most often ranch style. Three bedrooms, one bathroom, all on one level, with maybe, or maybe not, a garage. And there homesteads, too, recently established by a company in Iowa, that was developing trailer park style homes for the cheap new home buyer.

She wondered how she could bring a little of Boston's charm to this place where she was about to live next. Would this living experiment have been better in Boston? Should she quit and go home before she was in over her head? Part of her wanted to be part of the action but a part of her really wasn't sure.

One day Doug and Lacey found themselves in the heart of downtown Des Moines not far from the university on 7th Street. They had seen an ad in the Des Moines Register that very morning: *Seven bedrooms, two baths, dining room, living room, eat-in kitchen, finished basement on one acre of land. Widowed owner tired of upkeep. No hippies, please.*

They found the chalk colored, ramshackle mansion, circa 1870, with good plumbing pretty close to perfect for the group's needs. The only potential problem was the landlord who liked the idea of young married folks in his house, but not students, drop outs or activists, though he did not use those words. They finished up a tour of the house that had five bedroom on the second floor, room for a bedroom in the basement and a whole attic that was as large as an apartment. Lacey knew exactly who would want to take over the third floor. They stood on the steps of the pavement just beyond the steps that led to the front porch of the house. The landlord was taking down the FOR RENT sign.

"You're a nice young couple, not like those hippies who don't wash their hair. You'll want to have a family by and by like we did. My wife has been gone now these three years, God rest her soul, and the house has been empty and needs repair. You'll fix it up from time to time and mow the grass on a regular basis?" Mr. Hilgendorf half- asked, shaking hands and accepting the first month's rent of $150.

"I must tell you, Mr. Hilgendorf, this spring I am afraid you may be reading about me in the paper."

"I knew it, you and the wife are movie stars and you're making a movie here in Des Moines."

"Not exactly." Lacey whispered, giving Doug a look that said not to go on, to tell the landlord anymore, to let him think they were film makers. But he persisted.

"No, I am fighting a court case that's been brought against me and guys like me all over the country."

"You famous or something? Evade your taxes? He looked up at the house for a moment, then said: "You're not one of them damn protesters that know nothing and talk too much?"

"No, but I did protest." Doug was not going to elaborate but he wanted to be truthful. Lacey did not think the truth would serve them well.

"My three sons all served in the military, two before this war and the eldest just after the Korean War."

"I am sure they served our country well," she said, trying to end the conservation.

"Those damn kids are ruining everything. Not letting our president protect our people. That concert last August in the mud in New York State with drugs, the rock and roll and the naked people was a ruination. The country's gone to the dogs. I never seen anything like it.

"I can see you are concerned," Lacey stepped in, pulling on Doug's arm

"Thanks, Mr. Hilgendorf. We'll have the rent first of each month. And you'll let me know about the water bill. Thanks for your time." They shook hands with the landlord and watched as his 80-year old footsteps slowly carried him down the porch steps back to his car at the end of the street.

"I don't know how you kept a straight face," Lacey started in once they were inside H.O.U.S.E and out of earshot of Hilgendorf. "I just tried to follow your lead and not laugh. I kept thinking he would ask if we were married. We never mentioned the other five people who'll be in the house. Jesus, what will happen when he finds out? Or that we'll have an anti-war draft counselling office?"

"You'll see, Lacey, there are many men like him who need a little education about the goodness in people like us and others. You'll see. In the end we will educate him to a new way of looking at a new society."

"I dunno, Doug. He reminds me of Elmer Fudd. Looks just like that cartoon character with the grumpy face who scowls at the screen audience in his cap with its visor and his shot gun at his side. Not sure education's his game."

What they had just latched onto was a sprawling three story affair that had been built room by room over time in the early '30s as Hilgendorf could afford it. He had raised six kids there many years before in this family-friendly, suburban, neighborhood a mile from the center of downtown Des Moines. Gray-white aluminum siding the color of dirty snow covered the outside on all sides. It had no particular style except that it was truly rambling. Two sets of uneven planks led up to the front porch which was ample with wooden slats that that could buckle under too much weight.

The new roommates drew straws for room assignments. All agreed from the outset egalitarianism was a guiding H.O.U.SE principle.

Wayne drew the straw that assigned him to the attic. Even before he drew it, at first sight he saw the advantage of the top floor. It was one giant room stretching across the whole house with a high gabled roof that formed an inverted V. He took the poncho from his earlier digs and rehung it, minus the dart board, on the slanted roof over the double mattress where he would spend most of his time. In place of the dart board he hung a self-portrait sketched in charcoal. "Homage to me" to welcome visitors to the attic for a smoke or a salon.

Almost everyone Wayne encountered was invited to come and stay as long as they wanted, to listen to music and smoke a pipe or two. Homemade scented candles in tall brass candlesticks frequently lit up all night parties of mostly young gay men. It was a place of shelter for them.

The scent of the candles and the dope floated downstairs and lingered for days. Doug worried the cops might come and raid the attic for dope and illegal activity and that his case could be adversely affected.

" You know, Wayne, you may be having fun, but it's illegal fun, whether it's sex or drugs, and it could hurt all of us."

"Aw, Doug, you're just jealous, because you and Lacey don't do drugs and probably would have a lot more sex if you did," he said, blowing off Doug's concern.

The second floor had smaller rooms but more of them. There was one bathroom for all to share. There was a hook on the door with a painted sign that could be flipped to read, not men or women, but: HERE or NOT HERE, to reflect a genderless bathroom setting. There was an outhouse on the first floor just outside the kitchen by the back door with a shower for anyone who preferred to shower au naturel.

Luckily Doug and Lacey drew a kind of suite with two small rooms. These were at the back of the house on the second floor. They slept together in one room just big enough for a queen sized mattress on a floor covered in crumbling linoleum. The ceiling was so low Doug had to crouch to get into bed. There were two ceiling- to- floor windows that let in light very early in the morning because there were no shades and no curtains. A noisy radiator on one side of the bed cranked out heat at night overheating the sleeping couple sometimes waking them in the middle of the night. The walls were a kind of high glossy yellow after Doug gave them two coats of paint.

Lacey had asked for, and gotten, tangerine for the outer room. She did not get the other thing she asked for. One day, before they moved in into H.O.U.S.E., while they were looking for a couch for the living room, at the Salvation Army thrift store they found a piece of furniture they agreed they must have: A very large, wooden, roll-top desk.

It stood nearly five feet tall at the back, all blond mahogany on the sides with little flecks of light and dark embedded in the wood. Lacey was certain the desk was an antique and claimed it smelled like old wood and polishing oil. Doug researched it and found it had probably been made in the 1890's. The top could roll down to close the desk and just as easily recoil back like an accordion collapsing into itself. Inside the desk were a series of little boxes, two rows of them, inviting spaces that could store pencils or paper clips or erasers or buttons or spools of thread or sewing needles.

"This will look great in my office. It'll take up most of the space, which is good, because my clients will know I mean business."

"I think it would be much better up here in our room. I could use it as my special place for writing, paying, bills and a whole host of my favorite things. And when I roll the top down all the messiness will be safe inside."

"Come on, Lacey. You don't need a desk. You can write anywhere. I've seen you do it, on napkins, notes and legal pads at the dining room table."

"That's not the point," Lacey said, with an edge to her voice. You have your office. I need my own space. And the desk should be for me."

What she didn't know at the time, and couldn't say, was that the choice of who got the desk was really about something else.

That night, after dinner, she was sitting on the front porch in a second-hand rocking chair, one of two she and Richie had bought at the nearby

Salvation Army store. Richie came out of the house to join her. He lit a cigarette and sat down in the second rocker, sensing Lacey had something to say.

"You know, Richie, I'll be honest with you, that exchange today really bothered me." Of all the people in the commune next to Doug, she was closest to Richie. At times they could almost read each other's minds. Not this time.

"Okay, lady, what happened today? You look kind of blue."

"I don't know. We talked about the desk. Who should get it and why. We both made our case and I lost. I realize now I never made clear my real feelings about that piece of furniture. Wanting to have it was just symbol of what I have been feeling lately."

"Whoa, hold a minute, I don't get this. A desk as a symbol? It's just a dumb piece of furniture."

"I failed to make my real feelings known. What I was really feeling is that now that John and I are together, I feel a growing lack of equality in the relationship. What Doug wants comes first."

"You're making a big deal out of nothing."

"No, really. It was the same thing when we talked about children. He once asked me if I would ever get pregnant just so a guy would marry me. I said nothing when I should have screamed: "Are you kidding? That would be the farthest thing from my mind ever. Where I come from we don't do things like that!" Now I'm kicking myself and wandering what other times I have given over to silent submission."

"That's heavy stuff, Lace," Richie blew a double ring of smoke and went to get another glass of wine because he did not know what to say to his friend.

At the front of the second floor there were two large rooms with big windows that looked out on the street. Velta lived alone in the room on the left and came and went quietly to her job as a waitress. She held frequent feminist meetings there with friends on her days off, trying to educate the other waitresses as to their rights as women. She had even marched in a few demonstrations. The other room was vacant to accommodate visitors.

One night Lacey and Velta were on duty in the kitchen. It was their turn to make dinner.

"What the hell is moo-saka?" Velta challenged. She watched Lacey whisk the milk into sauce, spooning the finished product carefully between the layers of meat, eggplant and tomato sauce. "Is the 'moo' part from a cow, or what?" Said Velta turning her nose up at the unfamiliar dish.

It's a favorite dish in Greece, although it may have come via Turkey or Lebanon."

"Favorite dish in Greece," mimicked Velta, copying Lacey's voice and tone.

"Look, I'm not trying to impress you. I am just making dinner. I learned this recipe while on vacation in the Peace Corps."

"Maybe I should find a Greek wine to go with this," Velta shot back.

"Hey, c'mon, just because you're the resident feminist doesn't mean you have to give me a hard time."

"Lacey, you don't know anything about feminism. You cling to your man, ride on the back of his motorcycle and make his moo-saka-ah. What do you know about women's rights anyway? If you grew up with a mom who had to be the bread winner, you'd understand."

Now Lacey was mad. "I didn't grow up with a mother and had to fend for myself, so just shut up about women's rights. I've been on my own for a long time."

Lacey was still way too traditional and too much of a free spirit to find Velta's sarcasm anything more than merely annoying, but she was willing to co-exist with her as a housemate. However, she frequently reminded her and others at H.O.U.S.E: "I am not ready to join the movement, burn my bra, or go without one for that matter, or to stop shaving my legs and armpits."

On the first floor beyond the front door through the foyer, past Doug's office, was the dining room. Wayne and Doug found two large wooden doors discarded by neighbors, linked them together and placed cinder blocks underneath at each corner. The table sat two feet above the floor so diners could sit on the floor crossed-legged and eat Japanese style. It could seat as many as twenty on multi-colored cushions of all shapes and sizes and remnants of old couch cushions from Goodwill. The gentle beige walls suffered greatly from dinner guests who left their mark on them with painted signs and sayings based on their political persuasions or none. "Mankind must end war or war will put an end to mankind- JFK" leapt out of the wall in purple chalk at one end. Near the window big black letters warned diners: "in war truth is the first casualty." Plastic stars hung down from the ceiling on long thin threads, just high enough above the table so as not to distract people from exotic nightly dinners.

Dinner conversation might be low-level or lofty. Doug might engage a visitor in a conversation about "intentional communities," or Lacey might be heard defending the "Sounds of Silence." Simon and Garfunkel could start a dinner debate.

"Hey, baby, life's too short to sweat and fear," Wayne declared one night when Lacey started an album on the Victrola. Those whiny songs of "S and G," were Lacey and Richie's favorites. "I hate that urban angst thing. Homeward bound, the railway station, cigarette in hand, who cares? Whan, whan whan."

"Hey, I cry every time I hear Bridge over Troubled Water. She would begin singing: *sail on silver girl, sail on by. Your time has come….*" Richie joined her, though he couldn't carry a tune and didn't cry.

"Jeez, Lacey, how can you stand that stuff? Those guys are so depressing. 'And all the towns look the same to me, the cigarettes and magazines, hmm.' Reminds me of us on the road in Michigan. Don't you want to get away from that?" Wayne did a pretty good mimic of Paul Simon but Lacey was quick with a comeback.

"Wayne, you are a musical clod with no taste for poetry or great lyrics. "Slow down, you move too fast. You got to make the morning last.' Happy and gorgeous words about how to live life! So shut up already."

This could go on for hours about what was wrong with Judy Collins that she didn't write songs or that Wayne thought Bob Dylan had a lousy voice and that Joni Mitchell screeched through every song. Doug liked to listen to their frequent banter at the dinner table that made him laugh and took his mind off more serious matters.

The H.O.U.S.E nicknamed Denny Mr. Tie-dye. Although he was a VISTA volunteer, he became better known as the artist in residence because of the number of hours he spent and the methods he used tie-dying his many tee shirts. At dinner he would explain, ad nauseam, just how to make them.

"First you soak your shirt in a tub of sodium carbonate in water for an hour. Next you roll your wet shirt into one of several designs. You can knot, pleat or swirl your shirt into a shape to be tie-dyed like this," Denny said, turning his hands to show tablemates just how to do it. "Or you can place rubber bands around a shirt length-wise to create stripes. Next you put on rubber gloves like these, then mix the dyes...."

"Ah c'mon, Denny," Lacey interrupted, "you don't expect us to learn how to do that? I can't do any more than hem a skirt and you want me to dye a shirt?

Sometimes at dinner he extolled the virtues of another one of his talents, his recipe for recycling blue jeans into the popular pinto pants. H.O.U.S.E members often referred to him, not in his presence, as Denny the Dandy.

His tie-dying turned out to be no joke. Denny was tall and scrawny and rail thin probably because he liked certain drugs that left him without much appetite. Or maybe he didn't like the rich meals prepared at H.O.U.S.E. He had a small head covered in sandy orange hair and not much of it. He never mentioned what he had studied in college. But he was smart and artsy-crafty and in love with Velta from the day he met her. As it turned out, when Denny and Velta got together, at first it was all about sex. But later they would flourish in the clothing and tailoring business. With Velta's skills as a seamstress and Denny's talent for tie-dying in the 1970's the Constant Tailor would become a thriving and successful business in downtown Des Moines with branches in Ames and Iowa City.

H.O.U.S.E was off to a pretty civil and committed start.

Visitor

"Sure, we're happy to have you stay," Lacey said, giving the stranger the usual reply as the man pulled his travel bag through the screen door. The screen was beginning to rip and fray from the multiple visitors who stopped or stayed at the now locally famous digs.

"I'm a friend of Steve Bingham's," he said. "He went to Yale and I went to Harvard, but we were interested in many of the same things. I know he's never been here, but one of his friends said you're doing good things and would be open to my staying for a few days. I need to learn how the people in Iowa feel about what's going on in the nation."

Lacey offered him some Kool-Aid, took his bag, and, finally, asked for his name. Then she let him know that she was Lacey Rogers, married to Doug. The man had heard of Doug's case. Lacey saw that he was attractive: tall, thin and preppy looking in his corduroy jacket and jeans. She was pleased to have someone new to talk to from outside her limited circle. Like her father, Lacey "never met a stranger."

"Fred Slaughter," he replied. Then he added with a laugh, "Actually Frederick Elliot Slaughter, III. I guess I can't escape that." Lacey caught the phrase, recognized the familiar easy banter of one preppy talking to another. She instantly felt comfortable in his presence.

She invited him to join the housemates for dinner and took him to the attic to show him a free couch that could double for a bed. When he said no thanks to an offer of marijuana from Wayne in the attic, she liked him all the more. At dinner that night, she introduced Fred to the commune over wine and lasagna. Everyone was anxious to talk about the Chicago Seven, Steve Bingham's escape from the States to Canada, and Doug's upcoming trial.

Fred turned to Doug and asked bluntly, "So what are your chances of beating this?"

Doug, with measured his words, began slowly. "I'm trying to win my case on a technicality. It's not possible to win on the moral ground it deserves. I'm claiming that the date when I was considered draftable should have been based not on the day I received the notice—which took a long time because I was already in the Peace Corps in La Paz, Bolivia—not on the day it was sent. The case might be a little thin, but my lawyer says it's my best hope. I hate being prevented from pleading the real case, though—resisting the draft altogether or going all out like The Seven."

After the others retired from the table Fred pulled the pillow he was sitting on closer to the table. Lacey was sitting next to Doug, watching him play with the candle that was burning low over the wine bottle.

"Man, that seems like a tough one," Fred mused. "I've kind of decided to quit the bullshit and to give up trying to change the system. The only person I can change is myself. That's why I choose to leave the whole thing behind."

She had no idea what Fred was talking about, but she was intrigued.

"Right now I'm still the chair of the Sociology Department at a university back in Boston, where I've taught for the past ten years, but I'm thinking of leaving. That's why I'm out here. I need to feel the mood of other people, people who might be disillusioned like me with the system and the men running our country and our lives."

He launched into the story of his life, explaining why he was contemplating such a dramatic transformation at the age of forty-two.

"I've pretty much seen it all and tried everything," he told them. "I'm not bored, but I'm looking for a new path. In some ways I think music, theater, art, The Beatles, Picasso—they can all change the world more than the legislators in Congress. You know," he added suddenly, "I participated in those 'clinical experiments' at Harvard. They were definitely research, if not exactly clinical. I was one of about a hundred graduate students who took LSD to test its effects. And it changed my life."

At this point, Doug yawned, signed off and went to bed. He didn't believe in the use of drugs or anything more than an occasional beer. But Lacey was all ears.

"I'm developing the idea that the personal is the political—that our domestic arrangements and our foreign policy are the inside and outside of the same phenomenon. I believe there really is a connection between social ills and the average citizen's lack of involvement in the community."

Bingo! Lacey felt an instant connection to this man. She believed that things personal influenced views social and political. She was living in this place and this community because of Doug not because of her dislike of the government or even of the draft. She was only now coming to personally understand the wrongness of war that she would never have learned on her own, without Doug.

"Good night and see you in the morning," She wanted to hold this man close, be a part of him, to make him a part of her. It was more than just a physical desire drawing her to him; it was a real longing to get inside his head, his body, his mind, his spirit. She wanted to know why he wanted to leave behind the tug and turmoil of academic society. Wasn't that a selfish act? Wasn't Doug's struggle a more noble fight? She almost felt sick at the forces fighting inside her to make sense of both of these men.

Slowly, she forced herself to pull away and blew out the candle as Fred was telling her about his next endeavor. "I'm working on a book called *The Pursuit of Loneliness*. It's about what I've learned, and I hope it will be a relevant critique of America today. I'm going to try to lead the rest of my life based on what I've learned, outside society's ills as I see them."

Lacey took in those last words, scrambled them in her head as she climbed the stairs to bed and thought *that was a really odd and selfish thing to say. Whoever really lives outside of society's ills unless he's a hermit or Jesus or-- a criminal?*

Lacey crawled into bed feeling distant from Doug right next to him in the back room on the second floor. Her whole body felt heavy from the weight of the evening's discussion. She couldn't sleep. Unclear emotions bombarded her senses making her feel the way she did after taking one of those diet pills. The speed would race through her brain and body causing, like now, distortion in her thinking. Was she a dreamer like Fred or a realist here in this situation? Up to now life at H.O.U.S.E, the characters that inhabited the place, living among them, had been purely a fun trip. Now things were getting harder. There were choices to be made. If Doug went to prison the couple might actually have to live a life *outside society* when he got out. Felons can't vote. No insurance. No job. A husband labelled as a criminal. Could she face all of that? Possibly handle it alone? Dawn was breaking when she finally closed her eyes. Fred Slaughter would be gone before the sun or anyone else was up.

The next day marked a full month since the big move into H.O.U.S.E. Everyone agreed there should be a celebration of the date to mark living together happily in the new digs. A vote was taken and it was decided the event called for pizza from the local Italian restaurant run by the resident mafia boss in Des Moines. Lacey was glad Fred was not there.

Richie arrived with the wine and beer just as the three large oversized pepperoni combos arrived. Everyone plunked down around the dining room table sitting yoga style. Denny sat next to Velta on one side of the table, Richie and Lacey and Tom plopped down opposite them, and Wayne and Doug took their places at each end of the table.

"Let's have a toast, to honor our united front against the war and for a new and excellent, free society," Richie proposed. Every glass held high had a different shape: a jam jar, a sugar bowl, a peanut butter jar, a Mason jar, a creamer, and a coffee cup. Just like the characters at the table. All different shapes and sizes, hearts and minds.

All of a sudden Lacey burst into a mock rendition of the Mouseketeers' closing song: "Now it's time to say goodbye to all our company…." Lacey made a super cute smiley face like Karen, wiggling fake ears and indicating Wayne should join her as Cubby. Together they crooned: HOU- See YOU real soon! Then "SEY," adding the Y to make the song work out: "Why? Because we like you! H-O-U-SE!" Lacey ended the toast with "and that's us, *Housemates Of Unusual Sense and Excellence* here at H.O.U.S.E," light hearted but earnestly serious about the group. Over time the housemates would replace the word *housemates* with the word *hippies* as they got comfortable with the new age moniker.

Before the evening closed, the group took time to set up H.O.U.S.E rules. Beyond the collective commitment to activism and service, there were practical chores to be decided upon by mutual consent. Each member paid $50 a month for rent and utilities plus $20 for the telephone and utilities. There was a weekly collection for food by the person in charge of shopping for the month. There was a sign-up sheet posted by the member in charge of dinner for the coming week asking for menu suggestions. There were two well stocked refrigerators marked CARNIVORES and VEGETARIANS. The kitchen also had two yogurt makers for those who wanted either organic or regular.

Part of the upfront agreement of anyone joining the band of roommates at H.O.U.S.E was that everyone should contribute a personal "talent" or skill to the betterment of the whole group. That could be for a month or a year. Doug was responsible for paying bills and Lacey was chosen the best person to communicate with Elmer Fudd on most occasions. Others volunteered for trash duty or mowing the lawn. One person became the resident yogurt maker.

During the dinner Elmer Fudd stopped by to collect the next month's rent, referring to the group as his "young squatters." Lacey was gentle but firm when she handed him the check Doug had written earlier that day anticipating the landlord's unannounced visit: "Hey, Mr. Fudd, don't you know we're legit? We pay up and on time."

"Okay, but don't you forget my name is not Elmer Fudd," he shouted back. "It's Marion, Marion Hilgendorf," came floating off his tongue through the front screen door. "Family's German." Whoever'd name a guy *Marion*? She wondered every time he came to the front door, though she never said so out loud. Besides, he was almost too deaf to listen to what she had to say about anything. She preferred to refer to him as Elmer.

The Sentence

Doug sat alone in his office with Chez Guevara looking down on him from the poster on the wall. The afternoon sun was streaming through the front windows blinding Doug's eyes as he sat in his chair, his back turned away from the huge roll top desk. It was a lazy day, warming toward spring at the end of March. Everyone was out somewhere and he was alone in the house, feeling alone in many ways.

Lacey parked the Ghia and raced up the front steps of H.O.U.S.E to the rickety porch, let the screen door slam and burst into Doug's office.

"Betcha you have been thinking about me," she joked, "sitting alone here. Did you miss me?" Lacey asked playfully.

As soon as she saw the downcast eyes, she cut short her little flirtation.

"In truth, I have been thinking about you, about the way you are an asset in my life, feeling that I have so little to offer you now that things have come to a head.

Lacey slunk down in the seat reserved for clients to the right of the desk. As she moved, her shadow fell across Doug's sun-filled face, making him look all the more gloomy. She felt his mood and knew he was thinking about the trial set for the next day.

✦

March twenty-fourth. United States District Court for the Southern District of Iowa. Lacey and Richie and Wayne walked up the grand marble staircase and proceeded to the main courtroom on the second floor. The floor of the judge's chamber was pink marble, the walls were plastered gray to look like marble but didn't. The judge's bench sat on top of a slab of pink marble. Behind it was an alcove where lawyers could meet during interruptions in a trail or over disagreements. Lacey noticed the trash cans in the room were full and the room smelled of must and mayhem.

She had picked her outfit carefully for the day. She had given up pleated skirts in favor of bell bottoms. In fact, she mostly wore the pair Velta had made for her out of an American flag she had ordered from a catalogue.

Lacey liked the way the stars fell across her thighs. Today, however, she brought out the kilt, the Peter Pan collared shirt, held together at the top with a circle pin, the circle being a symbol in boarding schools back East of the wearer's virginity. *Oh well, she thought, it can't hurt.*

Lacey and Wayne and Richie sat up front on the left just behind Doug's lawyer, Gary Price. "The court will now come to order," the judge intoned with one loud bang of the gavel.

The three communards sat mute on the edge of their seats like the miniature monkey sculptures of hear-no-evil-see no-evil-say-no evil, praying for the best, fearing the worst. Wayne wore his everyday leather chaps and Glen Campbell fringed suede jacket. He constantly stroked his newly grown Fu Manchu mustache, making sure the hairs were straight and of equal length on both sides of his chin. Richie had on the same jeans he never washed and the red bandana, a signature necktie of sorts. He cracked his knuckles as if he were about the play the piano but never got started. Lacey was irritated by the nasty sound, afraid he judge could hear the crunching and gave Richie a look that said "shut up or else…!"

"Do you think he has a chance at this point?" Lacey whispered to Wayne. "The judge was Republican appointed, and, I have heard, is pro war."

The arguments were in. Gary had pleaded that Doug's draft notice should have been valid from the day he received it, not the day it was sent."

I don't know, Lace. The argument's a little thin. Doug did leave the States knowing he was 1-A. And the judge will site that," Wayne said unable to give solace.

Lacey looked around the courtroom to distract her thoughts from Wayne's reality check.

Everywhere was dark wood. The walls were wood, the tables and chairs for witnesses and visitors were wood. The witness box was wood. Much like a prison, Lace imagined. A place of monotony.

"Don't worry, Lacey," Richie consoled her, "they're not going to screw Doug by putting him in jail for a long time. Buck up, you'll see, things will be okay." Wayne wanted to believe what he was saying.

"Come on, Richie, what the Hell do you know? It's happened to others like David Harris and Joan Baez. I heard it took Harris three years to get out of jail."

There was a hush as the judge began to speak. "The Court has carefully examined and considered all of the grounds on which the defendant bases his motion for acquittal and finds them to be wholly without merit. The defendant, a well- educated individual, was fully aware of the requirements of the law and was accorded every procedural right available to him. In spite of this, the defendant chose to violate the law by refusing to submit to induction. The Court, therefore, finds the defendant, Douglas Rogers, guilty as charged in Count I of the indictment. Defendant will remain at liberty on his present bond pending the completion of a presentence investigation, after which defendant will be ordered to appear for sentencing."

But the conviction left room for an appeal, which might take a long time. Could that mean years. Years more could waste the important years of their lives. Free until then, but uncertain of their time together, they grew closer, as on this day in the quiet light of afternoon in Doug's office.

"You know, if I go to prison, for however long, you should be free of me, free to go, to be with someone far less encumbered than a so-called criminal," he said trying to be realistic and loving at the same time. He stroked Lacey's right arm as he talked and she kept it outstretched to him on the desk catching his fingers in hers as she listened.

"Look we can fight this together," she said, not really knowing what else to say, or if she believed her own words.

"You know, I can feel my optimism shrinking like dried fruit after the peach has had its day in the sun," Lacey broke a smile at this attempt at hyperbole. "I am not sure, now, if I am doing the right thing. I feel less certain each day. Distant from others, event from you." She rose to come nearer, kiss his lips gently and hold him, but he turned away, his feelings confused, dead matter inside him.

The words cut into her heart. Doug was losing confidence, in his case, in himself, in her and in their relationship.

"I can tell you are feeling abandoned by the courts by, by others who wanted to take your stand and didn't, by Gary who hasn't won your case, maybe even by all of us at H.O.U.S.E. You must not think like that. Never. Not one day." She wanted to sound emphatic and convincing but sensed she was merely coming across as dramatic.

"I like your passion, babe, but I am not sure you are on point. You may love me but that won't make it happen."

Just then, to break the intensity, Lacey started humming, then singing softly, the words of Joni Mitchell,

> *Oh, but now old friends they're acting strange,*
> *They shake their heads, they say I've changed*
> *Well something's lost, but something's gained*
> *In living every day.*
>
> *I've looked at life from both sides now*
> *From win and lose and still somehow*
> *It's life's illusions I recall*
> *I really don't know life at all.*

"A song doesn't do it for me, Lace. I am so much more guarded than you. It's much harder for me to reach my emotions and now they all seem to be leaving me. I had this feeling once before, when my mom died. I was sixteen and couldn't understand what was happening. And now I am grieving all over again a dead hollow pit inside me"

She wanted to do something, anything to ease his pain. Make love. Go for a bike ride. Run for a mile side by side.

Just then the phone rang, interrupting Lacey's attempt to change the mood.

"Hi, Dad. How's the new girlfriend? Doug tried to be upbeat. "I am so glad you have found someone to keep you company on the farm. She seemed nice enough when I met her. Not as big a talker as Mom was, or Lacey, here, but maybe that's a good thing."

"So, how are you doing son?" Hiram had been anxious for Doug every day since the trial.

"I don't know, Dad. I am not sure what I have done. Or if any of it will make a difference. I can't stop the war, all I can do is to try to keep others from having to go over there. But my chances of making a difference seem to be narrowing every day. It's hard for me to admit but I am sacred of being put away, my future shut down. Only now am I coming to realize that probability."

"Have faith son," was all Hiram Rogers could muster. And then he changed gears. "You've got that nice Lacey there with you. She'll cheer you up. I recall she tends to break into song every now and then just to keep you in good humor."

Doug put down the phone. A late afternoon shade was crawling into the sun's space. He pulled Lacey out of her chair and onto his lap. He stroked her hair, her cheeks, gently, as if for the first time. He could feel her warmth, even the restless energy in her body and it strengthened him, made him want her right there on the rug in the office.

Forgetting the sad thoughts of the day, he pushed the bell-bottoms down over her hips. She let him undress her, pulling the T shirt over her head, kissing her breasts as he inched her body down onto the rug. The rug was scratchy, some harsh Bolivian cloth but she didn't care. They kissed hard and rolled over each other until Doug was on top and inside her. He moved slowly, masterfully and Lacey knew making love was the panacea for the day. They came long and slowly and almost together, Doug first and Lacey catching Doug for the last of the pleasure together. Luckily the house was still empty, silently smiling on their stolen moment.

"Hey, do you realize we are lying on top of an American flag," she said, breaking the silence with a laugh. "Damn, that's right. We could get you arrested for defaming the flag, let alone wearing it," He joined in the joke.

They lay there content on the office floor until they heard the faint sounds of Doug's motor cycle out back. Wayne had borrowed it for the day. A late afternoon shade was beginning to crawl into the sun's space. A flag had lifted Doug's spirits.

Richie's Way

Lacey was reading a copy of Fannie Farmer's Cookbook at the kitchen table one morning when Ritchie came in looking for a beer.

By mutual agreement the kitchen was set up to accompany all kinds of gourmands and just plain eaters. There were two refrigerators. The sign on one read OLIVIA- VEGETARIANS ONLY. Inside were all kinds of vegetables sitting randomly on the shelves between cartons of raw, unpasteurized milk and plastic cups of yogurt flavored with vanilla or maple syrup. There were radishes, corn from Doug's family farm, celery, peppers in several colors from the garden out back, heads of garlic and broccoli, all staring at whoever opened the door looking to forage. Inside there was a blender full of carrot juice, a bottle of cider vinegar, jars of Green Goddess dressing, bottles of oil in different colors next to several canned beers and squares of cheese and mozzarella balls wherever there was an open space. The bottom tray harbored oranges, lemons, a pomegranate, whose origins were unknown to most in the commune and half of a very brown, unwrapped, overripe avocado.

The second refrigerator was OWEN, marked CARNIVORES ONLY. There were tubes of bologna and liverwurst, an opened can of spam, packets of hot dogs, several packs of bacon, leftover moussaka, a packet of chicken thighs in the freezer with several T.V. dinners. A dozen farm-fresh pork cutlets had recently been provided by Doug's dad and were waiting to be grilled by Wayne that night at the upcoming backyard party. The bottom half held bottles of wine, beer, hard cider, catsup, cranberry sauce, large jars of fresh sweet pickles brought in by Doug's sister-in-law, Thelma, the one and only time she came to visit H.O.U.S.E.

Richie opened OLIVIA and grabbed a Budweiser.

"Don't you think noon it's a little early to start?" Lacey said.

"Naw, it takes the edge off the night before. Have one, Lacey. It'll put hair on your chest," Ritchie deadpanned.

"Just what I need. No thanks. Here, read this for me. So I can get started.

Ritchie popped off the cap of the beer with his one good, front, tooth that made Lacey wince. "Ouch! Damn, you really do want a new set of pearls. Start here at the top of the page."

"'Indian pudding might not be pretty, but few New England desserts can rival its claim to fame as the most comprehensive of our regional sweet dishes. It evolved out of an initial British culinary tradition, which was then enhanced by Native American influence and finally, flavored with the fruits of New England commerce.' What kind of bullshit language is that?"

"Don't be so harsh. That sounds great to me," she said backing off slightly. " The mother of a friend of mine back home used to make it."

"You gotta be kidding, Lace. You think some dumb pudding is going to remind us of the Indians? You're a city girl, not a Pilgrim. Hostess Twinkies and ice cream would go over better with this crowd."

She took the cookbook out of Ritchie's hands. "It's made with cornflakes and molasses with a thin lemon sauce. It says right here, one quart of milk, and four cups of cornflakes. How hard could that be? God knows we eat enough of those around here. Corn flakes are boring by themselves. You just add a half a cup of molasses, a teaspoon each of salt and cinnamon, bake at 350 for an hour and…voila!"

"Voila, yourself," Richie mimicked Lacey. I'd say, keep the cornflakes for breakfast."

"Okay, okay, have it your way." Lacey liked Richie too much to argue over dessert. She closed the cookbook and put it down on the table. "Come on. Let's go to the supermarket and scare up some grub for tonight."

They headed to the local Hy-Vee in Wayne's beat up red pickup truck. Carol King was singing on the radio "you make me feel like a nat-ur-al woman," Lacey sang along with Carol until Richie interrupted her. "You know, Lacey, Janis has so much more soul. You gotta come hear her with me one day."

"Anything you say, my friend. Just know I love them all. Carol King, Janis Joplin, Joni Mitchell, Judy Collins, Dione Warwick, the Singing Nun and Kate Smith. Can't disappoint me with any of those great ladies—I mean women."

"You made your point, bitch." He turned the volume down to listen to Lacey hum the rest of the song.

H.O.U.S.E loved the Hy-Vee because it was an employee-owned supermarket where the workers shared in the company profits. Doug certainly felt that was a proper way for businesses to operate and Lacey agreed.

Richie chose to park very near the front of the store although it was hard for the truck to squeeze into a space more suited for cars than a big boxy vehicle. Lacey questioned why they had to be so close and wondered why he was carrying a blanket over his shoulder when the air was warm.

Inside the store Lacey headed for the molasses and an extra box of corn flakes and fresh lemons to make the syrup for the Indian pudding. Richie went for the potato chips, pretzels and packets of onion soup and sour cream to make the dip to go with wine and beer.

Half an hour later they met at the checkout counter. In addition to the pudding items, Lacey had filled her cart with flour, sugar, salt and other bulk staples needed to stock the H.O.U.S.E pantry. Richie had dumped the chips and pretzels in her cart and had headed off down another isle.

When he came back, she gave Richie a look that meant she was ready to go. "You go ahead and check out. I'll be right behind you," he smiled back. The checkout was always easy and friendly at the Hy-Vee.

Lacey proceeded to the parking lot and started to put the supplies in the back of the truck. As she finished, she turned to see Richie coming toward her, his thin body swollen in his battered army jacket. The blanket was slung over his shoulder but it looked bigger. "Look here!"

He placed the blanket flat on the ground pulling his arm out slowly. He unzipped his jacket. On either side stuck in the sleeve and under his armpits were cans of tuna fish, spam and sardines. In his side pockets were slabs of bacon, jars of pickles and maraschino cherries. He dumped out his jacket onto the blanket. From his pant legs he wiggled out several onions and one large sweet potato.

"What?" said Lacey, stunned at the stolen goods on the ground next to the truck.

"Whaddya mean 'what'?" Richie echoed. They're not going to miss a few potatoes or cans of tuna. Those Hy-Vee guys are nothing but corporate whores."

"I didn't get it. They don't deserved to be ripped off like this. Man you lost me on this one. God damn it! Are you crazy? I could have gotten caught with you. Not right. Not fair. I am mad as hell at you. She slammed the door of the passenger seat while pointing to Richie to get in the car and drive.

"I am sorry," he said, trying to calm her down. "I had no idea you would care or be so upset. I don't see it as so wrong to take a few things that won't be missed."

On the way home she wouldn't let go. "We don't rip off the good guys. Stealing is not a way to change the system. God damn, I am beginning to think you are just a free loader. You don't want to take care of, yourself, your teeth. You want to lose them all so some dental school will give you a free ride for new ones. That is fucking irresponsible, you moron."

She couldn't stop "Listen, man, I know about stealing and it is not a good way to go. Ever! When I was a teenager, feeling needy, I stole something big and when I got caught, I swore I'd never take anything from anyone ever again. I worry about you, Richie, getting caught in the future. Are you so needy that you feel compelled to steal and think you have the right to do so?

"Well, it's one way to change the corruption we live with," Richie said. He knew how mad she was and wanted desperately for her not to be angry.

"Well, it's not mine. I want to work toward change for our future not to tear down the entire system. That's way too far out for me."

Ritchie kept his hands on the wheel and his mouth shut the rest of the way home. Lacey sat in silence beside him. They both knew the closeness of their bond had taken a hit that day. They would have to work hard to heal the relationship going forward. But he commune was the glue that made that possible.

Hard Day at the Office

H.O.U.S.E. was a welcome walk-in for most of Doug's clients. They were young men, mostly just out of high school who had been drafted and who genuinely opposed the Vietnam War. Doug's office with the anti-war bumper stickers pinned to the bulletin board, a Bolivian poncho hanging on the wall and a funny looking coke machine instantly put budding dissidents at ease. Upon arrival they were greeted by Chez Guevara on the wall. Some knew who he was, some didn't, especially the farm kids.

"Hiya, how's it going?" Doug greeted them. "How can I help"? He knew how scared these young men were and he tried to put each one at ease from the start.

"My name is Lucas Wiley, sir. My number is so low I know they are coming to get me. I don't want to go. But I am scared. It's all wrong, you know. This country is breaking my heart. Lucas stammered as he spoke.

"First things first, my friend. Let's start with dropping the 'sir.' Just call me Doug."

"I don't want to be called no peacenik, but I will refuse to go. I'll go to Canada or Timbuctoo if I have to. Or prison."

Doug had a way of calming the fears of those who came for his help. He spoke slowly and listened carefully. He didn't want to scare clients with lawyer talk. He yearned not to just to help each young man but to change the system that made men go to war. He imagined a day when there would be peace again that he might run for Congress or the Senate. He believed in justice and the American way, Abe Lincoln and Mark Twain. His idealism was sound and unbridled, if somewhat diminished by circumstances. What gave him hope was counselling others the only way he knew how.

"We'll see what we can do. But it's up to you to choose. Where'd you say you are from?

"From Lucas, sir, I mean Doug. It's about an hour south of here. Population little more than 200. Lucas has two convenience stores and a Quilt With Us shop. But if you're looking for someone to quilt with, you're out of luck. The place is becoming a ghost town. It could disappear before I get done with this army thing," Lucas said, trying to make light to calm his nerves.

"Did you finish high school?" John was trying to gauge how to approach this case at the level Lucas would understand.

"Barely, but I got through. At first I wanted to sign up for the military so I could get more education. But when I got to the draft center here in Des Moines, I started to think about us killing all those Gooks over there and in my mind I saw those pictures in the papers. I got sick to my stomach right there and had to go outside to vomit."

"Pretty dramatic, I'd say. How did you find me?"

"When I got outside that day, there were a few people walking back and forth in front of the center carrying anti-war signs, "No, No We won't go." I met this guy named Tom Lesley or something like that with an L sound and he told me to come here."

"Tom Loesser. He lives here in the commune with us. Ex-Peace Corps."

"There are a number of things we can do. Together we can write letters to the draft board clearly stating your position. The letter will confirm your opposition to the war and that if drafted, prison would be a better choice than war. That is what you just said to me. Did you mean that?"

"Yes, I think so, because I feel sick when I think about killing someone."

"That usually works with the draft board unless the draftee is from a really small town in this state. Unfortunately, that applies to you. What do your parents say about all of this?" Doug wanted to know if he had support back home.

"Actually, it's just my grandmother and me. My parents were killed in a house fire on the farm when I was five. Grandma Wiley is a big Donna Reed fan and she started mothers against the war. So, yes, she is my best supporter."

"Did you try to get a deferment to take care of your grandmother?"

"They said it did not count because she is not my actual parent."

"Well, that's one down and several more games to play. And I do mean we will have to play some games.

"There's always the option to claim to be gay but for many that is unacceptable. Or one could become ill; develop ulcers after swallowing wads of tinfoil that could show up as ulcers on an x-ray. What do you say to that?"

"I don't know right now. I need some time to think, although I realize I have no time, really.

Doug felt like an unwitting priest, hearing confession from scared teenagers, absolving them of their guilt about not wanting to go to war. "In God We Trust." Only Doug didn't believe in God. Who should he tell them to trust?

Sometimes in the late afternoon Richie would wander into Doug's office when it was getting close to his cocktail hour, just to talk and ruminate with him. He would start gently with "How'd it go today? I heard you talking to that guy from Lucas?"

"Haven't you got something better to do around here than listening to me recite military rules and regs?" Doug teased.

"By the way, have you read that book I gave you, *Johnny Got his Gun* by Dalton

Trumbo? It's about a guy in a hospital who has lost his arms, legs, and all of his face. All he's got is his mind that still functions perfectly, leaving him a prisoner in his own body. His blob of

a brain winds up in a glass box and tours the country to show others the true horrors of war."

"Can't say that I have, Doug. But I've been meaning to talk to you."

"Hell of a read, Doug interjected. "I farm it out to all my clients in case any of them get cold feet about resisting to fight. I know you'd rather see a movie than read a book, right? There's talk of making it into a film next year."

"Ignoring Doug's comment Richie got right to his point. "You know, Doug, you may mean well, but you sound kind of stuck up or maybe a little 'holier than thou,' like you're talking down to these guys from some lofty place because you have been through it already, trying to break the system. Let each guy tell his whole story his way. I'm just trying to help, from my helpless point of view."

"Thanks, Richie, I'll take that under advisement. No doubt you have shared "this little wisdom" with Lacey, as well. Doug could be cold and shut off when taken to task.

Lots to Celebrate

One Saturday early in June the H.O.U.S.E. members decided it was time to celebrate their successful living experiment by announcing it to the neighborhood.

"I have this idea," Tom said, holding up a thin slab of wood into which he had carved H.O.U.S.E. in large, deeply cut block capital letters, each letter filled in with green paint. Green for the environment," Tom told the H.O.U.S.E members one morning in the dining room where several of them were reading the paper and drinking coffee.

"I didn't spend all that time in the Philippines making wood cuts not show you how great I am," he said with pride. "Denny, can you help me? Put up a ladder on that tipsy part of the porch in the middle, I can put up hinges and hang the new sign."

Up early the next morning, everyone ate cornflakes and yogurt, and took coffee outside to watch the hanging the sign. Families on the street were walking their children to Sunday services as a church bell rang in the distance.

"Glad to see you around in the neighborhood," shouted a man in a green leisure suit pushing a pram with a two year old.

"Glad I don't have to do church anymore," Doug whispered to Lacey. "We stopped going to church after Mom died. I think even Dad decided to give up on God,"

"I'm not so sure, Doug. Church is kind of a comforting place for me. Back home the church was always there for me, even when my family wasn't. That connection has always meant a lot to me, but I don't mean to get too serious." Not wanting to break the mood of the celebration, she left it at that.

"Hold it. Move a little to the right, Tom. That's it. Looking good," Doug was trying to be helpful. Tom was very proud of his creation.

"How about we add flower pots to the front porch on either side of the steps under the sign?" Wayne suggested.

"Now I know you're a fucking faggot, Wayne," yelled Tom. "What's wrong with just the sign? What's wrong with just plain green? Not colorful enough color for you? Go tie dye yourself someplace else!" All in good fun.

Just then Elmer Fudd showed up, beaming from ear to ear. "I like your style, there fellow, even though you been with them Filipinos. I'll forgive you. That's a damn nice sign. And you, Wayne Hippie, I like your idea about the flowers. Go ahead and dress the place up."

Wayne mounted the sign onto the prepared hooks high up in the center of the porch that formed the base of the second floor. "Welcome to H.O.U.S.E." There was laughter and clapping all round on the lawn from housemates and passersby. Even Elmer Fudd joined in.

✦━━━━❖━━━━✦

"Let's not wait for the judge's decision," Doug surprised Lacey one afternoon in the backyard while he was working on an antique car belonging to his dad that he had promised to repair. She was on the ground beside the car handing him each tool he needed for the repair.

"I am not sure which wrench you want." She said as she reached into to the tool box and pulled out the largest one.

Suddenly he crawled out from under the car, stood up and pulled her toward him. He kissed her head, careful not to touch her hair with his black greasy hands.

"No I mean it. Let's not wait for the judgment. Let's get married. Create our own celebration. I love you, Lace, and I want the world to know!"

She loved Doug surprising her and smiled up at him, kissing him and placing her hands in his until her fingers were black and greasy, too. She didn't care. Grease or grime, she loved this Iowa farmer and all he stood for with his life in play and in purpose. So what if he had to go to jail? There would be life after.

He kissed her again, holding her face between his hands. Black fingers appeared on her cheeks. "Now you've really done it. You've given me a black eye. I don't want to wash it off! Ever. I love you, too, my sweet mate."

"Did your father wear a wedding band?" Doug asked as he casually picked up the wrench from the ground where Lacey left it.

"Neither of us needs to wear a ring just to prove to the world we love each other," he said, assuming Lacey agreed with him.

His words stung. In that moment, she realized she had lost her chance to say what she really wanted: A WEDDING RING!

At her core she was a Yankee traditionalist, a woman who loved the lure of a good ritual, a fancy wedding, a Sunday morning communion in the Episcopal Church or big coming out parties. Her father had presented her to society in the grand ballroom of one of Boston's finest hotels. Lacey was one of 100 girls listed on the *Bird's List*, the genteel and coveted circle of girls "presented to society" that year: Loring, Hollingsworth, Baldwin, Chaffee, Cheever and Pierce. Not unlike her baptism in church when the whole congregation was asked to protect and guide her forever. The world of debutantes like the Episcopal Church, was a protective and exclusive society.

Lacey had loved the full length, off white, satin dress she wore to the Cotillion, even though it had been remade from her step sister's wedding dress. Her father presented her along with her classmate Molly, and all the other squeaky, clean, over privileged, eighteen year olds whose mothers watched intently from the balconies above, themselves decked out in evening gowns and covered in family jewels they would one day pass on to their daughters celebrating that night.

George Pierce wore a tux as if he had been born in it. The Brooks Brothers Patten leather pumps with the Mary Jane bows, so feminine, did nothing to tarnish his ultra- masculine image. Lacey adored him.

But now he was gone. She remembered how he tried to get her to marry that senior at Harvard.

"Lacey, he clearly loves you. He's headed for a solid career as a banker."

"I like him, Dad, but I'm not really attracted to him. I haven't even slept with him."

"You know what I always say, sweetie. Before you buy a pair of shoes, you better try them on."

But Fred was too effeminate for her. And there were others. The son of her father's best friend, the college hockey player. None of the trappings of Boston society were here. For Lacey, they had momentarily disappeared with her father and she no longer wanted reminders of that time and place.

Now she longed for something more, something bigger, than what would have been a predictable, comfortable life in Boston. She wanted adventure, risk even, some danger that would drive out the pain of missing her father. Something different. Is that why she was here in this commune now with a man facing jail? She sensed she might be wanting more of this man than he was willing to give. And this scared her.

"Let's gather up all these tools and put them back in the garage. It's going to rain soon, I bet you are sick of all this car stuff." Doug hit the nail on the head and Lacey was glad to go back inside H.O.U.S.E, to the comfort of music and the fun of making dinner with others.

After that Lacey was determined to show Doug how much she loved him and to do something that would make him more openly love her. All of the money she had earned and saved during in the Peace Corps at eleven cents an hour would just about pay for Doug's longtime dream of owning a motorcycle.

Friday afternoon in late June, H.O.U.S.E mates were preparing for a barbecue out back next to the garage. Doug was cleaning the grill to make way for burgers and buns. He had not mentioned his birthday to anyone but Lacey because he thought that was too self-centered. Growing up in the Rogers household, birthdays were acknowledged at dinner but not marked by gifts or goings-on that day.

Lacey was on the second floor looking out of the bedroom window when she saw Wayne slowly rolling into the backyard on a shiny new, black and red. BMW motorcycle.It occurred to her he would have loved it if Lacey had given him those wheels.

"Jesus, man, where'd you find that that mother of a bike? Did you steal it or 'free' it from somewhere? Jeez, it's a beauty," Doug whistled.

"Hey, buddy, don't look at me. Whaddya know, this one's for you!" Wayne hooted ecstatically in his high pitched voice.

"Happy Birthday, old Man!" You've reached the age when I can' no longer trust you. You know what the poster says. Never trust anyone over the age of 30!"

"What is this, Wayne? Where'd this come from? Where'd you get the cashish?" Doug was clearly clueless.

"Dummy, this is for you! From Lacey. Isn't it spectacular?"

"You must be kidding. This can't be." Doug was almost speechless. He banged the kitchen door as he ran up the stairs to the bedroom.

"Lacey, thank you. But you shouldn't have. Did you spend all the dough you made in the Peace Corps on this bike?"

She didn't answer. "I am glad you like it. It was Wayne's idea," she lied. "I hope you'll let him use it."

Doug nodded "of course, any time." He didn't say more. He didn't kiss her. All he said was "now can go anywhere on it. Even to Boston."

"I Hope you don't think I am going to Boston on that thing anytime soon," said, half joking, half serious.

That night at the barbecue, the beer flowed and the wine made everyone merry. Denny and Velta announced they were getting married and everyone congratulated them with toasts and friendly barbs.

"What did you have to do to snag her, Denny? Wayne cajoled. Congratulations, man!"

"I thought you said you might go off and live with only women," Richie pointed out to Velta.

"Come on, Richie, don't give me a hard time. I am as surprised as you are."

"Come on, you all, don't give us a hard time," said Denny. "We are happy together. And besides, now there is one more free room to bring on a new H.O.U.S.E member."

"Here, here!" Cheers and clapping all around.

"Come get your burgers and dogs," Doug shouted into the air. Lacey followed with the buns. The condiments were on a table cloth spread on the hood of the Ghia parked out back for the occasion. Everyone sat on blankets enjoying the night air and the food.

"Oh, dear, look who is here." Wayne said, clearly not expecting the newest visitor.

"I invited him," Lacey said, shaking his hand and handing him a beer. "Why not? He's been good to us."

"Nice of you young squatters to invite me," said Mr. Hilgendorf as he came into the back yard. "Okay, you may not be squatters, but in my book, you sure are Hippies. No religion and a lot of nakedness, if you ask me, even if you do pay rent and keep the place clean."

"Beside collecting our rent and calling us hippies, do you have any other interests?" Lacey asked, trying to steer the conversation in another direction.

"Well, yes. Since my wife died, I've taken up with flowers. I like to plant in my garden. All kinds. Petunias, lilacs, roses and such."

'That's lovely," Velta said. "Maybe one day you will bring us some."

"Hold on, little lady, you'd have to be pretty special in my book. But maybe I will if you all stop calling me Elmer Fudd. My name is Marion."

The partygoers looked at each other trying not to smirk.

"You know it's Marion, Marion Hilgendorf, and don't you forget it. That contraption over there looks like a new motorcycle. Did you steal it from somewhere?" he asked, talking to no one in particular.

Doug chose to respond. "Lacey was kind enough to buy it for me so I had to pay her back by asking her to marry me."

"Wonderful, wonderful. Congratulations to you." said everyone through mouths full of food and wine. At the time, so much in love, Lacey cheered, too, completely missing the sexism in the remark. Later she would realize the wedding plans were started by a motorcycle.

Janis Plays Des Moines

Every night Richie turned to the God Bacchus and usually passed out before dinner was on the table. When he sat down he was so thin that his jeans often slipped down to the crack in his behind but were held steady there by the black leather belt with the peace sign on the buckle. His signature red bandana sometimes adorned his skinny neck, sometimes his waist and occasionally was used as a snot rag.

Lacey was ever mindful of her rescuer tendencies since high school when she gravitated to the bad boys in the class who needed a friend or a mother to pull them through a bad day or a bad exam. Known as the "morale gal" back then, she fell hard for Doug as an adult and for his legal challenge. She was also equally hell bent on saving Ritchie him from himself.

"You know, Ritchie, we have a lot more in common than the East coast and our jokes about quaint Iowa towns. We love the same music. We love Simon and Garfunkel, even though Wayne doesn't, and we've sung every song in Hair together-at least twice.

"How about that?"

"Burst to earth, womb to tomb, as the gang says in West Side Story." Lacey couldn't resist.

"Too bad you don't share my love of dope and drink" Ritchie said but we manage to make us work."

"So how about we go see Janis together when she's in town." Lacey was all smiles and willing to buy the tickets since Ricthie's pockets were always empty.

The chance to hear her came one night in early July. Lacey wanted to break Richie's habit of getting drunk every night before dinner by going to a conceret.

"So why not do it with a concert?" she said to Doug one night before bed. "You don't know this, but I have always wanted to be in a rock band. Ritchie is the only one I told. And I don't much about Janis Joplin, but I know he and I love her rebel girl attitude and the voice laced with Southern Comfort. So I want to go see her with him. Besides, the tickets are only $4.00."

Wayne had gone to New York City to join the protests in the wake of a police raid on the Stonewall Inn a few nights before. The Stonewall Raid and its aftermath would mark the birth of the gay pride movement. That same night, Wayne got to hear Jerry Lee Lewis and Pacific Gas and Electric play a music festival in Central Park, while Janis Joplin was preparing to play the Veterans Auditorium in Des Moines.

Lacey got to the ticket booth about an hour before the concert and was surprised there were no long lines. There was only one person in front of her, a small woman so short she had to stand on tiptoe to speak to the ticket master. She had long, streaky, muddy brown hair down to her waist and her face was covered in greasy pimples. Chains of cheap Indian beads dangled from her neck. The pattern on her bell bottoms exploded in a kaleidoscope of color, and she wore them long over her barely visible high heeled platform boots that disguised how really short she was. Thick huge dark sunglasses covered most of her face, so big they fell half way down her nose, no longer shielding her from the sun or strangers.

"Hello," Lacey ventured, "where are you from? That's quite a colorful bag you have there," looking at her rumpled army backpack with all the stickers on it. "My friend will be joining me shortly." She wished she had better opening line.

"Port Arthur, Texas, originally, but all over," came the faint reply.

Just then Richie slid into Lacey's side. He tried to get her attention, but she was still making small talk with the woman.

"This is going to be a fantastic concert. I just love Janis Joplin's voice and all the things she tries to stand for. "I can sense the rejection by her own family in her songs, the need to prove something to them," she continued, speaking almost too knowingly about someone she had read little about. Richie poked her hard in the ribs.

"What are you doing here?" scowled the ticket master as he opened the booth window and leaned forward.

"I am the entertainment here tonight." The voice was low, quiet and polite.

"I'll bet you are, lady," the man barked "but not on my watch. And you can't carry those bottles in with you. Hand them over."

There was disgust in the ticket master's voice. Lacey saw the wound in the woman's eyes through her glasses, realized it was Janis and was ashamed to witness this attempt to humiliate such a great talent.

She looked at Janis, nearly four inches shorter than herself, and felt sorry for the enormously talented songstress. All the fame in the world could not make her feel secure and confident, even in front of this obnoxious man in the booth.

She couldn't stop herself. Lacey bent slightly toward Janis and put her arms around her, not holding her too close, out of respect, but holding her with a gnawing sense of a shared insecurity too deep to address with words.

Janis let her hold her for a moment, not knowing whether to move or stay. Then she stepped back, wrapped a feather boa twice around her neck, and adjusted the glasses on her nose.

"Thank you, my friend."

Luckily, Janis' stage manager came out to the booth, gave the ticket master a hateful smirk and $200 and ushered Janis into the auditorium without a word.

Lacey was furious at the guy in the booth and shot him a really dirty look. "So what if Janis brought a little Southern Comfort on stage?" How could you treat a guest artist like that?"

"Look, you wise-as Hippy, I didn't know who she was, so shut your wise-ass mouth."

Richie pressed Lacey's arm to stop but she went on. "Forget that she's a star, you shouldn't treat anybody like that. Who the Hell are you anyway? Some little jerk treating people with no respect from inside your little box of power!" She had clearly lost it. Richie pulled her away from the booth and guided her in silence into the auditorium.

As usual, Richie came stoned, having had a bowl of marijuana at H.O.U.S.E. Lacey hated any substance that might blur enjoyment of the music that night. She bought the tickets because she wanted to share the evening with him.

"Seems like I'm having to rock this concert on my own. You're stoned. I worry about the ride home on Doug's motorcycle but I am determined to enjoy this, with you or without you."

Janis did not disappoint her or anyone else that night.

Toward the end of the concert Lacey leaned over to Richie as Janis started a mournful *Summer Time* from *Porgy and Bess*. "Don't you just love her?" she purred. "I love everything she stands for. And now I am not sorry I got to speak with her, however dumb that was." *"And the livin' is easy isn't it Richie?* Aren't we all having a grand time together at H.O. U. S. E.?"

"Sure, Lacey, sure. Anything you say goes. I just love being around you. It keeps me healthy. She had heard him say that more than once before, but what he didn't understand was that it was H.O.U.S.E, not Lacey, that was keeping alive.

The BMW seemed to drive itself home that night without incident even though Ritchie was still slightly stone. "Babe, I could drive this thing with my eyes closed," Rictchie said as he drove around the corner to the side street entrance to the garage."

"I think you just did," Lacey said, only half joking. "I mean it, don't do that to me again.

Remember, we're friends." She kissed him on the cheek, slid in the back door, shutting it noiselessly and left him standing, still stoned, under a full moon.

That night, lying next to Doug, thoughts of the concert and the strong moonlight coming through the window kept her awake.

She identified with Janis and imagined they might have had similar childhoods. She flashed on cruel slights in her childhood by thoughtless grownups on school visiting days and at dancing school when parents sat around and commented on other people's children.

"That Lacey could lose a few pounds. She so chubby it's a wonder she can run." Once, when she was four, in a ballet class at the Waldorf Astoria, the teacher suggested she find some other form of physical activity since she lacked the body and grace to do ballet. Later, on the hockey field in high school, she could still hear the coach yelling at her "faster Lacey, faster, you are too slow! You can't score from back there."

A week later Lacey read that Janis told an interviewer that her favorite audience was in little old, homey Des Moines. The magazine said she had given her all that night in a wistful *"Me and Bobby McGee* "and the playful Mercedes Benz song. All this while sipping through two bottles of Southern Comfort. Lacey and Richie thought they would share Janis for a lifetime but only too soon she'd disappear, gone at the age of 27.

The Wedding Planner

Wayne got the guidelines for weddings from Waterworks Park in a letter that summer and read it to the other H.O.U.S.E members.

"It says here weddings are allowed at the fountain and gazebo areas. Reservations are made on a first-come, first-served basis and are not confirmed until our office receives payment. The user is permitted three hours of area use. No tents allowed."

"Too bad about the tents," Wayne said, "that would have been fun. But it's the perfect setting for you two and all of us. I'll get my friend to lend me his hearse and I'll greet your folks at the airport, Lacey! It will be such a gas,"

"Just think. We can have an unlimited number of friends and family come and we can celebrate with a great outdoor barbecue in a vast green and wooded space," Denny said, already excited by the project.

"Harmony and understanding, peace and love abound.....!" Lacey sang to herself but wondered how harmonious it would be on that day with her Eastern relatives and stepmother in attendance.

Early on she enlisted her commune colleagues to help design a wedding invitation that could appeal to free spirited friends as well as straight laced family in Iowa and Boston. It was Richie who came up with the final design.

"I got it!" he declared with tipsy pride, well beyond his limit of wine for the night. "The symbol of the Twins signifying Doug's Gemini birth sign inside a circle of a sun that was Lacey's sign of Leo. Lacey loved the idea and asked Tom to make a woodcut of the design that could be used to print 150 folded pieces of parchment inviting folks to the event at 5:00 on Saturday, August 30, 1969.

"Lacey, let's do the ceremony in the Quaker tradition. I'd like to show respect for those folks because of my work with them at the American Friends Service Committee," said Doug. "I guess that goes along with the no ring plan," Lacey said not without irony, thinking of the fancy nuptials she had witnessed with pleasure back home.

"The good news is we can get married in a park. There are 1500 acres there for us to revel in and you and Wayne can have a field day planning the ceremony."

The next week Lacey and Velta headed to the Salvation Army store in search of a dress for the occasion. They found something even better. "Hey, come here, look at this," Velta said digging into the bottom of a bin full of fabric," a whole bolt of orange raw silk that's never been used. This is perfect for you!"

"I've never been a fan of orange anything," said Lacey. "Besides, that color will make me look fat."

"Lacey, that is pure shit, I mean, ridiculous. A color doesn't make you fat. You'll see, I'll make you look great. Audrey Hepburn waist, empire, cut high in Breakfast at Tiffany's. Little flecks of gold in the orange. Super! "

Velta wasn't listening to the protest.

"One day I hope to have my own shop. That's how good I am. I'll call it the Constant Tailor. I really appreciate you lending me the Singer sewing machine Doug's grandmother gave you as an "engagement present," although it's a little late for that since you've been together for a while. Does she know you guys sleep together?"

"I doubt it. It's just as well. She wouldn't like it if she knew and Doug's not about to break her heart."

"I know I'll put the machine to good use. Heaven knows you'll never use it. I'm proud to christen it with your wedding dress."

"Okay on the color. Let's get out of here."

That night at dinner, after the others had left, Lacey asked Wayne to help her plan the ceremony. "You know Lace, don't laugh, but I am planning to marry a woman one day, as a way, I hope, to reunite with my parents."

Lacey picked up the last of the dishes, and stacked them one on top of the other, and carried them to the kitchen.

"I am not so sure that will work for you," she yelled from the kitchen sink. Come on here and keep me company." Wayne got up from the table and leaned against the kitchen wall while Lacey washed the dishes. She liked talking while her hands were in warm water and soap. It made her think better.

Will you continue to have relationships outside your marriage? That could be tough and stressful."

"I don't know. Would depend on who I marry. Maybe she would be open or have her own *other* relationships. I am just glad to plan your wedding as a practice run."

"I am happy to leave the details to you. Just don't go overboard with a grand welcome to Iowa for the out-of-state wedding guests. I am not sure that would go over with my stepmother, Jane, with whom I had always been at odds."

"Okay, my friend, we can talk about *my marriage* another day. Right now I am planning yours. So good night, my friend," Wayne said, blowing Lacey a kiss as he went up the stairs to the attic.

Lacey lay awake for a long time on the mattress, not moving so as not to disturb Doug's sleep. She thought about her father. What would he think if he could see her life, look down on the events leading up to the wedding? Was it possible he knew? She wished he could be there on her big day. She missed him terribly. It was always there. The hole in her heart.

Slight Tensions

Doug's enthusiasm for the wedding was somewhat more measured than that of the bride and the wedding planner.

Another late afternoon of rumination in Doug's office. Lacey appeared with a glass of papaya juice and a beer.

"Your choice. Pick one or both. I am happy either way and I'm all yours," she said. He took the juice and she put the opened beer on top of the roll top and eased into the chair next to Doug.

"Cheery little thing you are today, what's up?"

"Nothing much. I was upstairs with Velta. It was a fitting day for my dress. She is really serious about this design stuff. She barely lets me look in the mirror to see what she is doing. This could be a disaster, you know, and then I'll have to cancel the wedding!" Lacey, joked.

"Seriously, Lace, I do see our wedding as more than one thing. Most of all, it's necessary because I really do love you with all my heart, not just for the fun we have living here with others in this commune we are building. But also because in my compromised legal state, I need an ally, an event that might make me look good before a judge, capable of being a family man. You are my asset in this. I am clear on this point."

"And so am I. Okay by me. I like the idea of being an asset for you, for us. Maybe it will keep you out of prison, maybe it won't. We have to hope for the best."

"I am sorry if I seem cold and calculating."

"Not that, more like distant. Like you are changing," She didn't want to say *less sure of yourself.*

"That day I met you on the side of the football field you seemed vibrant, outgoing, and almost debonair in your Shetland sweater and corduroys, no hint that you really didn't like clothes much or dressing up. Now you seem weighed down. Like the daily routines of living seem silly and unimportant to you now in the face of all your challenges."

"I can't help that I feel cut off and remote. It's almost surreal. Why should I care about some dress code for weddings or follow the rules of etiquette, like you, or placing my fork to the left and knife to the right. Nothing like that really matters."

"Ouch, sounds like you are dumping on me."

"I am not really sure what I am saying. Maybe I am just a minimalist at heart, no frills and no fancy. My authenticity, if that's what you call it, comes from my ideas, not the niceties of life. Even in the courtroom, when I try a case, I stick to the basics of dress and discourse. I've got my uniform: worn-out jeans and cowboy boots. I never try to sway a judge's opinion with anything but the basic facts."

Doug's words stung. She had no comeback. Did Doug think her manners and style were insincere, lofty or worse, throw-aways? At that moment she wanted to escape.

"Right. And I would never try to change you. But I need to be at a class in twenty minutes. She leaned over, kissed him on the cheek and was out the door in a flash." She jumped in the Ghia and drove away as fast as possible. There was no class. Lacey stopped at a gas station and called Wayne back at the house. Luckily he was in the attic next to his phone."

"Hi, Wayne, can you turn down the music? I don't need the Fifth Dimension right now. I need you. I worry about Doug. He's acting different, almost closed. I feel like he is becoming aloof, a bit of a stick-in-the-mud in his own way. He judges me. I can't help it if I like good manners and sharp dressers. That doesn't make me look insincere. Does it? Please. Can you talk to him? I can't. I don't know what else to say." She hung up. Wayne knew what to do.

That night Lacey stayed at school in the library and tried unsuccessfully to concentrate on Edmund Burke. She knew she didn't want to be there when Wayne talked to Doug.

For dinner that night Tom had made a Philippine dish called lumpia. The lumpia was a kind of wrap filled with ground pork, minced onion, carrots, and spices with the mixture held together by beaten egg. Tom had mixed in green peas, cilantro and prunes.

"Mighty tasty," said Richie, grinning ear to ear, already in his cups.

"Do you know what prunes can do for you?" Tom started in about to give a health nut lecture.

"Cure my constipation?" Ritchie said with a laugh, aiming at his butt, sitting cross-legged at the table.

"They are loaded with iron and other things you need, especially when you are trying to quit smoking."

"That's cool, if you say so, though I don't believe it. Nothing can help you quit smoking except quitting smoking, "Velta said with conviction.

"You'll have to teach me how to make that," said Ritchie, "even though you know I don't know how to boil an egg."

Did you say you made those wraps, the lumpia, or someone sent them to you?" Velta was curious.

"A Philippina gave them to me to make the dish. Someone I've been dating who is new to Des Moines."

"Whoa, now there's a story, Tom, what's up with you?" Velta was ready for show and tell.

"None of your business."

"Let the poor guy alone, will you?" Denny said helping himself to the pork dumplings and the rice on the table.

While they bantered back and forth, Wayne turned to Doug at the end of he table and whispered so the others could not hear.

"How's it going, Doug? I have been thinking about you lately. How are you coming with your case and your lawyer, Gary Price? Is there a date yet set for the appeal? I got to say, you don't seem much like your old self these days."

"Why should I? I am not my old self," he said testily.

"Do you ever think that maybe, in your own way, you are becoming a little straight-laced, maybe up tight, for an avowed radical, my friend?" he said half joking, half chiding his friend.

Doug knew instantly Lacey had talked to Wayne. He didn't really mind. He knew he had hurt her feelings with his outburst. He pushed his fork around the empty plate and waited for Wayne to continue.

"Do you ever think your future wife might like to see you dress up occasionally?"

"She can wear whatever she wants. I have no need to dress up. She can take me as I am, the same as I take her."

"Listen to yourself. Are you so judgmental?" he said trying to be gentle but firm.

"She loves ritual and comfort and the tradition of community," Wayne said with conviction. "And I do, too. I'll do it and whomever I marry will, too. You and I are very different in that way. Lacey's more like me."

"Then maybe you should marry her."

"That was cruel, Doug. But I do love her in my own way."

Doug pinched the flame of the candle in front of him with his fingertips, signaling the conversation was over. "As part of our generation, I want to push the envelope on nuptials. No ring can tell the story of true love. Lacey goes along with my final decision," Doug was adamant.

When he heard those words, Wayne began to worry about Lacey. He watched Doug go to bed and waited up for her to come home from the library.

As usual, she banged the screen door, on the way in.

"Will you never learn? Some people are sleeping while you ignore the need for quiet. You are never quiet!" Wayne said, glad to see her home safely, but not resisting the barb.

"Judging by your comment, I can tell you missed me," she said with a flirt and a smile.

"Listen I am just worried about you. And Doug, too. You are so playful, the one that likes to dance, dress up, play word games and drink wine. It annoys me, and probably you, too, that every time someone offers Doug a glass of wine he says, 'no thanks, I have no need of a toque or Tokay." That's cute, but supercilious or whatever you call it."

"I call it holier-than- thou." Lacey said, turning serious and looking at Wayne hopelessly. "I've tried to tell him how that sounds. I've at least tried marijuana several times. I must admit I prefer wine to weed. Whenever I smoke dope, I either want to make love to the guy next to me or to go to sleep, not cool either way, but at least I am not a prude."

They parted hoping a new day would lift Doug's mood and bring him brighter spirits.

The Wedding Party

When Jane Pierce emerged from the Des Moines airport terminal, Wayne was ready for her, perched on the hood of a newly polished, blue-black hearse emblazoned with silver lettering: "Dolan's Funeral Parlor, Home of your Best Last Trip."

Lacey had not chosen the hearse as the wedding vehicle of choice. Wayne presented the idea to her after he rented it. "Isn't it awesome?" Wayne began persuasively. "I rented it from a gay friend of mine who has been a funeral director for many years and is dedicating his life to bury victims of some unknown virus he fears will become an epidemic in the coming decade. He wanted his hearse to have its final fun run. He converted it into more or less a limousine, putting three passenger seats in the back where the corpse would have been and adding a bar so traveling mourners could bury their sorrows with a few drinks on the way to the funeral."

At first Lacey was peeved to have been tricked into having this monstrous black coffin on wheels greet her family entourage. But then, sitting inside in the back seat, looking out the window, she was happy about the darkened glass, which enabled her to size up the family situation without being seen.

On either side of the hearse's hood, Wayne had attached flags on metal sticks about a foot high. The flags—black with a white peace symbol in the middle—blew freely in the wind when the hearse moved. The air was humid, it was ninety degrees, and the heat made the black hearse gleam in the late-morning sun.

Lacey stayed inside the hearse in the back, glad to be shaded by the blackened window. Wayne hopped out of the hearse and rushed forward to shake Jane's hand as he took her small suitcase. "Hiya and welcome to Iowa. I know you Easterners often call it Ohio, but we're from I-O-W-A."

"I have been to Ohio and Des Moines is not Cleveland," Jane said, making clear the joke fell flat. Wayne turned to greet Lacey's brother, Bret, who was grinning at him, appreciating Wayne's discomfort.

"Nice to meet you, Wayne," the fifteen-year-old said. "My sister is quite the adventuress."

Jane was wearing an off-white business suit purchased for the occasion from Boston's best women's clothier, Bonwit Teller. Clearly she was expecting a fancier, more formal affair than the one the commune had planned. She sported a gold pin just below her left shoulder and wore her signature charm bracelets— three of them. Her charcoal hair had bounced up into curls in the humidity. Her large bosom, pressing against her suit jacket, gave her the look of an aging Elizabeth Taylor in a low-budget movie. The painted lips and nails glared a frosted magenta in the afternoon sun light.

Lacey could feel the nightmare coming. When her father was alive, Jane conveniently managed to be absent or ill for most of Lacey's big teenage events, like her high school sports events and graduation. Would Jane pull out once again—leave tomorrow on the first plane out of Des Moines? For a brief moment Lacey wished she would.

As soon as she saw her brother coming toward the car, however, she brightened up. Bret had just come home from his first year at boarding school and was looking fresh and young in his khaki pants, blue shirt, Brooks Brother's jacket, and red and blue "rep" tie. He looked like a teenage version of their father, and Lacey felt a wave of pain and joy. When he got closer she saw that he had grown his hair long and pulled it back into respectability, for Jane's sake, in a ponytail. The guitar Lacey had given him was slung over his left shoulder. She couldn't wait to sing the Simon and Garfunkel tunes with him, or maybe even "Lo, How a Rose Ere Blooming," which they had practiced the last time they were together.

Hanging on to Bret's right arm was Clara, the only product of George Pierce's marriage to Jane. Clara had been born with mental challenges, and at nine years was becoming too much to handle for her free-wheeling mother, who was more interested in finding the next man to take care of her than in taking care of her daughter.

As Jane approached, Lacey jumped out of the back of the hearse onto the pavement.

"Hi, Jane, so good to see you, so glad you could all come," Lacey blurted out too quickly, her nerves cutting short the family friendly hug.

"Hey" was the only word Bret uttered, and it was enough for Lacey to open her arms wide and to wrap them tightly around her little brother's chest. He was coming home to her after a long time away.

"You know our father died two years ago at Christmas," Clara said in a non-sequitur to Wayne which was not unusual in her often one sided conversations.

"Yes, Lacey told me. So sorry to hear."

By now Wayne had opened the back seat door for Jane and put her bags in the way-back. Clara got in beside Jane, and Lacey stepped over Clara to sit in the middle. Bret was thrilled to be offered a place in the front seat with Wayne, so he could see the flags flutter on the trip back to H.O.U.S.E.

A sliding glass window separated the driver's area from the passengers sitting behind. While Cam and Wayne turned on Carol King at high volume in front, behind there was stony silence. The passengers stared at the three decanters in front of them offering whiskey, scotch and soda. They looked all the same, in their leather cases in the velvet box facing them. Seated between Jane and Clara, Lacey felt like one of them, bottled up, glasslike and rigid stuck between two people from the same family mix but very different on the inside. Lacey sensed their personalities had never fit together. Never would.

The thought suddenly made her feel sick. The smell of smoke in the car didn't help either. The ashtrays had been used, probably, by the last passengers. The lids were wide open, jutting up from the arm rests on either side with nasty little butts peeking out of each one. Lacey sat back and tried not to throw up.

"This is quite a rig," Jane commented as she lit one of the Salems frequently dangling from her magenta mouth.

Lacey did not respond. They rode the rest of the way to H.O.U.S.E in silence.

The H.O.U.S.E. members had mowed the lawn, scraped the graffiti off the refrigerators, put flowers in every room, and cleaned the living room by moving the furniture around and taking down the Che Guevara poster on the wall behind the TV. They thought the other posters, particularly Peter Max's LOVE, issued that year looked "positive and neat" on the wall.

When the hearse arrived, Jane stepped out self-consciously into the afternoon sun on the sidewalk in front of the house. She frowned as she looked up at the welcome sign on the porch.

"Hiya. I am Lacey's official dressmaker," Velta said, chuckling at her own joke as he spoke. "And this is Ed Tinker, a new member of the commune who's just returned from Waterworks Park, where they are getting ready for the festivities for tomorrow."

John came down from his office to greet everyone. Lacey introduced her stepmother to her future son-in-law. "How nice to finally meet you, Jane said, looking over the young man about whom she knew little except that he could go to prison for "evading" the draft. Or was it "resisting?" As she shook his hand she couldn't quite remember, and realized she didn't know the difference.

They walked up the stairs, together, Doug carrying Jane and Lucy's suitcases. "How are Edie and Joe and Peter and Rachel?" Jane asked hoping, like Genesis, to list each of her fifteen first cousins. This way she could keep Jane occupied and avoid too many questions that might lead to the old tug of war between them or maybe an insinuating comment about Lacey's current life style.

"You know, Rachel got married to her boyfriend, who is an only child and a psychiatrist," Jane started. Jane had a way of linking things together in a lump judgment in a single sentence. Upstairs, as they moved from one shabby but immaculate room to another, Jane commented on the flower vases and the nice furniture the group had acquired, though she knew perfectly well where it had come from. "Cousin Edie is a speech teacher of sorts and Joe is an investment banker. Doug, being a lawyer, what kind of a practice does he have? Is he with a firm?"

"Right now his office is here at home. You see he, or I should say, we, not just Doug and I, all of us here are trying to stop this war by keeping young men out of the draft. That's how Doug got into this. He got drafted untimely back from the Peace Corps. That's the case he is fighting now for himself. And no, Jane, he is not a deserter or an evader. He is resisting military service. He hopes to become a conscientious objector, by winning his case on appeal."

"You know George wouldn't have approved of this," Jane said, pointing to the surroundings with a judgmental wave of her right hand as if she were dismissing a servant.

At the mention of her father tears welled up in Lacey's eyes. "How do you know what he'd approve of?" Lacey said. "He wrote to me in Tunisia saying he wanted to find a way for me to go back to college. He made me promise not to tell you since you didn't want me to go." Lacey couldn't stop herself. She didn't care. She lashed out at her step mother: "And why didn't you ever tell me he was sick until he was already dead. I never got to see him. I need him here now!"

Jane turned red, thoroughly embarrassed and stunned by Lacey's violent outburst. "I don't believe you," Jane said in defense. Even Lacey was shocked by her own words, not knowing how so much pent up hate could come out of her.

At that moment, Bret came bounding up the stairs two at a time, guitar in hand, to save the two women from further verbal combat. "Hey, Lacey, let's give her some time to freshen up while we sing *April Come She Will*, like we practiced last Christmas. She can rest up in your room. Okay?"

Thank God for Simon and Garfunkel, Lacey thought. Out from under the upstairs confrontation, she was sorry for being a part of it. Cameron and Lacey retreated to the porch to harmonize while Jane powdered her nose and took a nap on the mattress on the floor in Doug and Lacey's back room.

An hour later it was nearing six o'clock. Jane came downstairs "refreshed."

"How'd it go up there?" Lacey said. "Did you find everything you needed to freshen up? I found some beautiful old lace hand towels in the thrift shop and put them in the bathroom just for you."

"Don't know how you sleep on a mattress as hard as that and so flat on the floor. Like it was just thrown down there in that airless space of a back room," *Clearly she's not refreshed Lacey said to herself.*

"Well, come now, have a drink. We don't' have martinis but we do have good wine and beer, whichever you like. And can Cam have a beer, too? Just one?" Lacey asked.

"I have prepared a great meal for us. Greek moussaka and Indian pudding for dessert," Lacey almost squealed with pride at the thought she would impress her stepmother.

"You had no culinary skills the last time I checked," Jane was quick to say. She glanced at the sunken level of the dining-room table with the cushions neatly placed all round. "There's no way I could ever get down there, that low, to eat a meal." A clear signal to Lacey that Jane and Bret and Clara would not be staying long.

Wayne drove the threesome to their hotel so they could rest before the wedding. Before he dropped them off, he invited Bret to come back to H.O.U.S.E for dinner and to help out with preparations for the grand roasting of the pig for the reception following the wedding. After dinner Bret accompanied Wayne first to the airport to pick up Lacey's childhood friend Molly Bradley. Later they would head out to the park for the night.

The Wedding

Lacey heard the screen door slam and ran to greet her friend. She and Molly Bradley hugged and laughed with no words, and then they stood back to take a long look at each other. The past three years had led them onto very different paths.

"I am so excited for you!" Molly said, throwing her arms around Lacey, giving her a huge hug. "I can't believe it! Can't believe I am here with you. Mom asked me to give you these, first thing, when I got here." Molly's mom and dad had supported Lacey through many of her high school trials, and they wanted to send Lacey love and support in the form of proper wedding gifts from back home.

There were two gifts, each in a large box wrapped in shiny white paper tied with a large, silk bow. One bow was silver and the other gold. They were so beautiful that Lacey almost didn't want to open them, but Molly insisted, brimming with her own excitement. Lacey ushered Molly into a corner of the dining room where they could sit down comfortably on the plush colorful cushions Lacey had rearranged for the visit.

"Oh my, Molly, it's gorgeous! So decadent!" A filmy, white, chiffon negligee fell out of the leaves of tissue paper in the silver bowed box. A matching silk peignoir accompanied it. *What was Mrs. Bradley thinking, Lacey wondered? Did she think Lacey was still a virgin, soon to make love for the first time with her knight in shining armor?* Lacey certainly hoped that Mrs. Bradley would never know about her less than pristine past. In any case, it was a lovely gesture that made Lacey smile in gratitude.

The other gift was equally gorgeous and unmistakably Yankee. Two beautifully cast silver candle sticks tucked in tissue paper inside the gold bowed box marked SHREVE, CRUMP & LOW, BOSTON. Lacey gushed over both gifts, aware their presence in the commune might confirm her roommates' suspicions that Lacey and her friend were products of a privileged, elitist class where all those "people" come from-the East Coast.

With Jane no longer there to put the young people on edge, wine flowed freely at dinner, and there were many toasts to each other and to the day ahead. Lacey's cinnamon-laced moussaka was a hit, and all agreed that the pudding must be "real Yankee", because they had never heard of it before in Iowa. The molasses dessert was the crowning glory of the evening.

Molly and Lacey stayed awake long into the night reliving their high-school days. The whole H.O.U.S.E was quiet except for the hum of a quirky refrigerator they could hear from the dining room where they still hovered, curled up on cushions in front of the candles that were burning low, the wax slowly dribbling down the sides of the wine bottles where they had been set earlier. A light rain was beginning to fall outside. It was almost 3:00 a.m.

"You know," Molly said, "I kind of knew on that trip to the U.N senior year that Mary was depressed when we stayed at her house in Yonkers. You couldn't see it, 'cause you and Bitsy went off and got drunk at the other end of the house, but it was pretty clear to me. So I wasn't surprised when she killed herself after that first year at Vassar.

"Man, I have had times when I was depressed. And just like Mary no one ever knew and I didn't tell anyone. Weren't we all at Middleford at one time or another?" Lacey said. "When the head mistress wouldn't recommend me for college, I wanted to shoot myself. Correction. I wanted to shoot her!"

"But when D'Arcy died, wasn't that was a real shocker?"

"Tell me again so I get it straight," Lacey said. "D'Arcy was living in Greenwich Village with the drummer from the Thelonious Monk band. There was some jealousy incident. She shot him, and then he shot her? Or was it the other way around?"

"I am not sure. And it sure won't show up in the alumni magazine. I do know that D'Arcy's parents are raising the two children. D'Arcy was amazing in class when it came to history and she sang with us in the Madrigals, remember? Such a shame she died so young."

"You know, it's funny," Lacey said, "how I can remember so much about so many of classmates in high school. I remember because I was so often jealous of them." The late night admission seemed to crawl out of Lacey's voice.

"How about you, Molly? I have been so full of talking about me and my life. Is there someone special in your life right now?"

"Well I am not as ready to marry as you, but I've met someone I am getting to know slowly. He's an ex-priest I'm really drawn to. We have lots in common, our values, interests and our career paths. In teaching, I mean.

I have decided I am not cut out to be a performer as a violinist, but I can have a long career as pretty good teacher. You know?"

Lacey didn't know. She had given more thought to the excitement of the moment than to any thought about shared personal interests beyond her and Doug's united struggle in the public eye for an end to war and discrimination.

"*Career?* A word I seldom heard growing up and never used. I am back in college five years behind all my high school classmates who by now are married or have jobs. Was her career going to be Doug or was she supposed to do something on her own?

"I dunno, Molly, you seem to have so well thought out what you want to do in life. Me, I just arrived here, fell in love with Doug and three months later we are getting married. Doug is going to do great things one day and I will be there with him. But I haven't given much thought to what I will do when all this war stuff is over. I did think about going to law school here, but then I realized I only wanted to do that to compete with Doug, not for myself, and that didn't seem like a good idea. About the only thing I like to do is write…and that's just for my course."

"You always wrote well in school, even if your ideas sometimes seemed, you know, a little "quirky." Maybe that's just another word for "creative." Remember that senior paper you wrote on the "Psychological and Emotional Wounds of Ernest Hemingway?" Whoa, you went way over the top with that one! What kind of grade did you get on that?"

"B-. I was always a B- in just about everything except languages. I was good at French. That's why the Peace Corps took me, thank goodness! Even then I didn't give much thought to where I was going. I didn't even know where Tunisia was the day I accepted the assignment- had to look it up on a map. I've never really planned ahead. And even now I don't know what the future will bring either way, win or lose the case."

"One thing I know about you, Lacey. You have always landed on your feet. You had a few rough years in high school, but we laughed through most of them. Remember that time you came to our house when you shaved one leg in my bath tub and you were going to go home and ask your poor single parent dad if you could shave the other? That was hysterical! Some plan you had. But the trick worked. And I'll bet you've known how to wing it ever since. Don't be hard on yourself. I love you just the way you are. And so do Mum and Dad."

In a late-night, tipsy moment, Lacey felt the slight chill of a mental wind blow over her leaving her in unsettled weather. A cloud of doubt was forming inside her sleepy head. Unlike her more traditional and cautious friend, had she been perhaps too unguarded in her initial attraction to Doug? Molly had planted a seed that made her vaguely aware she had not given any thought to life beyond the present moment.

The next morning Lacey came down stairs for some coffee and calm on her wedding day. She came into the dining room wearing the icy white peignoir and nothing else and sat down drowsily on a loose cushion, crossing her legs carefully as she slid them under the dining room door/table.

"Oh my God! Who gave you that?" It was Richie up early from too much to drink. "Does your friend think you are a Vestal virgin as yet untouched by the carnal world?! That is a hell of a gift," he chortled, clearly amused by the sight of the filmy negligee.

"Her mother does," Lacey was quick to reply, already giggling. "Shhh, Molly is not up yet, so don't make fun. It's a beautiful gift even for a *faux* virgin like me," Lacey continued dragging the French "oh" for emphasis. "Listen, Richie, I need some alone time before this afternoon. Can you take Molly on a tour of Des Moines so I can gather my thoughts? I know you think I don't actually have any, but trust me, I am full of thoughts about this day.

"Hey, babe, a tour of Des Moines will be over in fifteen minutes flat, but okay, I will find a way to keep her engaged and occupied."

"Richie, you can be such a gem when you're sober." Lacey, cracked, wishing instead she had just said thank you.

Late that night, while Molly and Lacey and others went to bed, Wayne and Bret were in the park with the pig. By the time the night guard let them into the park grounds it was already past midnight.

They parked the truck in the empty parking lot as close to the front gate as possible even driving over the crosswalk right up the entrance so that they could more easily make the move from the truck to the ground with lawnmower, hedge clippers and other garden tools needed for designing the "altar." Cam was in charge of the wheel barrow that carried tools, breakfast food and a pan and a kettle to heat water for camp coffee in the morning. They walked along under a blue black sky dragging their load until they came to an open meadow where the wedding would take place next day. They made a second trip back to the truck to pick up sleeping bags. A quilt of stars covered the sky guiding them as they walked back and forth from the truck. Luckily it sent down enough light for the man and the boy to carry out the prenuptial activities that Wayne had begun the very day Lacey and Doug decided to marry.

Wayne wanted Bret to stay with him by the fire to tend the spit so the kid could hear the first crackle of the fat splitting open the sides of the pork. Bret had eaten lots of bacon in his life but never seen that much pork turning over a spit in the middle of the night.

"God, this is so good, Wayne!" Bret burst out after about two hours of frequent turnings of the roasting swine, "I wish my dad could see this. I wish he could be here for Lacey. They were so close. My brother George and I always thought he loved her the most. But I don't know. I am much younger so I wasn't there for a number of years."

"What do you mean you weren't there?" Wayne was quick to probe.

"When I was born our mother flipped out. It wasn't the first time. They had to put her away. I don't know for how long. All I know is that when she got out she came to Boston and took George and me away on a train to go live in New York near her mother. I never really saw my sister until I was three. That's when Dad came to get us."

"How did that happen? Did he know where you were? Why didn't he come sooner or try to see you more often."

"I am not sure. I was too little. I don't remember. Later I was told that he came to get us in a place in Brooklyn that was once an air raid shelter. We were there for three days after they took our mother away. As she was being put in the ambulance, she told us never to tell anyone our names. Finally George told. So the people there contacted Dad and he came and got us," Bret said slowly, very tired by now and not wanting to say more, uncertain how much Wayne already knew about his sister's family.

"The fire is dying down now. We'll start her up again in the morning. And we'll carve the Gemini twins in the grass and mow a Leo sun in a circle around it. Play me a song now to sing me to sleep, kid," said Wayne gently to the teenager.

In the distance the night guard could make out the silhouettes of Bret and Wayne by the light of the fire. He heard Wayne's coyote laughter and Bret plunking out Simon and Garfunkel one note at a time on his sister's old guitar. That night the hippy and the preppy slept soundly on the grounds of Waterworks Park.

Wayne got up long before Bret was awake. The morning sun was still asleep at 5:00 am on August 30th. While the steam squeaked in the kettle on the fire still burning from last night, Wayne took the chalk from his knapsack and carefully set it aside until he could down his first sips of coffee. He made the coffee with care, pouring hot water into a pan, dumping ground beans into it. He jiggled the coffee water in the pan over the fire until it was properly steaming. He was meticulous. After drinking the first dark roasted cup to make sure it would taste right for Bret, he picked up the chalk and proceeded to the second task of the day.

He found a perfect patch of grass next to the camp perfect for the ceremony. First he cut down the high blades with the mower from the truck making a swathe about twelve feet wide as he walked the machine round and round Next on the cut grass he chalked a circle, the start of the Leo sun sign, for Lacey. Inside the circle he drew a Roman numeral two, the sign of Gemini, for Doug. The wedding would take place inside the circle late that afternoon, after assigned commune members scattered flowers strategically around the chosen spot.

In his mind Wayne had already planned the whole thing, where the vows would be taken and how the guests would move from the ceremony to the reception, all happening at the same site. Quietly he clipped and tweaked until gradually there appeared in the grass the semblance of jagged little triangles etched around the outer rim of the circle. These were the rays framing the Leo sun. He sharpened the two straight lines in the center of the circle to symbolize the twin minds of Gemini. By the time Bret was up, Wayne had completed the touches on his hippie altar.

"Hey, Cam, come get your coffee and take a look at this," he yelled, "Pretty damn good, I'd say." In truth, Wayne did not suffer from either a false sense of humility, or any real hubris. He was happy to share his abundant talents with his favorite friend's little brother.

Back at H.O.U.S.E Doug and Lacey were making their own preparations for the day. They had decided to approach the altar together, foregoing the usual fanfare of the bride's march down the aisle. Indeed, there would be no aisle to march down.

By early afternoon the commune was empty, deserted by the H.O.U.S.E mates who were out in the park, setting up folding chairs borrowed from the local Quaker Meeting place. They brought flowers, donated by florists who loved the idea of Des Moines' first hippy, to scatter on the ground the altar in the park. It was rumored the local TV would be on hand to film the event.

Lacey and Doug tried to stay calm throughout the morning, lying in bed late, not talking much, not up for making love, but affectionately, holding each other close. They had coffee down in the sun-filled dining room and knew the weather would smile on their big day. "That's one thing out of the way," Doug joked. "We won't have to fight the weather. Let's hope everything else goes as planned. You never know what Wayne has up his sleeve."

For a while Doug worked on his BMW out back by the garage and Lacey tried to concentrate on writing a letter to thanks Mrs. Bradley to thank her for the negligee. Neither escaped a mounting sense of excitement and nervousness as the day moved on. Their wedding might be different from others but the feelings were pretty traditional, even for a modern couple.

Lacey was thrilled that for the wedding Doug had picked out a gray and white, pin-striped suit. He had trimmed his mustache neatly, slicked back his sandy hair with Vitalis and all in all made himself stunningly handsome for the day.

"You scared?" Lacey asked timidly, as they dressed. "Why is a mouse when it spins?" She let out first a chuckle, then a full laugh. "As a kid whenever I got scared by something, my dad would ask 'why is a mouse when it spins?" There's no rhyme or reason to it. And so there's no rhyme or reason to be scared. Get it? I always remember it when I feel frightened or unsure of myself." She glanced at Doug. "It's going to be a marvelous time—I mean life, Doug, isn't it?"

"Here we go!" Doug declared with obvious joy in his words. On this day, optimism was in his heart whatever else the future might bring. He would say it again later in that same reassuring voice.

It wasn't so much that she was actually scared. She definitely wasn't afraid of the sacred covenant of marriage. It was more that she was thinking about the awesomeness of the adventure on this day and in this time and place with Doug. She was about to go to a great party, and she and Doug were the hosts. That's what scared her. Should she have given this more thought before jumping into the fire?

She was still tripping over her thoughts when Doug interrupted. "You look lovely. And I love you right now and forever. So don't be scared." His words sank deep into Lacey's core like a drug feeding her nerves with calm. She admired the way he could be so sure for her this day and every day they were together.

Even if she didn't think she was good-looking, Lacey felt beautiful that day. The shine in her deep brown eyes and her childlike smile greeted the world with wondrous expectation of the future. The orange silk dress that Velta had made fit perfectly, and gave her extra confidence. Her dark brown hair shone like polished mahogany and fell loosely over her bosom. The brief bangs, brushed to one side, gave her a saucy look.

When they got to the bottom of the stairs near the front door, Doug pulled on Lacey's right hand and leaned in close to whisper in her ear: "Promise me that you will never change for my sake and that you will always be the person you are now."

Lacey, in a flash, wondered if that were possible, but in her excitement simply nodded yes. "I will always be here for you," she said.

Doug had polished the BMW until the chrome shone like silver and rolled it into the street in front of H.O.U.S.E. ready for the wedding ride. Lacey and Doug had written "getting married" in fluorescent orange letters across their helmets, though Lacey refused to wear hers on the ride over. The orange paint matched Lacey's dress and would later shine in the dark on the return ride from the ceremony. She managed to lift her dress up just enough to hop onto the back of motorcycle, where she sat side-saddle, though she knew it was dangerous. She would rather be cool than careful that day.

They rode slowly through the streets, like royalty in a horse drawn carriage, heading to the park, each conscious, for a brief moment, of the seriousness of what they were about to do. At the edge of the park the bike slowed in the thick grass, crunching pine needles and dirt beneath its wheels. When they came to the "altar," the astrological circle of flowers where the wedding would take place, the BMW came to a halt. Doug hit the kick stand, then dismounted and came around to lift Lacey down from the hot black seat. He took her hand in his and brought her sandaled feet to the ground, looping one strap back onto her right foot.

"Here we go," came Doug's simple words again bringing a smile to Lacey's lips that everyone sitting in chairs around the circle could see. They saw the love in her eyes as she took Doug's hand.

"Hang on tight because it's going to be a long and beautiful ride." Doug knew the right words for this moment.

Hand in hand, they walked to the front of the wedding circle. As they passed the guests, sitting in mismatched folding chairs, Doug leaned down, picked up a yellow daisy, and placed it behind Lacey's right ear.

From behind one of the oak trees, a trumpet sounded the bold notes of the Voluntary from the Wedding March. For an instant Lacey thought it was too much for this crowd, but she loved the classical sound so much that she soon forgot her fear and faintly hummed the melody to keep her nerves under control.

As the couple reached the head of the circle, Lacey could hear "oohs" and "ahs" from the guests seated around the rim. Most prominent were Lacey's stepmother Jane, her little brother Cameron, and her half-sister, Clara. Across from them were the members of Doug's family: Doug's grandmother, Henrietta, his dad, Hiram Rogers, his brothers, Walter and George and their wives and young daughters. Some of the H.O.U.S.E members were seated, but most preferred to stand and move with the couple as they approached. The lone bridesmaid, Molly, was seated in front. As Doug and Lacey approached, Molly rose and moved in step with them, then stopped next to Lacey so that all three stood side by side in front of the waiting minister.

The minister, Reverend Holmquist, a Methodist, and one of Doug's anti-war colleagues, greeted them with a peace sign. "Please stand, as you are able," he began. "We come together today to honor these two people, who live in harmony and unity as social-change agents in a turbulent time. Their stand in opposition to this dreadful war is a beacon for all of us."

The words were not exactly capturing Lacey's thoughts. She wondered if Doug had written those them. She hoped a lighter tone was coming.

"God bless them this day!" someone shouted from the back of the crowd.

The Reverend continued, unfazed by the interruption. "Doug, please step forward. Do you take this woman as your partner in progress and poverty, and in peril as confronts you both?"

The words broke cold over Lacey's joy. Wasn't this a little harsh, a little humorless? But she kept her eyes peeled on her betrothed and exhaled visibly in relief when Doug said "I do," followed by a nervous "I mean, I will."

When Reverend Holmquist posed the same question to Lacey, she responded with a more than emphatic "I surely will!"

Once they were declared husband and wife, the couple kissed, turned, and walked back through the guests, rising to greet them as they passed by. Wayne had given handfuls of pale orange paper flower petals to the guests to toss over the couple. And then there was wild clapping and cheering for the newlyweds.

Only Jane remained in her seat, too stunned by the non-traditional service to rise and greet the couple. Lacey could see out of the corner of her eye that Jane was picking at her magenta nails and self-consciously retouching her lipstick. The expression on her silent mouth screamed, "No Hippies, please!" She was alone in this alien place. Her husband had been gone now for nearly two years. She knew he probably would have given Lacey his blessing but she found this whole event embarrassing. Couldn't Lacey have married a Harvard guy with money and breeding and brought some decency back into the family? Even the Peace Corps had seemed to her a idea. After that brief college stint she should have gone to typing school and gotten a job.

Behind the tree the trumpet rolled out a serious Bach Chorale and then Lacey's lighter request for John Denver's "Leaving on a Jet Plane," which she had asked for because it reminded her of all the times in the past year she had to fly away leaving Doug in Iowa.

"Thank you, Doug and Lacey, for being the really first wedding I ever wanted to attend, or I guess I mean, to plan," Wayne began. Laughs all around came from the H.O.U.S.E members who had dubbed him the "wedding wizard." "May you topple the government with your love and bring us home a better life for all. God Bless!" Plastic cups raised high for the toast as Wayne shouted out "let the pig party begin! " Paper plates loaded with pulled pork, coleslaw and beans were passed by Cameron and Richie to the salivating guests. Hiram had brought other offerings from Scranton including the church supper favorite, ambrosia salad, made with Jell-O, whipped cream, miniature marshmallows and peaches. Guests dipped homemade biscuits into the juices from the suckling pig and swallowed down chunks of pork with long swigs of beer and soda pop.

The pig came in just behind the wedding couple as the most popular guest at the reception. People returned for second and third helpings moving from chairs to seats on the grass as dusk spread its cloak over the park.

The high point of the reception was the presentation of the cake, a six layer monument as wide as a tire and about two feet high that arrived on a wide wooden platform (actually a door) wrapped in a U.S. flag carried by two waitresses from Velta's restaurant. Their entrance happened just as the paper plates from dinner were being dumped into waiting trash cans appropriately marked for the occasion: TRASH and COMPOST.

The cake was tall, with a wide layer at the base topped by six other layers, each one smaller than the one below, each an eggshell white swathe of butter frosting, covered in roses and peace signs, appearing on all sides of the layers of the confection. The cake came to a standstill in front of the couple. Velta handed Doug a large machete with a steel handle. The onlookers began to laugh until someone joked, "You may need that one day, Doug, don't just waste it on the cake!"

Doug and Lacey didn't know that during the month before the wedding, H.O.U.S.E members had made cheese-cakes in several flavors and sizes, which were then mounted on top of each other to form a giant wedding cake. "You really never knew I was hiding these cakes in the freezer?" Velta asked in pleased astonishment. "I even hid some at the restaurant to keep it a secret from both of you."

At the last minute, one of the H.O.U.S.E members admitted that he had stolen a plastic bride and groom from the front window of a Mac truck and placed them on top, two perfect icons symbolizing this modern-day union. Lacey and Doug carefully cut down through the layers of cheesecake, their hands cupped together on the machete.

Doug kissed Velta and thanked her for the huge cake and knife saying: "It's big enough to feed the mess hall of an army. Just the place I hope I never go, but delicious for all of us here today. Thank you, again, Velta, for being such a great roommate to all of us and thank you all for coming to witness our little ceremony today."

Doug's father and his son George and wife Amy looked at the wedding couple and the lively reception in front of them. "Too bad Walter couldn't be here and had to be off in the National Guard this weekend. Maybe it's best anyway on this occasion," Hiram suggested to George.

"Right, Dad, George echoed, "I wouldn't want Walter to spoil Doug's day with a lecture about loyalty to Uncle Sam. But you know, I wonder if Doug knows what he is getting into. Lacey doesn't seem stuck up or anything, but she does come from a different world. I bet she's been around the block a few times, if you know what I mean," he said without getting into any specifics.

Hiram came to his eldest son's defense. "Ah, George, don't be so hard on Lacey. The kids seem to be committed to each other. Even if I am in favor of the war, I am not against them wanting to make the world a better place or wanting to get married. Actually, I'm surprised they are getting married at all given their hippie views," he said, speaking like a true gentleman, soft spoken and at the same time accurate in his assessment.

The reception lasted well into the night, first in the park and then back at H.O.U.S.E. Lacey and Doug thanked Jane for coming. Wayne waited in the hearse to return the family visitors to the hotel. Lacey hugged Clara but saved the biggest hug for Bret. "Take care of yourself next year at school. Always remember I love you and you can call me whenever you need to." And then they were gone.

Lacey replayed a movie of the wedding in her dreams. Everything was perfectly choreographed and could be replayed at any speed day on any night. Doug was mainly just glad they had gotten through it with a job well done. Now there was a more important matter to consider: how to face the long wait before the rendering of the appeal in Doug's trial.

A Boston Engagement

Sights and sounds of Boston calling up memories for Lacey as she and Doug sat side by side bumping along on a bad train ride like it was a bus on a dirt road back in Tunisia. No matter, now that they had landed safely, they were both enjoying the ride. Molly had invited them to come east for her engagement party. It was good timing. They were calling this their "honeymoon trip." Molly greeted them at the train station just outside Boston on Route 128.

It had been five years since Lacey left Boston for the Peace Corps in Tunisia. She wondered what it would be like to see old friends. Would she feel the old tension with family?

Realizing that she was too absorbed in her own thoughts, she turned to Doug. "How are you doing? This is a real first for you, isn't it? Not us, I mean this, Boston?"

"I came east once with the debate team but we never got past Rochester, New York. People are pretty much the same everywhere I guess. I am just glad the judge allowed me to travel with you, he said with sincere relief.

She did not want to contradict him, but on the point about people being the same everywhere, she disagreed.

"New Englanders are different, Bostonians especially so, and Middlefordians are downright provincial and particular. We are headed right into the eye of the storm in my home town," she warned Doug.

They would be in Middleford for three days over the Columbus Day weekend for the engagement party and Lacey hoped it was going to be a good time to introduce Doug to the world she came from. They were staying at Molly's parents' house since Lacey's stepmother and brothers were in New York for the long weekend. Lacey was grateful and thought the timing of her family's absence couldn't have been better.

As the train pulled into the 128 Station, Lacey could see Molly on the platform waving to wildly to her from the other side of the track. She could feel a hug from her best friend even at a distance.

"Hi, Doug, Hi Lacey! This is Jonathan whom I told you about at your wedding. So here we are ready to do the same thing. And to have you here with us is such a treat. Mum and dad can't wait to see you!"

They packed into Molly's ancient, green Chevrolet wagon with the fake wooden panels on either side she had lately inherited from her parents. It was the same one Lacey remembered parked in the Bradley's driveway all through high school.

"Hello, hello and come on in," welcomed Mrs. Bradley at the front door. Black Sambo, the curly black poodle had died while Lacey was out of the country and a new little cocker spaniel lapped at her heels to greet her.

"And this must be Doug. We have heard so much about you. But let's not talk about war on this of all weekends." That was a gentle signal that there would be no discussion about Doug's current "problem" while they were there.

Mrs. B served tea, English style, in the late afternoon and everyone had a cup cake or a scone, a ritual Doug had never seen before and had only read about in English novels. That night friends and family joined Molly and Jonathan to announce the engagement at the Union Oyster House, Boston's oldest restaurant. On occasion Daniel Webster had been known to sup and lift a glass there.

Lacey was in her element at the restaurant, seeing classmates she hadn't seen since high school graduation: Susie, who lived in Newfoundland and Betsy who had gotten married and moved there, too, and Molly's older sister who had invited her classmates, some of whom Lacey recognized. It was good to be back home.

A number of the guests knew Lacey had joined the Peace Corps instead of going to college and asked why she had chosen to do that. She was still insecure about not having a degree so she preferred to talk about returning to college that fall rather than the good work she had done in Africa. No need to brag or upstage Doug in front of people he did not know.

The room where the party took place was much more than the label above the door which read "function room." The room had been a warm and inviting space and the epitome of American décor and the choice for many diners since the mid 1800's and was now the perfect setting for the engagement of the daughter of an old Yankee family.

During the cocktail reception oysters on the half shell were passed by waiters in stiff white jackets wearing gloves and holding the tray at an angle so that guests could easily scoop up a slithery mollusk with a tooth pick and neatly return the little brown stick to the tray.

"Disgusting! You mean you swallow that slimy thing raw?" Doug barely kept the question to a whisper.

At one point during the evening Mr. B, no one called him Howard, clued Doug in on the history of the toothpick. "The toothpick was first used in this country right here at the Union Oyster House. An enterprising man named Charles Forster of Maine first imported the picks from South America. To promote his new business he hired Harvard boys to dine at the Union Oyster House and to ask for toothpicks. Pretty interesting story, don't you think?" Mr. B was clearly pleased with this piece of arcane knowledge he had just imparted to Doug.

While others found the historical tidbit interesting, Dough decidedly did not.

"B stands for boring in my book," he whispered to Lacey.

"Shush, shhh," Lacey pleaded under her breath.

After the hors d'oeuvres came the dinner, equally unfamiliar to the guest from the Midwest. Doug had never eaten lobster and Lacey offered to help crack open the crustacean with the clackers and to scoop the meat out of the claws and shell with the tiny fork and slender silver pick.

"That's a ridiculous way to eat. Why don' they just prepare it in the kitchen and bring you the lobster ready to eat?" He whispered to her at the same time rejecting any help with the utensils.

"It's part of the ritual, the way you eat lobster, silly guy. It's the way it's always been done." She was aware when she said that how shallow her words sounded. But damn it, she was back home and she was going to enjoy it, even if Doug didn't.

"Well, not where I come from. I am glad we don't have lobster. Hell, we don't even have salt water in Iowa." She could tell he was feeling defensive and insecure because he didn't know how to eat the thing in front of him. She had not seen this side of him before and the first time was not a pleasant surprise.

She turned to him with a cold ultimatum: "Straighten up and fly right here. This is my home. In your home I do what you expect of me. A lobster is just a lobster. You don't have to love it but you do have to have good manners." Her face, now growing red, went unnoticed amid the pleasant conversation of the evening. No one suspected how uncomfortable she was or how hard she was trying to hide her feelings. She was beginning to realize Doug might not travel well—on many levels.

The others at the table were having too much fun to notice Doug's consternation. They were sucking the legs and dipping chunks of lobster into cups of hot melted butter and swallowing everything down with more and more white wine. Everyone was having a grand time except Doug. The only thing he ate was the corn on the cob, now stone cold on the plate next to the uneaten intact lobster. Lacey ignored his discomfort for the rest of the evening.

The next day everyone gathered in the Bradley's kitchen for brunch and farewell. Mrs. B had made finnan haddie, a food almost completely alien to anyone not from Boston. She had risen early to mix the heavy cream and eggs with the haddock and to make the toast points on which the rich traditional dish would rest.

Doug was cordial but quiet. He drank three cups of coffee before he could attempt the offering much too rich for his tastes. He couldn't wait to get home to plain old bacon and eggs.

Lacey was glad they had come to share the joy of the coming marriage of her best friend. But this was Boston not Iowa. They were going back to the land where Doug was most comfortable and that she had learned to embrace, but she could feel a shadow of differences that hung in the air and separated them in social settings.

Spaghetti Fight

Doug enlisted Lacey to be his first lieutenant, his voice in a protest against Spiro Agnew, in a speech in Des Moines. While Agnew exhorted the crowd inside the convention center to beware of the television news media's coverage of unsavory issues, Lacey and her comrades stood outside in the cold, alternately singing *Give Peace a Chance,* and shouting together in lock step rhythm: "Hell, no, we won't go." A slight rain misted over the crowd on a cold, windless afternoon. It was Thursday, November 13, 1969.

Lacey wore the coonskin cap she had picked up at the Salvation Army the day she bought the wedding dress fabric. Velta bought one, too but she was not there because she was working her waitress job. The red, white, and blue striped bell bottoms and tee shirt were not enough to keep Lacey warm and she stood in front of the convention center freezing but holding her candle steady. A guy in the crowd was playing *We Will Overcome* on his guitar for the crowd for the second time around. Richie was standing next to her, warm in his army jacket. He couldn't carry a tune and didn't try to sing along with Lacey and the others. He was busy rubbing Lacey's back, trying to keep her warm. Half way through the song Lacey stopped singing and noticed Tom Lesser, on her other side, had stopped singing.

"What's wrong, big guy?" He was not tall. Lacey called him *big guy* to build him up.

She could tell he was sensitive, at times often going out of his way to help fix a roommate's bicycle or show a friend how to set up a recycling plan. When Lacey shared stories about the Peace Corps he listened and encouraged her to write about them. He even offered to show her how to tend the garden he was digging out back beside the garage. She was sorry that she had no interest.

"Hey, Tom, what's up, man," she asked, a little too casually before she realized Tom was in pain and it was not the rain that made his eyes wet. Noiseless tears fell onto his parka before Lacey turned to him and said "What's wrong? Don't you think this is beautiful? So many of us here together to protest the "nattering nabobs of negativity' himself."

"It's not that," Tom said, wiping his eyes. "It's just that there's so much work to do. In our whole lifetime we'll never get it right. Why don't we quit all of this? I think that's what we're both meant to do. All of this chanting will go nowhere."

Lacey didn't understand why Tom's reactions were so different from hers in this moment. Wasn't their protest meaningful? Wasn't this fun? An adventure? She was caught up in the spirit of the crowd that day. She was there for Doug because he couldn't be. Tom seemed too depressed for her words to help. She said nothing. She knew he felt her insensitivity.

A heavier rain began to cut into the cold air, matting her coonskin cap and her long brown hair hanging limp down on each side over her breasts. She could see the drops running down Tom's face, blending with his tears as she tried to move closer to him so they could ward off the cold together.

❖

"You doing all right, now, Tom? I was worried about you today.

Back at H.O.U.S.E., when there was no more crowd and Spiro Agnew had flown off to Florida, the thought of Tom's words stayed with her. They had separated when the crowd dispersed. But his words would not leave. Why was there too much work to be done and why should she quit?

"Thanks, Lacey, I'll be okay. It just makes me sad when I see talent like yours, wasted, that unless used, will shrink and die. The same goes for me if I don't make some changes. That's all."

Whoa! There he goes again. Right out of the blue. She thought they had been done with the subject of her writing. He had only seen that short story she wrote one time. But what if he was right? Would she do better to write about the world around her instead of trying to change it? She thought about the short story she had written and never published.

When Lacey was nineteen she met Hal, who was then twenty-six. He was tall, blonde and charismatic and had been tossed out of every prep school he briefly attended. He was missing a middle finger on one hand. And he was probably crazy. The one constant in his life was the carnival with the game booth he owned on the midway.

"Under ten over twenty-five, win yourself a cupie doll." Lacey's imitation made Tom laugh.

"His behavior was often erratic, but at the same time exciting to me always. I hated my job as a nurse's aide in a hospital. Who wouldn't be thrilled to leave that scene for the midway?"

Lacey put her arm around him. "This will pass for you, you'll see. And maybe one day I will write. Just not now. Things are not hopeless. You'll see when you get back to the farm. Is it going to be soy beans or corn?" She held him close before the last of the sun disappeared after the rain stopped in the early evening.

She headed into the kitchen to put the pot on the stove to boil water for the pasta. The pot was a great steel caldron she had found at the Salvation Army Store used to boil bandages for the wounded Confederates on the front lines in the Civil War. "This is one old pot," said aloud to the empty kitchen.

Tom was the first to wander in, restless, and looking not to be alone after the day's trauma. He cast his eyes in the direction of the two refrigerators that stood side by side at attention waiting for orders.

"Come on, let's get started," Lacey said, intending to keep Tom busy but not pre-occupied with life.

Tom did as he was told, and started to rummage through OLIVIA, the fridge for vegetarians only. He pulled out a head of lettuce, washed and dried the leaves and cut it carefully, placing neatly shredded pieces on the butcher block table in the center of room. He found a jar of artichokes in the pantry and placed then on the cutting board he had engraved with H.O.U.S.E across the top. "I like looking at my handiwork. It makes me feel better to know I can at least do something," he whispered to Lacey.

Richie came in. "Enter, oh great carnivore!" Lacey teased. "Here comes the king of beef. Or should I say beefcake?!" Lacey frequently commented he had the best "bod" in the H.O.U.S.E.

"We gotta have more than tomato sauce for the pasta," Richie said. "How about a little crumbled bacon for the salad or a few meatballs?"

"No dice, it's vegetarian night," Lacey said, interrupting Richie. "We need a calming influence tonight, a comforting meal, not one full of the meat that brings out aggressiveness in us."

Tom rolled his eyes and continued with the lettuce and artichokes.

"Hiya, can I help?" Wayne chirped, coming in with Velta who contributed a loaf of fresh bread baked by a friend who was a baker and a jar of tomato sauce from the restaurant. The bread was already sliced and still warm.

Lacey was in her element supervising her staff and creating culinary coups in the kitchen. She never read directions. She was, by her own admission, and that of others, an "experiential" not an "experimental" cook in the larder and in life.

Lacey had already filled the pot with water which was now boiling and ready for the spaghetti she and Richie had made the day before. They had mixed and pounded the dough into smooth balls then pushed it through a machine that resembled a meat grinder. Out came strands of whole wheat pasta ready to dry on wooden laundry racks by the kitchen back door. She had dumped the brown, squishy, mess that looked like the head of a floor mop, into the pot. And now it was ready

Richie and Tom were waiting for their orders.

"Tom, with a fork, take a few strands of spaghetti out of the water and throw them against the wall. If they stick we'll know the pasta's ready."

Thwack! The spaghetti hit the wall high above the stove and stayed.

Wayne took the fork from Tom and conducted the same exercise. Splat! Bullseye again.

Velta, who was finishing slicing tomatoes suddenly hurled a wet, juicy one against the wall next to the spaghetti. The seeds dribbled down the whit wall.

"Whaaaah?! Exclaimed Lacey as she shut off the stove, clinging vainly to the idea of preparing a beautiful meal. She reached into the pot, pulled a wad of pasta up and threw a softball pitch against the wall.

Richie threw a slab of mozzarella against another wall. Velta responded hurling a spoonful of the red pasta next to the mozzarella. More mozzarella, more sauce, more tomatoes.

The shredded lettuce became the next prospect for the wall. Tom threw the still wet leaves so hard that they stuck for a few moments before falling on top of the stove, some into the pot of spaghetti which was now cooling down. Lacey reached for another handful of pasta and flung it hard at the wall.

Everyone was laughing. Everyone found a vegetable or a handful of pasta or a spoonful of tomato to pitch wherever there was a space on the wall. It wasn't exactly Jackson Pollock but it was deeply satisfying. They were letting go of the tension of the protest that day.

They didn't hear the sound of the engine stopping outside the back door. They were still laughing when Doug appeared in the doorway still in his helmet, the strap hanging down from his face. All culinary activity stopped. Wayne was the only laughing. The others suddenly looked sheepish, waiting for what Doug would say.

"Jesus! That was fun! Wayne proclaimed after several moments of silence. "Guess we really needed to blow off steam," he said wiping the tomato paste off his face as the others did the same.

"Jesus, that was childish," Doug said sarcastically mimicking Wayne's attempt to put a positive spin on their antics. No one spoke after that. The kitchen crew began picking up the remnants of their food preparation off the wall, cleaned up the floor and the stove and got ready for the evening meal. Lacey was left alone in the kitchen with Doug.

"I heard it said sometimes you can be a real prick," Lacey said flatly as if she were merely reporting a fact. She turned her back on Doug, making clear she wanted nothing to do with him.

Dinner was a solemn affair. The food was tasty. But there was no flavor in the conversation at the table and they ate in silence watching Lacey sad sitting low in her seat, not hungry. Later that night Lacey slept alone in the empty room at the front of the house.

D.C. Bound

Two days later Wayne, Lacey, Denny, Velta, Richie and Ed Tinker, a new member of H.O.U.S.E, left Des Moines at 5:00 a.m. in a used VW bus formerly owned by a town florist. The flower shop's purple lettering still showed through the fading lavender paint on both sides: Frannie's Florals. H.O.U.S.E. mates had stenciled waves all the way around the truck and then painted the bottom half an aqua marine blue. They were proud of the new design until someone pointed out that the truck could be easily spotted when speeding or trying to escape police or protesters.

Denny drove the bus. He had moved out of H.O.U.S.E and taken up with Velta who had left shortly after the wedding because she had saved enough money to open her own seamstress shop, the Constant Tailor. By now she and Denny were business partners, as well as lovers.

Ed Tinker had taken the place of Doug who had to stay behind—he was now not allowed to travel until his trial was over. Lacey missed him, of course, but was glad to be on the road for a few days, able to feel free again and unattached. The feeling was a secret that she shared only with Richie. She was glad Ed Tinker was along so she could learn more about his family's case against the government.

Ed Tinker was the older brother of John and Mary Beth Tinker. Earlier in the year the younger brother and sister had won a very important legal case involving constitutional rights. Lacey was embarrassed she knew so little about the subject of constitutional rights. What if Doug's case was upheld in the Appeals Court in Saint Louis? Would the case go to the Supreme Court? Lacey was glad there would be plenty of time to talk with Ed on the twenty hour ride to D.C.

Well over six feet tall in his big rusty brown leather cowboy boots, Ed was a standout in any crowd and a potential landmark if they got separated in the crowd in D.C. He had a thick shock of blond hair, almost albino like. He was shy and quiet unless he was talking about his siblings of whom he was very proud. Barely an hour passed before Lacey asked Ed about his family's case.

"In December four years ago some students, along with my brother John and sister Mary Beth met in the home of another student to plan a public showing of support for a truce in the Vietnam war," Ed began. "They decided to wear black armbands during the holiday season and to fast on December 16 and New Year's Eve. The Des Moines school principals learned of the plan and said that any student wearing an armband would be asked to remove it and refusal to do so would lead to suspension."

Just as Lacey nodded, Ed said: "You guessed it. They got kicked out. They sued all the way to the Supreme Court and won. No one can take away the right to free speech. Damn proud of them, I am." Ed reclined, as comfortably as his huge frame would allow, into his seat and took a nap.

Though the story was not really relevant to Doug's case, still the idea of facing the appeals court or the Supreme Court, and losing, scared Lacey. "Do you think judges are really fair minded and objective or just mouthing the views of those who appoint them?"

"I don't know, Lacey. You ask a fair question. You're beginning to think like Doug. He wonders that same thing I am sure. All I know is we won. I can't say more."

"Hey, buddy," Richie weighed in, "it's not WE WON, it was your brother and sister."

"I know," Ed admitted, "but I was there to support them the whole way and feel we did it together."

"For sure," Lacey said, distractedly as she looked out the window wondering what would happen when Doug's trial became a reality and not just and unscheduled date.

Denny's turn at the wheel came in the afternoon at around 4:30 somewhere outside of Philadelphia. After about twenty miles he began to sweat, get cold and shiver. Then he went white as a sheet and started to faint. From the front passenger seat, Wayne grabbed the wheel, got his foot on the brake and pushed Denny into the window. He guided the van off the highway down a ramp onto a narrow deserted side road and pounded the brakes to a full stop.

"What the fuck?! Did you drop just before we left Des Moines? You wanna kill all of us?" Wayne screamed.

"I dunno, I'm sick, Wayne. I didn't think this would happen. I need water. Please help me. I think I'm going to throw up."

Wayne put his canteen to Denny's lips and immediately Denny barfed all over the van's steering wheel and Wayne's lap, an empty stomach kind of barf, gray water and guts and last night's pizza.

Lacey and Ed were in the second seat, and Richie and Velta were in the way back. "Let me out, I've got to help him. Leave him alone. He'll be all right if I just get to him," she pleaded to have the back door opened.

"We've got to get to a truck stop to get him some water and a bathroom to clean him up— and the van," said Wayne.

Wayne pulled Denny out of the van and he and Velta dragged him around to the front and then stuffed him into the passenger seat. He slumped in sick exhaustion, his head flopping against the window.

Velta got back into the way back and Wayne started the motor. Within a few minutes of being back on the highway they spotted a truck stop up ahead. A billboard to the right of the highway read *Eat this way*. About two hundred yards further on, the next one beckoned *Dolly's Dugout Diner next right*. Trees and telephones lined the highway. Gray afternoon clouds loomed overhead. Lacey noticed the birds flying south for the winter in perfect formation.

"Why the hell did this have to happen?" Lacey said to no one in particular. Then immediately "I mean I am sorry Denny is so sick." She was not sorry. She was not fond of druggies. "It looks like now we may not make DC by night fall."

Wayne got off the highway as quickly as possible, drove right into the diner and parked as near as he could to the front door. Other truckers were in the parking lot waking up from sleeping in their cabs all night. They'd soon be heading into the diner for a hearty Dolly breakfast before taking off to deliver their ton of bananas or furniture or whatever to retailers in cities on the East Coast.

Ed and Lacey and Richie and Wayne found seats at the counter just as a bunch of truckers were leaving. Wayne headed to the bathroom with Denny, who, at least now, was walking, though still not steadily.

Wayne ran the water in the faucet, cold as he could make it and splashed some on Denny's face. "You know, we could have died right out there on Route 66! God Damn it, Denny, you gotta quit that stuff, not just for this trip but for good. I can't have a friend who does that stuff."

"Bug off, Wayne," Denny said with a weak smile, steading himself by leaning over the sink and away from Wayne, still making little gasps for air. "You can't preach to me. You've done this a hundred times up there in the attic. I always come back. Mostly it's a great trip, just not this time."

"But not while you're driving, you jerk. Listen, man, Velta will leave you if you don't quit this stuff for good. Grass is one thing but that acid is bad all the way around. Damn right she will go. And I'll leave, too, even though you are kinda cute at times."

Wayne took off his shirt, washed his chest and hands and found one of Denny's shirts in his backpack, printed with a cluster of bunched up colorful stars he had made a few months before. "Guess I'll have to wear one of your cockamamie crazy shirts for the rest of this trip. But I'll never wear another one until you quit that business. You hear?"

"I hear you," Denny said, in a whisper, barely audible to Wayne. He picked bits of barf out of his teeth and swallowed handfuls of water in great gulps.

"Okay, now let's get back out there and get something to eat. And promise not to barf on me in the future. No one in the bus knew Denny had taken something powerful, but only Velta knew he had dropped acid, because she was used to these episodes. After eggs and coffee and Texas toast they each took turns walking Denny around the parking lot. He recovered after several hours, making trips back to the diner to get fluids and lying down to rest several times in the back of the van. The group had lost several hours of vital time by the time they restarted the van.

Ed took over the wheel while Denny slept off the drug in the back. Lacey turned on the radio and started singing softly with Carol King. "You make me feel like a nat-ur-al wooom-man." Ed and Wayne joined with their squeaky falsettos. "I bet you do feel like a natural woman," Lacey said as she blew him a loud smacking kiss from kiss from the back seat.

The rest of the passengers took turns at the wheel until they arrived in D.C. around 9:00 that night. Wayne had a friend named Glen who worked in the D.C. Peace Corps office who lived on the hill at Third and A Streets South East behind the Shakespeare museum. And there was a church across the street from his friend's apartment where, as a last resort, they could sleep in the van in the parking lot.

Wayne parked the van in the church lot and went to knock on Glen's door. No one was home and the sign on the door asked the mailman to keep the mail until November 20.

"Guess we'll have to sleep in this hotel tonight," Wayne said pointing to the van as he came across the street." They all got out, shaking their legs for exercise, glad the evening was warm and that this end of town was not crowded. "Let's head over to the top of the hill and find some pizza and maybe a beer before it's too late," Wayne said. By midnight they were back in the van, everyone trying to sleep sitting up their seats. The sunlight woke them early on Friday, November 15, 1969.

The sexton had come on duty early to clean up the church for the services the next day.

Lacey saw her opportunity. She jumped out of the van and walked up to the man opening the door with his key.

"I hope we didn't inconvenience you by parking here last night. We drove all the way from Iowa to join the protest today."

"It's not my church. It's God's place. I don't think he'd mind."

"Do you think he'd mind if we washed up in you restrooms before we walk down to the mall?"

"Can't say as he would mind that either. What I do think he minds is this damn war. No sense in it."

"You are right about that and we appreciate your kindness. We'll be quick. Any place you suggest we get breakfast."

"There's Roland's across the way. Mean and ugly waitresses but the food's damn good."

"Thanks, we'll take you up on that, waitresses and all."

The group cleaned up, changed into new tee shirts and put on jackets. The sexton was right about Roland's and they each had a hearty breakfast and packed a few extra rolls for later that day.

They missed the opening rally the day before but they read about it at breakfast. Richie read to them about it at breakfast. "The March on Death was led by three drummers followed by eleven coffins containing the names of 40,000 soldiers who had died or Vietnam Villages that had been destroyed. They placed the names in a coffin out in front of the Capitol. Pretty powerful stuff."

Ed Tinker picked up where Richie left off. "And there was a man who carried a three-hundred-pound cross, proclaiming that if Christ were alive, he would impeach Richard Nixon. Banners and placards were everywhere. Signs made references to Spiro Agnew and the Silent Majority. Over and over the crowd sent up chants of "One, two, three, four. Tricky Dick, stop the war!"

The day was cold and clear. Busses lined the side streets on the Hill and everywhere else. Denny, now fully recovered, took charge. "We're gonna leave the bus here on Capitol Hill. Soon the group was walking dawn Capitol Hill toward Union Station and then down Pennsylvania.

"Although I can't tell, I think I can see Army and Marine Corps behind every column in Fed buildings along this route. It's creepy and I'm a little scared." She knew from the news there were two thousand metropolitan police on duty for the march, and the Pentagon and the Justice Department were swarmed with paratroopers.

"Don't be scared, Lacey. Be happy! Be glad we are here." Wayne shouted, hoping to boost her confidence, but merely agitating her nerves even more.

She felt better as they got closer to the White House when saw the sheer size of the crowd. "Wow, there must be half a million people here!" She wondered if Doug was watching on TV back home or if the feds had kept the whole thing off the air waves. "Doug would really love this if he could see how many people are here with him against this war." She felt the collective pulse of the crowd moving with her in solidarity. "Someday what we are doing is really going to matter," she blurted out to a teenage girl walking in step with her mother a short distance from Lacey.

Performers and speakers alternated throughout the afternoon on the podium below the Washington Monument. It took over an hour for Lacey and the others to make their way to the front of the crowd. Some people were smoking marijuana, but drugs were not a big part of the event. Music hat day ran the gamut from the sounds of a symphony to the schmaltz of Mitch Miller.

"Look up there," Lacey said to Ed and Wayne who were with her and Velta with Denny behind them. "There's George McGovern and Eugene McCarthy up on the stage. Funny how McGovern is all side burns and thinning hair while McCarthy looks more like a banker with a crew cut."

"But they share the same politics," Velta was quick to say. "My mom back in Minnesota worships him. Says it was the best thing for the state when he got elected senator. She wanted him to become President last year. Too bad we got Nixon instead. But it was McCarthy who kept Johnson from running again."

"When I look up there at George McGovern, I just see seriousness and sincerity written all over his face. He looks kind of like an older Doug Rogers."

"Who's pretty serious and sincere, too," Velta added. "Doug's got those same sideburns."

George McGovern was tall and lanky and from South Dakota. The senator smiled openly, waving to the crowd, his right hand raised with a peace sign as the crowd welcomed him.

The two were speaking together as one voice, urging everyone to be of good courage in this struggle to end the war. Lacey had no inkling that just two years later she would be helping George McGovern run the biggest race of his life.

The cast of *Hair* had come down from New York and were singing "The Age of Aquarius," releasing a host of doves into the air above the crowd. Lacey was close enough to watch the doves fly over her head and to sing along. *Harmony and understanding. Sympathy and trust abounding. No more falsehoods or derisions. Golden living dreams of visions. Mystic crystal revelation. And the mind's true liberation Aquarius, Aquarius.*

Lacey knew all the words. She began to sing and cry all at the same time, letting her voice ring out loud and clear with the *Hair* cast until she had belted every last note of the song. Richie's saw Lacey in tears and put his arm around her.

"It, okay, my friend. I am crying tears of happiness. I believe music has the power to move multitudes and if it can do that, maybe it can move Congress, too, to end the war.

Some people in the crowd began dancing to banjo tunes played by Earl Scruggs. Demonstrators and all the H.O.U.S.E members joined Pete Seeger in singing the words of John Lennon. *All we are saying is give peace a chance.* At the end everyone raised hands in a giant collective peace sign.

By now the H.O.U.S. E. gang were experts in the right way and the wrong way to wield a peace sign. They made the peace sign by turning the palm facing out, folding the pinky finger and ring finger toward the palm, holding them in place with the thumb. They used the peace sign in greetings and good byes; in all photographs to be remembered; to another driver after making a traffic violation; when faced with members of the armed forces, especially now in DC, and when passing other hippies. They knew not to employ the sign when being questioned by police.

All the great musicians of Lacey's personal hit parade were there that day. It was a free concert with all of her favorite musicians: Arlo Guthrie; Mary Travis of Peter, Paul and Mary; Leonard Bernstein; and playwright Adolph Green, who wrote one of Lacey's favorite musicals, *The Bells are Ringing,* starring Judy Holliday. Even Timothy Leary, whom Lacey had only recently discovered through Fred Slaughter, was on hand in a buckskin outfit, looking more like Daniel Boone than a contemporary hippie. She thought fleetingly of giving him her by raggedy coonskin cap.

Lacey sensed she was on a mission in the nation's capital. She was there for Doug but also fully for herself. She felt a kindred spirit with every person on the mall that day- a oneness- with- all and solidarity that welled up inside her bringing tears again and a catch in her throat as she tried to sing along with Pete Seeger. Her tears surprised her as she croaked into the wind, not because of the nearby fumes of tear gas, but because she at last understood what this was all about. People could make a difference- now, not some day in the future. She felt proud and privileged to stand as one with hundreds of thousands of others who were making a difference.

The Appeal

Across the yard on the other side of the lawn H.O.U.S.E. stood a huge oak tree with a trunk as broad as a baby elephant with thick gnarly branches. Ed was tall enough to hurl a very thick rope over two sturdy branches that hung side by side. He drilled holes in a thick wooden board, put a rope through them and tied knots securely on the other side. "Voila, my one and only swing for you, my friend," he boasted. Lacey loved it and often went to swing there when she felt anxious as she did that day in May.   It was two days before Doug's appeal.

They and Doug's lawyer spent the next night in a cheap hotel outside of Saint Louis. They arrived at the 8th Circuit Court of Appeals early to decisions would be read from 10:00 to 11:00 am.

Doug sat up front in the first row on the left. Lacey took her seat directly behind John in the second row. It was already 10:20.

Doug leaned back as best he could in the rigid chair, "What's taking the prosecutor so long?"

"I don't know. There are three on the panel and they have to hear both sides. They must be holed up in the back room."

"You make them all sound like cronies."

"They are, so far as I am concerned. They're probably all Republican appointees."

"Nice. I appreciate your sarcasm. I am more sanguine about all of this. Whatever happens, happens. There is nothing more I can do now. I do know I love, you, Lacey, even if I get put away."

"Will the court please rise," the judge intoned, speaking slowly with the emphasis on the "rise."

Please understand no evidence is presented here today and there are no witnesses. The three judges have met en banc and have reviewed the arguments on both sides in our first case, Douglas C. Rodgers vs. The United States.

As they listened to the lead judge, Lacey wanted to hold Doug's hand, put her arm around him, to not feel awkward standing behind.

"Why is he talking like we're stupid and don't understand?"

"Lacey, shut up, stop talking. Just wait. That's what I am doing."

"It is the opinion of the court to allow the defendant, Douglas C. Rodgers, to initiate application to become a conscientious objector following pursuant to entering the U.S. Military."

Dan threw his hands in the air so excited about the decision. He and John shook hands and the almost but didn't hug. Dan stepped aside to let Lacey congratulate Doug with hug.

Doug didn't move toward her. When Lacey put her arms around his neck, Doug pulled them down to her sides.

"This is not a victory yet. I feel very measured. I have to go into the army, not what I wanted. I'll have to go away, enter Fort Leonard Wood, be a soldier until they can process my claim. Who knows how long that will take? No I am not satisfied yet."

Lacey managed to hold back hurt tears and her tongue until the ride home.

"I am sorry I overwhelmed you. I am so happy you get a second chance instead of four years in jail."

"I am sorry, too. I am just not capable of the kind of emotion you experience. I do appreciate your support. I do love you. In my own way. I am just not demonstrative."

Lacey had no words. What good would it do to tell him now how much he hurt her? He didn't get it. She needed affirmation. He had delivered rejection.

"How about you take over the rest of the drive home? I'm done in. Exhausted. Need to rest."

For once, she couldn't wait to take the wheel.

"Let's stop just ahead at that diner."

John slept while Lacey counted trees, then gas stations and finally cows until they reached the outskirts of Des Moines that night

"Let's make love one more time, to be inside each other now, to remember this time while we are apart," Lacey said softly, leaning over to kiss Doug's ear from the other side of the mattress. A candle glowed its last light.

"No, I can't. Not tonight. I don't feel like it. Can't you see I a distracted? I don't feel close…to anyone or anything. Look at that candle. Time is running out," Doug whispered.

Lacey said nothing for what seemed a very long time. She did not know what to say and was not used to being speechless. "Good night, sweetheart," was all she could muster. She rolled over and pulled the sheet up on her side. Better to sleep, she warned herself, than signal her sadness to this man so filled with his own sense of loss.

Several days later Doug bought his bus ticket to Fort Leonard Wood, Kansas and was as ready as he could be to be inducted into the military. Lacey drove him to the bus station.

"You need to take care of things while I am gone."

"Right. I'll be sweet to Elmer Fudd."

"That's not what I mean. You be sure the bills are paid and Wayne doesn't burn up the attic with his dope."

"Sure, sure, sweetheart. The main thing is I will miss you so much. I wish I could go with you."

He gave Lacey a peck on the cheek. Lacey's insides screamed to hold on to him, to

capture his face for the last time to protect herself from the absence she was going to feel.

"You seem so calm, I can hardly stand it." Lacey began to cry.

"Lacey, these are tough times. I love you because you are strong. So be strong now, for me."

But I feel so weak and wounded. I cannot tell him now. Just smile and say good bye.

"So long, sweetheart, the bus is boarding now."

She watched him mount the three steps into the bus and stood beside it until it took off. She waved until the van disappeared from sight. "Good bye, my love, good by my love."

Rejection

With John gone, Lacy focused on those around her for comfort and companionship.

A former client of Doug's came to stay at H.O.U.S.E to whom Lacey was drawn.

Larry Fernstrom had been a medic in Vietnam. He had been awarded a purple heart. His mother had come to see Doug to ask him how to help her son.

"He wants to be an artist and now, courtesy of the G.I. Bill he is enrolled in drawing classes at Drake. But he can't seem to go to class. He is having nightmares of aiding soldiers in the fields in Vietnam, of pulling boots off of soldiers as they got wheeled into the make shift operating room where he was stationed. If they died he feels responsible, if they lived, he still feels he didn't do enough."

Now Larry was living at H.O.U.S.E in the empty bedroom up front on the second floor. He came and went but no one asked if he was going to class or elsewhere. With John gone, Lacey wanted to learn more about life in the army from Joe who had been through it. Joe seemed to be on the edge of losing it and she was worried about John's sanity. She had not heard from in more than two months. Why?

"I have to go there. Now. He must feel so alone, like you."

"Lacey, anything is possible," Joe started in. She hadn't really talked to him about much of anything so far except that she was curious about his art classes because she wanted to take them, too. The only thing she really knew about him was that he thought the only reason to be in a room with a girl was to make out with her. But on this day he was serious and opened up to her for the first time.

"Every part of war is Hell. The training, the barracks, the shouting sergeants. I made it through only to face those poor helpless gooks who just kept on coming. We aren't fighting to defend democracy. We are there for the aluminum and other resources. They gave me an award for saving lives that should never have gone over there. Now I am all torn up inside. I can't talk to anyone any more. I keep having sweats at night and

I wake up from dreams punching the air with my fists and attacking my pillow. It's even hard for me to say these things to you. So, yes, anything could be happening to Doug and his mind inside that place." Joe seemed momentarily spent from these admissions. Lacey reached out and put her arms around him, shedding tears of sorrow that matched the mist in his own eyes.

"Joe, I know it must be so hard to put your feelings into words after all that you have been through but you must keep trying to do that with all of us here to listen to you. We are here to help."

Lacey could be insensitive, even bitchy, at times, but this man's story hit her hard at her core. The war had clearly wounded Joe even though he came home without a scratch. She was deeply troubled by what she heard and turned to Richie for advice.

"I really don't know what to say to Joe. I think you are headed for a crash if you keep things bottled up inside much longer. Doug's not here to talk to you but you do need real help. None of us know what it was like to be in Vietnam. I have got my own worries. I need to go see Doug now. I am worried he could be on the edge himself."

Lacey and Doug spoke once a week on the phone but only briefly. In the third week in August Lacey received a letter.

Dear Lacey:

Well. Tomorrow I will have been in the army two months. I have found my way to one of two typewriters. What do I have to show for my time here? Nothing. I am going to have to stop thinking I guess because the more I think the more I want out of here and the more I feel I made a mistake. I think that it is wrong for me to be here. I am gradually feeling that it would have been more honorable (if there is such a thing as honor in the world) to be in prison. I would rather have people see me in prison than here. This place violates the very thing I believe in. I hope there is a chance of me getting out of here soon.

I will call my lawyer Dan this afternoon and see what is happening and maybe why. Thinking seems to get me in trouble. It makes me not want to go along with this stuff. When I think I wonder why are officers treated better than enlisted men? It just does not make sense to me.

Lacey stopped there and turned to Joe. "I think he may be really depressed. He's so bent on his conscience being right. It's scary, he's so isolated."

Lacey continued reading aloud to Joe.

"They may say this stuff is not dehumanizing but why do I have reactions that are violent and have to restrain myself when I did not have so violent a reaction in civilian life? Sometimes I am close to violence. There is no reason I should be this way. I have never been as close to this as I am here. That bothers me. Here I do not really give a shit about people or anything else. I do not trust other guys. I have contempt for most of the drill sergeants and pity for the rest of them. I find myself not being able to respond to the situation in a civil and human manner. I try but it is difficult. I know that I am strong enough to survive this and be normal again when I get out but here I do not like my reactions.

I had a feeling yesterday that I do not want to have you visit me here in this place and see me. I want very much to see you but not here. There is something about this place that makes me ashamed of being here and of violating my conscience and everything that I stand for. Here I see nothing constructive I can do but survive until I get out. I do not like this position. What can I do?

When you come down I will not stay here on the base at all. I want to get away from it. This may be the pride thing Wayne was talking about. I do not know. All I know is I do not like what I am feeling.

I love you and would like to talk to you about this.

Doug

"Let me go with you," Richie pleaded with Lacey. "Even though my license got suspended over that drinking thing, I could go with you to keep your spirits up and make sure you drive safely."

"You? Make sure I drive safely? A guy who can't drive is going to protect me on the road? You must be kidding!" Lacey laughed openly at Richie's suggestion.

"Richie, you can't come with me. I have to go myself. I need time with him alone," she pleaded to her friend. *Won't you let me go with you? No, my love no.* Lacey could hear strains of Peter, Paul and Mary in her head as Richie pleaded his case. But unlike the song, she wouldn't change her mind.

"I dunno, Lace, you are not the best driver on the planet and the fort is three and half hours away from here through some treacherous windy roads down there in the Ozarks. You need me in shining armor to protect you." Richie had a way with words when he wanted something.

"Thanks, sweetheart, but I gotta do this on my own. Doug would want it that way. I am excited to go see him."

⬩⸺⸺◆⸺⸺⬩

The wind and rain battered the windowless Karman Ghia most of the way before Lacey reached Fort Leonard Wood.

When she saw Doug walking toward her from the barracks, she ran to him, throwing her arms around him as if to greet every part of his body all at once.

"Don't ever do that again!" Doug barked, pushing her away from him.

Lacey was stunned even before she could feel the hurt. The touch of his push was icy cold, his hands almost frozen in the motion. His voice was a dry rasp. His whole body seemed to reject her presence. She had no frame of reference for this sudden alienating outburst. Was it the realization of what he had done in opposing the law? The fear of being a felon? Regret? A rejection of their marriage and of her? She was afraid all of the answers might be yes.

She said nothing in response, just walked alongside him until they found an empty picnic table where they could share the food Lacey had brought from H.O.U.S.E. She laid out a red and white tablecloth on the table, which was anchored to the ground. She put down the homemade bread Wayne had made and the cheese and fresh grapes she had bought on the trip. Doug picked at his food. Lacey wasn't hungry either.

"Why is this table chained to the ground?" Lacey wondered, picking a conversation out of the air. "Do the guards really think a prisoner would make off with a picnic table?" The joke

went unanswered.

Doug made no comment for quite a while and even then gave no reason for his coldness toward Lacey. Lacey was the one to ask.

"What's wrong? She didn't want to say "with me" but was clearly thinking she had done something for him to reject her.

"You coming in this cold and ugly place is too overwhelming for me. It's not like me to hug and gush like you. My family doesn't do that and I don't like it."

And there it was. Lacey was crushed and embarrassed to have been so excited to see her husband and Doug couldn't handle so much emotion. But what was too much? In any case, she would show him. Never again, she promised herself, would she be so effusive.

Eventually their discussion picked up tempo, and they talked about H.O.U.S.E and the upcoming appeal. When the time was up, Doug barely kissed Lacey goodbye. It almost seemed as if he would have preferred a handshake.

Theirs was not the kiss of familiar lovers, but a quick peck on the cheek before she drove away. Both were distracted, engulfed by the empty feeling of an unknown future. Soon Doug would come home and Lacey would tuck that feeling away in the closet of her mind to protect her from remembering the hurt of that day.

Hanging by a Thread

Lacey banged the screen door on her way in. She liked doing this instead of announcing her return with a loud yell. She thought it more civilized to make an entrance unannounced. After six hours on the road she was famished and ready for a glass of wine. She knew a number of the "apostles", as she called them, would be waiting around the dinner table. In her absence they all ordered pizza.

"What a cop out! Pizza? Can't any of you guys cook?" She joked-- glad to be back.

Soon Lacey left the dinner table to seek solace on the swing. *Why, why is it so hard? I love John, but he is so distant, fighting his battles alone, leaving me out. Is it my fault? Does he not trust me? Why can't I ask him? When haven't I heard from him?*

She often headed outside to swing with her thoughts about friends or food or politics or thoughts for the day. While one would never accuse her of being a deep thinker, she could be reflective. As she pumped the swing she thought about her relationship, mostly with John, but on many levels. She felt almost free, swinging back and forth in a comforting rhythm as the night set in and the constellations began to look down on her from above. She loved the Iowa night sky because it was not yet blotched by the smoke from manufacturing so common back East. Out here cows and corn on the ground left the skies clear at night.

Several nights later, Richie and Wayne and Ed Tinker and Lacey were sitting cross legged around the dinner table waiting for Lacey to deliver another moussaka to the table. Danny and Velta were visiting, bringing news of their new design company.

This is going to be some awesome eats," Richie said, setting empty jars on the table and filling them with red wine.

Lacey came into the dining room with the moussaka an accepted the accolades of "ooh and ah" as it was placed on the table. Wayne brought in the salad.

"Rubba, dub, dub, He gives us grub," Wayne said, delivering the blessing as a joke.

There was much chewing and not much conversation for a while. The candles on the table were going strong though it was still daylight outside and the evening was warm and drying.

At one point Wayne casually looked out the window. The look on his face turned a warm wine smile to a look of disbelief.

"Oh my God. He's hanging there. I can't believe it. " she heard Wayne whisper, as if he were far away.

Richie turned his head seeing the noose, picking at his words. "Oh my God! He sure knew how to put a good rope to use," he said, not hiding his cynicism. "He was always just hanging by a thread." Richie's words were intentionally cruel. He had been close to Joe, but he knew, not close enough. He was angry that his friend chose to go.

"Oh, no, God Damn I it, I was afraid for him when I left. Did any of you try to talk to him, even ask him how he was?" Lacey was becoming distraught than sad, her face turning red as she grew more agitated.

"What do we do? Ed, can you get him down from the tree. Lay him on the ground and I will call his parents." Lacey was searching for answers, any answers, no matter how incoherent she sounded.

"His parents will come and take him away," Richie began, his words slurring. Lacey's immediate was just as cynical as Richie's. *Being stoned sure takes the edge off death.*

"They will say it's all our fault. He was under the influence of quote 'heathen hippies' like us. They'll ask us not to show up at the funeral. Just you wait."

Lacey bolted from the dining room in search of a phone, leaving her comrades in stunned silence sitting on the floor with the half eaten pizza. She wanted to reach Doug, let him know immediately, she wasn't sure why, she just needed to. She should have asked him about that when she was at the stockade but was afraid to after their altercation.

It took a long time for the guard to find Doug and bring him from his cell to the phone. Now holding the receiver she was suddenly paralyzed, afraid to say-what?

"Hi, Lacey, what's up? Hey, I'm sorry about the letter. I didn't want to alarm you. I feel so jumpy in here. I'm not myself. Or maybe I am myself. I'm not good with so much duress. I dunno. I know I must have hurt you."

"I understand. I love you. It was the pressure, the uncertainty for you. But now we are talking. Holding the phone is the closest to holding you." She knew that probably sounded like too much.

She began slowly, taking all affect out of her words.

"I want to let you know Joe hanged himself tonight using the rope on the swing. Got up on the ladder and kicked it clear out from under his feet. Oh, God, this is so awful, Doug. If only I could have done something. Could I have done anything?" Lacey almost pleaded for an answer.

"Cut it out, Lacey! He was on a mission. Don't blame yourself. There was nothing you could have done. That's what war does to those sensitive enough to be touched by it. It ruins them," came Doug's sobering response.

"Joe had been watching the tree for a long time. He watched my joy swinging on it. It only gave him pain. Oh, God, I wish I could have done something to help. Joe put the noose in place with enough coils to do the job as quickly and as painlessly as possible. We're the ones who are left in pain."

"Hey, the good news is I'll be getting out of her soon and you can come get me." Lacey was full of relief and remorse.

Homecoming

The sergeant in charge of releasing Doug looked up from his desk and down over his glasses with sour parting words. "Young man, you are very lucky to be out of here before the winter sets in. I hope no more of you get sent this way. You are a disgrace to the military and your country." The "fuck you" in Doug's eyes was silent but sharp.

Lacey was relieved. Doug showed no visible emotion or reaction, but she could tell he felt no victory either. Lacey had learned her lesson this time. She hugged him loosely and greeted him with a simple "hello."

Sitting in the passenger seat in the Ghia next to Doug for the ride home, she could feel through the leather the tensions mounting in Doug. The lack of affect in Doug's voice came out a slow drone. "What did I miss? How could I have changed the course for others? I just don't know." She knew he felt he had been rendered powerless, forced into a place where he would now have to find a way to have his voice heard. He was not going to be one of those guys who spent two years as an orderly in some rural hospital.

Doug was still is his uniform. Lacey had to admit he looked so all American and gung-ho which he was not. She knew he wouldn't want her say how handsome he was. She felt very uncertain on the ride home.

Doug took his right hand off the wheel and pull Lacey toward him. "I know this has been hard on you, having to worry about me so much. I am sorry I have been so self-absorbed. I will do better, especially when we are in Tokyo."

"What?!" Lacey was in shock,

"That's right. The ACLU and the American Friends Service Committee have gotten together to fund a two year position for me to be civilian counsel in military courts martials on the U.S. bases in Japan."

"Oh, my God. How great. You have pulled off a great opportunity." This time when she kissed him from the passenger seat, he welcomed her touch. She rejoiced in his touch, the smell of his skin again and the tickle of his sideburns to her cheek. All resentments gone.

When they reached H.O.U.S.E in time for dinner everyone was on the front porch to greet them with a barbecue on the front lawn and Tupperware pitchers of Sangria and cheap Bali Hi wine. "Congrats! You made it. Welcome home. Man, we've needed you to get back home," Tom Lesser waxed on, obviously thrilled to see his friend.

"Look at you in that faggy uniform," Wayne said, clapping Doug on the back and handing him a jar of Sangria."

Denny and Velta were there in matching tie-dyed T-shirts. "I see you have your own uniforms," Doug said greeting both of them with a smile and a handshake.

"It's good to be home and be with you all. It was pretty lonely in Kansas on the base."

Just as the evening was ending, Doug made his announcement. By now everyone was seated around the table in the dining room watching the candles dim and the sky outside grow dark. "Lacey and I are going to Japan. I'll be working with the Quakers, hoping to help GIs who may need legal help. We'll miss you guys, but it's time to move on."

The faces around the table looked stunned, even hurt. "What, how can you leave now, when you've just come home?" Wayne was almost angry at his best friend.

Richie was just plain sad and was quick to say, "I am going to miss the only girl I have ever really loved." Lacey hugged him close and hard in the sadness of leaving him.

"Congratulations," said Ed. It is probably time for a new adventure for you and for us. For a while Ed had been wanting to take over leadership of the commune and to bring in new members.

She caught the vibes in the room and jumped in to rescue Doug. "Now that you guys have decided that new members, Alex and Andy, can have their baby born here at H.O.U.S.E. with a midwife and are ready to raise a child collectively, I have to say Doug and I are not ready to participate in child rearing for others, let alone ourselves." Doug smiled at Lacey for stating the case so openly and honestly, even if she was stating *his* case not really *hers*. They were both glad she had been the one to make the admission ensuring they were a united front. No children, no, thank you.

That night they lay on the mattress upstairs in the back room. Doug was starved to make love now that the tension was gone and he could focus on the future. A bunch of condoms in little packages lay on the floor next to an empty bottle of water. Lacey saw that as a good sign. Doug was coming alive. She opened herself completely to him. He kissed her gently, then ravaged her body and came hard late into the night. She loved it. The farm animal in Doug returned that night.

PART II: JAPAN

New territory

"Let's not do research. That'd be too easy," Lacey said the next morning. "I don't want to know everything about Japan before we go," she pleaded, when Doug suggested they go to the library. For once she got her way. Doug got permission to leave the country and the Quakers and the ACLU agreed to fund his alternative service as civilian counsel in military Courts Martials at any of the 44 U.S bases in Japan. They were on their way. It was September, 1971.

Lacey fidgeted in her seat as the plane hung over Hanada airport waiting to land. "I can't believe we are here. I never thought about where we would go, didn't want to came to the Far East but now that we're here, I'm on board. Oh, that was a silly pun, but you get what I mean," Lacey laughed, unrestrained and ready for this new adventure.

They spent the first few nights with a Japanese Methodist minister who had trained in the states and had come home to convert his folks from Shinto to Christianity. On morning after breakfast he told the new arrivals with a bit of a smile, "honestly I am having a harder time competing with the Mormon missionaries than my own countrymen. The Japanese are fascinated by them."

The sights and sounds of Tokyo assaulted their senses in different ways. "I have no clue about those tiny characters," Lacey complained as she tried decipher the signs hanging about the shops lining the downtown streets. But she loved to shape the phonetic sounds in her Learn Japanese Quick Book until she could get "Kon-ichi-wa", good day, just right.

Lacey loved the honking cars and the noise and lights of the Ginza. Her Japanese sputtered through the first week, imitating those who greeted her.

Doug, on the other hand, chose to attempt to understand the signs around him by trying each day visually to interpret the characters overhead in the shops and storefront restaurants in Tokyo. It helped that restaurants placed live samples of food menu in the glass encased windows so that the first week they could just point to selections until they learned to say "kore wa ikura desuka?" "How much is this?"

"Konichi wa. Geigin, desuka?" greeted them at every turn. "Are you a foreigner?" It was pretty obvious they were and it was pretty easy to understand "konicha wa" simply meant "good day to you" after they had heard it enough

After reading through the ads in the English newspapers, the Yomiuri Shimbun and the Asahi News, Lacey made an appointment to visit an apartment for rent in a house just outside of Shinjuku on the major subway line, the Seibo Shinjuki sen.

"Konichi wa. Watashi wa Lacey Rogers, desu."

"Yes, yes, come right in," greeted the smiling man who opened the sliding front door to the house. Lacey could not believe the good karma standing in front of her.

"I am Watanabe, Kenji. My name means "healthy second son" so I guess I should be grateful," he chuckled with a line Lacey was sure he used often with geijin. She knew the Japanese always smiled even when they weren't sincere so she felt a bit uncomfortable at that moment.

"I graduated from the University of Pennsylvania. You know the Wharton School, Yes?" Lacey was learning that all Japanese questions ended with the positive-yes? "And this is my wife, Yukio. She went to school in the States, too. You know the girls' school in Mass-a-chusetts-a, Dana Hall?

Another deep breath and Lacey could not believe her good fortune. The two little boys peeking out between their parents' knees were adorable. She wanted to hug them both immediately but restrained her enthusiasm mindful of Japanese formality with strangers.

An hour later she paid the "key" money two month's rent in advance rent and after a quick tour was given the keys to the upstairs apartment. The two room suite came with a tatami mat and a hibachi grill built into the floor of the main room. As was the custom in Japan, there was also a kind of fish tank built into the floor next to the single window that overlooked the busy street below. In it was a full grown, orange-spotted, carp trying swimming in a space not much bigger than he was. Lacey and Doug were to look after this resident as long as they lived there. She was clear she was going to "give" the fish to Doug on the day they moved in. Her part in the effort was to name the carp "Tony" for Tony Orlando, the not so great singer of the day back in the States.

Lacey didn't know what she would do in Tokyo, but she was open to almost anything. Most of the time she was too busy to keep up with her journal but she found time to make her first entry since leaving the States. "Our trip began a month ago-or did it really start two years ago in Iowa? Anyway, it began at least a month ago because that was when we flew over the international dateline on Valentine's Day after stopping for a week in San Francisco. *I left my heart in…..* Why do I always hear a song? It must be genetic. Doug was so matter of fact right when I was hoping for a romantic moment on that day at that point when we crossed over.

Since landing in Japan it has been a mix of personal agony and impersonal curiosity. I am fine when we are sightseeing, but after, or in between times, I am riddled with strange images of the past and future. At night I have dreams of hanging from a noose coming out of nowhere, hanging from nothing, in a black sky. I think I am coming to grips with my own insecurity for the first time. I am a bunch of spare parts without a whole. I am fractured in many ways. The absence of anything to identify with in this huge anomic metropolis isn't exactly helping."

In another entry, oddly written in smaller handwriting, perhaps out of timidity, she wrote "my relationship with Doug is beginning to fracture as well. I am beginning to withdraw from him and hide my feelings. I can bounce back from most things without regret but need more excitement, more passion and affection from my husband." Her Leo birth sign indicated her big ego needed lots of praise, even flattery to keep her happy and interested. She was too proud and too insecure to express her needs to Doug outright.

One night, after they had moved into the apartment, Lacey heard Doug coming up the steps, removing his shoes and closing the sliding door. She had been writing a letter to her friend Molly back home to thank her for sending old copies of Sports Illustrated and the past months' scores of the Red Sox games. She put her pen down and bounced down on a pillow in the living room.

"How'd it go today in Yokuska?

"He's going to get screwed by the JAG's office. He's no more gay than I am, but they are trying to get rid of him on that score. He just hates being here like most of the other black soldiers who are made to go on the front lines."

Lacey popped open a bottle of beer because she knew it must have been hot and dry on the train that day.

"Some days I wonder if this war will ever end. It's gone on too long and too many innocent lives are being ruined not by death, but by living through it."

She sat patiently through Doug's, by now, diatribe.

"I think when this is over we should go live in Israel, not go back to the States. Whaddya say, Lace?"

Lacey gathered her courage by looking at the carp trying to swim in the all too small tank.

"I say we can't live anywhere together until we talk about our relationship."

Doug was quiet for a long time. Then simply "what do you mean?"

"You know what I mean. We don't really talk. I don't feel I can get close to you. I don't feel intimate with you. I don't mean about making love. I mean about really being with you apart from your work and your heady ideas." Doug didn't look hurt at hearing this outburst from Lacey so much as irritated.

"I am pretty smart, but unlike you, I am not so cerebral. You can't be in your head all of the time and never in your heart where I need you to be."

"What do expect from me? I am not stuck in my head when it comes to why I am doing this." He wasn't shouting but his voice was rising.

"I need more spontaneity in my life. And I need it from you. I can't always be the spark. It's a two way street and I don't think you are on it." Lacey wanted to stop but she couldn't help herself.

"If you are so passionate about ending war, how come you aren't more passionate about us? You are so measured all the time. You never even get riled up…when maybe you need to."

"Dammit, Lacey, it's hard enough to go out there every day to defend some dumb luck GI without having to come home to this kind of harangue! Besides, you're just frustrated 'cause you haven't found a job yet and you're taking it out on me. So just get busy, please!"

That was enough. Lacey looked at the fish swimming round and round in puddle of a pool and felt very sorry for Tony and her.

Language Lessons

Lacey spoke French and some Arabic and wanted to learn Japanese so she could get a job. Even now she spoke limited Japanese better than most "geijin." After the brief confrontation with Doug, she wanted to quell thoughts about her marriage by concentrating on finding work.

One night when Watanabe San came home from work he came upstairs to see Lacey. Even before he slid open the door and took off his shoes, he was smiling. "We are looking for someone to teach us advanced English at the Okurasho (Treasury Ministry). Do you know of anyone interesting?"

"You mean interes-ted, not interest-ing," corrected Lacey, "and yes I would be. I'm your man, I mean your woman," she was quick to self-edit, chuckling with glee as she did.

And that settled it. Lacey was soon spending two hours three times a week teaching the highest officials in the land how to use a knife and fork at formal state dinners in Geneva, how to talk about Impressionist paintings in Paris and how to play poker in Monaco if asked, by a Royal. It was great fun, paid good money and relieved stress while she looked for fulltime work.

At home Yukio Watanabe who had gone to Mount Holyoke College wanted to improve her English language skills. What began as mutual language learning became a friendship over time.

One day Lacey and Yukio were having an English lesson in Yukio's kitchen downstairs. Lacey pointed to each implement and appliance she could find in the small space. "This is a whisk, this is an eggbeater, this we call a mixer, this a "flipper" She spoke slowly, like the announcers on Radio Free Europe that she listened to nightly as they tried to reach new English speaker converts to the West, with careful intonation of each syllable in every sentence.

Then Yukio turned the tables on Lacey and taught her one of her first cultural lessons. She asked her if she knew about the two kinds of spoken Japanese: male and female.

"No. And why are there two different ways to say the same thing?"

"So that there is no misunderstanding," Yukio replied. "When a man says 'Hara-hetta-des' he may mean, 'I am hungry, I am desirous, I want you, I crave,' et-a-cet-era. A woman must say 'No-naka-wa-sui-te-imasuyo,' meaning 'my stomach is empty,' so as not to be confused with a sexual or dark meaning." This startling division of the sexes, built into the culture of the country since ancient times, she guessed, was something she would have to learn fast if she was going to make her way in Japan. She also had to learn the lesson of being a "shufu" in a foreign country.

"It means 'housewife' in Japanese," Yukio began. "It is much more common in Japan than in America. Here it means that when a woman marries she must quit her job even if she doesn't have kids. You must know this because as a geijin you are much more free and independent. If you work here you must be "dareful" to explain American concept." "You mean 'careful', not 'dareful'," Lacey said. "Thanks for the tip. In English that means thanks for the advice, not the 'tip' of a pencil."

While she was getting her bearings—learning to shop, going to the public baths, fixing up the apartment—Doug traveled to the numerous US bases all over Japan that supported the American war effort in Vietnam. As civilian counsel, he was there to defend dissident GIs brought before the military court on "trumped up" charges by the higher ups for minor infractions of military code or outright false accusations.

When the editor of the *Yomiuri Shimbun*, the largest Japanese newspaper, advertised for a French tutor, Lacey got the job. Her copy of Japanese in a Nutshell went everywhere with her as she tried to learn the vocabulary, simple conversations and idioms of the language so that sooner or later she could be accepted as more than a *geijin*. Soon it was covered with fingerprints and coffee stains as she stayed up night after night to learn new meanings. Doug began referring to it as her Japanese Bible.

Every day she and her fellow co-workers happily debated the American versus the English way to spell or pronounce a word. An English "harbour" was a "harbor" in America, a "colour" became a "color," "advertising," was "advertizing" to Lacey. It was all such fun.

She loved the fact that she was the only woman among thirty men, some Japanese, some Hawaiian, and several English. Each with different English accents British. "Seiji San, how'd you learn English? Lacey asked her Japanese colleague. "By your accent I'd say you learned from someone from Chi-cahggo. You've got that Midwest accent. I love it. I love guessing how and where everybody here learned to speak English."

"Me, I spent time in the States at Brigham Young University. One semester. That was enough for me."

"I bet. Did you go to any Mormon services?"

"Yes, the family I lived with took me one time. That was enough. I am Shinto, not Mormon. I very polite though."

"You bet. Once would be enough for me, too. Mormon has its own language and vocabulary some might say."

Lacey loved her colleagues, who returned her affection and liked this American girl who acted more like a brother than most women they knew. They didn't know many if they weren't married or not engaged in an official "omiai". They were glad to have Lacey there to practice their "women skills" for their future, arranged marriages.

Lacey began to feel an undertow, a further shifting in her relationship with John, but not in the direction she had hoped. While she reached out to colleagues and immersed herself in Japanese culture, Doug began to tire of his unrewarded attempts to curb the war effort.

One night after night he admitted "I feet lost in here in Japan, travelling month after month to one U.S base after another- Iwakuni, Sasebo, or Yokuska- with little support from JAG officers or even the dissidents who needed my help." He turned more and more to reading the silent street signs, less and less to talking to the locals in the cities he visited.

Little by little Lacey felt him withdrawing from those around him and from her. She began to spend hours away from the apartment, playing Risk or Monopoly with the neighbors, who wanted to learn English the fun way while he stayed behind upstairs.

She loved teaching the couple downstairs to play Risk in English. Considering the country was an island nation, and almost completely homogenous, except for the indigenous Ainu up north, the idea of trying to conquer the world as a tiny nation through a board game seemed an ironic but playful teaching tool for Lacey. She didn't realize how competitive the couple would be. Yukio and Kenji loved acquiring territories on the board and trying to conquer each other's. Lacey understood that Japanese women were said to be ruled by their husbands' wishes, and, especially in public, stayed out of sight and cared for the children. But at home things were different.

"I take your terri-to-rorey these time," Kenzo was clearly pleased and smug.

"Chotto mate," Yukio started.

"In English," Lacey reminded her.

"Toki doki, Lacey san," Yukio came back in Japanese.

"I take my turn now. With re-inforce- aments, I attack and cap-tu- you terri —to rories.

"Right on! That's what we say when we mean 'good job'.

"Anata wa ii shigoto wo shimashita ne!" Yukio echoed.

After the game Lacey stepped outside the first floor apartment for a breath of fresh air. The scent of the cherry blossoms filled her lungs and cleared her head from the tenseness of the game. Lacey was happy to be in Tokyo in the springtime because it meant that the cherry blossoms were everywhere: in all the public gardens and right here outside the door.

Returning upstairs she found Doug listening to the Stars and Stripes radio. She could hear the replay of the ABC telecast from the day before of the start of the Watergate hearings, May 17, 1973.

"We are beginning these hearings today in an atmosphere of utmost gravity. The questions that have been raised in the wake of the June 17th break-in last year strike at the very undergirding of our democracy. If the many allegations made to this date are true, then the burglars who broke into the headquarters of the Democratic National Committee at the Watergate were in effect breaking into the home of every citizen of the United States."

It was the first of many nights Lacey found Doug lying on the tatami listening to the voice of Senator Ervin from North Carolina who was leading the Watergate hearings.

"That guy is amazing," Doug sounded more excited than he had in months. "We've got a chance. If we can get Nixon, this goddamn war can be over! And Ervin's quotes like this one from Mark Twain's admonishes, 'The truth is very precious; use it sparingly.' "That's great stuff."

Lacey was glad to see Doug excited about Watergate, obsessed even. But she was worried that he was losing interest in the fight again the war on the bases, not in the radio.

"Whatcha been up to. How did it go in Yokuska today?"

"Same old, same old, the Judge Advocate wouldn't give us the time of day."

"I am sorry. You've got to find a way to make this Japan gig work for you before the time's up." Lacey said.

"God Damn it, Lace. You always start right in with *what have you done today?*" Don't you know it's hard enough just being here, let alone winning a case for one of these poor, fucking GIs?"

"Sorry. I am trying to be supportive, but you seem to be losing interest in the life and culture here. And in me." She said.

"Oh, for God's sake. Don't be so egotistical. Of course I am interested in you. You're the successful one here. You've got friends, you speak the language, you are making a ton of money and I am just nursing my ass."

The words stung. "I am sorry. I don't know what to say." Night was falling and she needed air again, to be away from there, from John. She bolted down the stairs, not knowing where to go. Then she saw that the public bath was still open.

"Kom-ban-wa," Lacey said in her best accent to the lady at the desk.

"Ogenki desuka?" The lady asked if everything was fine with the new customer.

"Genki desu, Lacey said, trying to leave thoughts of the uncomfortable scene with John behind.

"Kore wa ikura desuka?" She knew how to ask what something cost, but in those early days she didn't know how to count in yen, so she just handed the woman all the cash she had and hoped not to get ripped off.

"Arigato dai gozaimasu!" The attendant squealed. Lacey knew she had been had but didn't care. She was ready for the bath she hope would relax her.

She slipped off her sandals and placed them next to the front desk beside the others lined up in a row and took the towel offered to her.

The female attendant opened the sliding door and a waft of steam greeted her inside in front of the sunken pool filled with ten Japanese ladies all staring at once up at her.

She saw an empty space in the row of little stools along the wall opposite a pool the size of a tennis court. Taking her cue from the other bathers, she tried to shuffle delicately toward the space but the pigeon toe in her step got in the way and she felt clumsy. Reaching the empty stool she sat down so low and so hard that her knees shot up into her face. Forgetting to take her clothes off, then realizing she needed to change, she went back to hang her dress on the wall on the other side of the pool. She took a large clean towel from the pile next to the clothes hooks and wrapped it tightly around her. As she sidled awkwardly back to the stool, the heat and the steam from the pool made her feel queasy and the weight of the towel was becoming as heavy as a winter coat. Regaining her spot in the row of stools, she picked up the white bowl and wash cloth beside it, unwrapped her winter coat and stepped naked into the waiting water.

The bath was warm and she sank easily into it dropping down to her knees to cover her arms and chest. The pool was only four feet deep. No matter where she was she was self-conscious about her body. Especially here, where none of the Japanese women seemed to have any body fat or breasts. She began to wash herself with the bowl and cloth.

"Konicha wa. Anata wa Geijin desuka?" Said the first lady, inching closer to Lacey through the water.

"Hai so des," Yes. Lacey wanted to be as polite as possible not knowing what might be next.

Very soon she begin to feel she was on another planet. She didn't know what the second lady was asking. She couldn't translate and tried to keep still in the water and not cause any ripples that might draw attention. The woman pointed to Lacey's stomach. What? What? How to answer?

Suddenly she got it. No words needed. She flashed on all the times John said he didn't want children. That time when they were leaving H.O.U.S.E and she had the members that neither of them wanted kids. Was it true then? Was it true now? Would she want to have kids, even if she wanted kids now, with this man, seemingly so disgruntled with the world?

"Iie. Iie," Lacey blurted out. Then in English, "I am not pregnant!"

In a way, did she wish she were?

The American Reporter

By December Lacey was speaking to visiting Western reporters and dignitaries on a regular basis. One day a reporter from The New York Times stopped by her desk to gather some views of the war from Americans abroad for a story he was writing under a deadline. He wore a classy, double-breasted, navy blue suit, a paisley handkerchief and a tie that matched the paisley patch in his breast pocket. His thick, sandy hair was a giveaway, and Lacey identified him immediately as a thirty-something preppie on assignment. Nevertheless, she was a willing to meet him at her desk for an interview, which would go to print the next week in the States.

Thirty small desks hunkered together in a large rectangle that took up most of the space in the main Yomiuri office in downtown Tokyo. Everyone looked up as the tall American entered the office and made a bee line for the only other American in sight. For a moment all typewriters went silent as the reporter approached Lacey's desk in the back of the room.

"Hi, my name is Harry Spence, New York Times. They say you're from Boston, married to a draft dodger."

"No," she explained. "He was never a draft dodger. He was a draft resister who was granted military status as a Conscientious Objector. We call these people pacifists, in case you haven't heard the term." He was granted military status as a Conscientious Objector. He's actually here to defend GIs in court when necessary."

"I see." Harry took out his steno. "Could we talk about this over lunch? I understand you're quite the activist too. I'm told you've been raising money among the American ex-pats here for the McGovern/Eagleton campaign. Is that so? I'd love to hear about that too. My treat."

That was how it started. Harry was sophisticated: New York family, Saint Mark's, Dartmouth undergrad, Columbia Journalism School. A member of the social set she had left behind. On the one hand the Leo in her was enough of an egotist to look forward to being interviewed for her opinions. On the other, she liked Harry's cologne and that he bothered to wear it.

Lacey suggested lunch in the company cafeteria to get right to the interview and not waste time looking for a restaurant in the neighborhood. They ordered soba noodles which, as time went on, neither of them seemed interested in finishing.

By three o'clock Harry had invited Lacey back to his apartment in Roponghi, a part of town where the wealthy foreigners lived. Apparently he was also a photographer, and he wanted to show Lacey his photos from the battlefields in Vietnam.

His apartment, on the second floor of a modern Western style building in Roppongi, the suburb where diplomats and wealthy foreigners and businessmen lived. Two bedrooms, a sunken living room, windows, sunlight on three sides and a full bath tub with a bidet. Harry was living like a king while she lived in a two room shack on the second floor in an out of the way suburb of Tokyo.

"I came here once to meet an old friend, a classmate from Middleford, who is still here, married to a Japanese business man."

"I have had this place for a couple of years. Here please, come sit down." He moved some books off the sofa and motioned Lacey to join him."

"When I am not here, there's a Swedish camera man who stays her who works for Japanese television filming commercials."

Beside the sofa was a low book case filled with framed family and other photos.

"This one I took from the deck of a sub in Danang. I captured the planes taking off. I really liked this. I entered in a contest I didn't win, but it was worth the try. I'd really rather take pictures than report on our dying troops."

"I had a boyfriend who served in the Navy in Danang after NROTC at Harvard. He wanted to marry but I joined the Peace Corps instead." Immediately Lacey felt stupid for saying something so irrelevant.

"And this one is of William Calley. On this point Lacey was all ears and well aware of this, the worst incident in the entire Vietnam War.

She knew the whole story but didn't want to let Harry know that she could recite chapter and verse about the whole violent disaster. She and Doug had been over it many times and read all the reports they could get their hands on before it became public.

"This one is of my family back in Greenwich. There's Mom, typical of her to be photographed in a tennis dress. And Dad in those ugly Pulitzer pants. Missy, my little sister, who's not so little now, at 23, and her pooch, Abigail. Feisty little thing--I mean my sister"

Harry put down the photograph of his family and looked straight into Lacey's very deep set eyes. She was still seeing the tennis dress, the pants, the sister and the dog when Harry all at once Harry was so close she could feel his touch even without it. A huge homesickness for men like him back home welled up in her. She missed New England and the ugly plaid shorts, the Lacoste shirts and the tennis matches. The picture of his family sent her back to a place she had not been in a long time. She missed her Dad at dinner in those silly Brooks Brother patent leather pumps that looked like a grown-up version of the Mary Janes she wore to dancing school.

"You are very attractive, and I am drawn to you, even if you are a little bossy for my tastes." He chuckled as he leaned, held her chin with the touch of his finger and gently kissed her on the mouth." His lips felt soft, and Lacey thought and wondered if he cared that she did not wear makeup.

Very quickly it happened. Harry put William Calley back on the book shelf beside the sofa and led Lacey to the bedroom. He sat her down on the bed, saying nothing but waiting for her to signal to stop or go. She sat at the edge of the bed trying to look prim and innocent.

Harry leaned and kissed her gently on the forehead. He began to push the silk covered buttons through the slits in the front of her blouse. The beige silk sheets matched the color of her blouse and she luxuriated in the smooth, slippery feel of them against her body as Harry removed first her blouse and then her skirt, sliding it gently down over her ample hips.

He touched her many places and seemed to know all the zones that were awakening sensations she had never felt before, with Doug, not even with the Carnival man, the sex obsessed Hal. She was fully aroused now, kissing Harry hard, then openly, her mouth in his. It was too late to pull away now. Lacey let go and felt herself scream inside, a small joy and then a bigger one with Harry coming right behind her.

Lacey knew there was no way to say no to this. There was no need to say much. It had been immediate strong, fulfilling and over.

This is not right. I mean, thank you. No. I have to go," she excused herself and bolted before Harry could stop her.

When she got home, Doug was already there.

"I've got to talk to you," Lacey began, sliding her shoes off outside the door.

Doug was cleaning the fish tank. The carp floated, unable to move in the tank. A low table sat in the middle of the living room, doing double duty as a dinner table and a desk for Doug.

"A reporter from New York, from ABC news, showed up in our office today. He asked to interview me about the war, about being married to a CO and what I thought about life in Japan."

"So what did you tell him?" Doug kept his head turned away from her, swirling the water in the tank with a wooden spoon so that the fish would try to chase it.

"It's not what I told him that matters. Somehow, over lunch, it came out that he was originally from New York, went to Saint Mark's, and knew some of my classmates at Middleford…. He just seemed very nice. He asked me to come to his apartment to see the photos he'd taken of soldiers in the field, and I went. One thing led to another…"

"So what did you tell him about the war?" Doug asked.

"That's not the point. I was very attracted to him, and I nearly let myself go. It really bothered me, but it bothers me more that I wanted to be with him. Even now."

"Well, Lacey," said Doug, sucking in a long slow cautious breath, "you have to do whatever you feel you must do. I won't stop you."

No trace of expression in his words or affect his face. Though she didn't know it, what she wanted was Doug to do was jump up, get mad, and sweep her off her feet.

"How can you be silent? Not care enough to be angry or tell how much you love or hate me? Your indifference is frightening me!"

"I am not uncaring, Lacey. I love you enough to never hold you back or tell you what to do. It's your world, too, and what you do is yours to do." John reached out to take Lacey's hand but she pulled away.

"You don't understand. I feel more frustrated than guilty. I need you to be more passionate, to overwhelm me from time to time, to surprise me, with your love. I can't stand the lack of emotion."

She began to cry though she wasn't sure why. And it was hard at first because she hadn't cried since her father died. The tears started slow and then flowed hard and long. She went in the other room to pull out the tatami mat for the night, then changed her mind. She went outside and smoked a cigarette at the top of the steps. It was early evening, warm for December.

"Maybe there is still time for a Monopoly game downstairs," she said to herself, hoping, for now, to forget the confrontation upstairs.

Bonenkai

It was December, and for every company worker in Tokyo, that meant just one thing: bonenkai. Bonenkai literally means "gathering to forget the year" where all troubles and confrontations are forgiven and wiped away by a lot of alcohol.

Lacey called John to tell him about the plans. "The party committee" in the newsroom has been planning for months and are adamant that I attend this all-male event. No wives are ever invited."

Lacey grabbed the flyer with the description of the party site and the map on her desk as she headed for the Seibo Shinjukusen line at the end of the day. On the way home she read Hoshi Ryokan was located in the town of Minakami in the Gunma prefecture of northern Japan.

She raced up the steps, slipped her shoes off, dropped them inside the door and stepped inside the apartment.

"Look at this, Doug. This inn was founded in 718. It's practically as old as Jesus! This is going to be a blast. Come, let's eat and talk about it. I am able to go that last weekend in December."

"I don't know, Lacey. This sounds like an evening of debauchery."

Lacey opened her bento (snack box) and set the sushi down on the hibachi. She mixed some miso with hot water and placed the soup in cups on the table. Doug looked at the brochure and for a while they ate in silence.

"The event is going to take place in this fancy resort two hours from here. A great chance for me to get away and see some countryside."

"You're not going to that drinking binge alone. You know those guys want a piece of you in some way. I'm going with you or you are not going. I want to make sure you don't get into trouble. You know I don't drink and probably won't enjoy this boo-nin-kay," he said, mispronouncing the event. "But I'll go."

"They want to watch you get drunk on beer or sake and to dance around with you to Western rock and roll until you would fall down and pass out."

"Don't' be silly, Doug, I'll have a few sips and just dance long enough to have some fun.

Doug said nothing.

"Okay, then come with me. I'll do my part and then we can retire to enjoy the resort, tokidoki (okay)?'

"Okay."

"You'll see. This is the right thing," Doug said as he fell off to sleep that night. Lacey got up as quietly as she could, slid open the door enough to pass through and seconds later was standing over the square of water staring at the carp, unable to move, in the pool that was too small for him.

"Good night, Tony Orlando, good luck trying to swim in your pool. I'm having trouble swimming in mine." she whispered and crawled back to her place on the tatami beckoning her to sleep.

The day of the event came and Lacey and Doug took the train to Minakami to meet the other Yomiri team leaders as well as the team players. The guys from the newsroom were on the train along with the. They were the real party animals, the guys who worked the printing presses in the basement.

"I actually like the men on the lower rungs of the paper's pecking order," she told Doug, "more than some of other colleagues. For one thing they don't speak much English, and this gives me a chance to practice my Japanese. They have been less exposed to Western culture and are more open to telling me about ancient Japanese customs and about their own family life. I feel more included, less geijin. I am grateful for that."

Lacey worked hard at her editing job and had really earned the right to a bonenkai. Not only did she write play reviews and a social column about foreigners living in Tokyo, she learned to set type for her articles from the guys in the basement who were the company typesetters.

"Let's set this one in 12 point Bodoni and then do the subhead in Times Roman 12," said Lacey, not really sure, looking at the first cut of the article on her visit to the reconstructed site of Hiroshima. Her next piece was going to be about the custom of arranged marriages in Japan and she felt ill-equipped at this point to write about "omiai," especially in light of her own marriage.

"So, what's it like, Kenji, the arranged marriage thing, the "omiai?" Does it work? Am I being to forward to ask?

You know, Lacey San, you can ask me anything. Omiai is a great and good custom. It honors our parents who choose our correct partners.

With everything planned there are no, as you say, "false expectations," no worries. I am right, yes?

"Silly, why do you always ask a question with a yes at the end?" Lacey was trying to be playful to get a serious answer. She could tell Kenji was a true believer and not about to give her a few negative pearls about the custom. She was beginning to wonder if Kenji might be right.

"Are you coming to the bonenkai?" Lacey asked, really just to pass the time once she saw Kenji was done with his comment.

"You bet! This will be the last big outing before marriage ceremony in the spring when the cherry blossoms will be in full bloom."

On the train Doug read aloud from the brochure. "Minakami is a small, hot spring, resort in Gunma Prefecture, not far from Tokyo. It used to be a lonely isolated outpost surrounded by mountains. After a tunnel was built in the 1930's, it became a popular spot for day trips from Tokyo. The resort offers skiing in the winter, rafting in the summer, beautiful leaves in the fall and hot springs the year round."

The setting was gorgeous, with wooded slopes all around. The bit of landscaping that had been done blended perfectly with the natural backdrop. Lacey knew they were in for an unforgettable stay and she planned to relax and savor every minute of her time there.

Entering the inn they saw in front of them a fire pit where visitors were sipping tea from a kettle gently simmering above the coals. The main section of the ryokan was all wood and there were photos of some of the ryokan's many famous historical visitors dotting the walls. Some of the rooms were of a more recent vintage and equipped with phones but the very oldest rooms welcomed guests in the same simple way as they had hundreds of years ago, bowing to each one.

"Here you are, Rogers san, this is your kimono, take sash," the man behind the reception desk offered Doug. And you, Missy Rogers, here is your own. Tokidoki? Your rooms are ready."

"Rooms not room? Wonderful! Oh, yes, very tokidoki, and beautiful," Lacey was delighted and was careful to say so, knowing someone in the office on the committee had gone out of his way to make her and Doug especially comfortable.

"When you are ready we will begin in the large room for the dinner." Politeness and formality filled the air at all times.

In their suite on the bedside table next an explanation of the history of the inn right was a Gideon's Bible. "Guess the missionaries got here way ahead us," Doug said with a laugh as he began to read a tourist pamphlet to Lacey. Lacey was already changing into her bathing suit and motioned for Doug to do the same.

"Let's go get in the water!" Lacey said excitedly. "It's really cold outside and we can sit in the pool and watch the snow drifting off the barren trees while the steam rises around us! Can't wait. Wahhdya say?"

Doug changed the subject. "Can you believe this?" Doug said noticing the insignia on the pocket of the Turkish towel robe as he put it on. "I'll be damned! It says Hilton Hotel. Guess the corporate reach is everywhere, even here in the mountains."

"Oh, c'mon Doug, you are becoming too cynical. So what if they have Hilton towels. Honestly, the world is not such a sad place. "C'mon, let's go."

Doug had never ventured into the public baths in Japan and wasn't so sure he was ready to do so now.

In their slippers they inched outside the sliding doors and walked down the narrow path to the hot springs in the cold night air.

"What if there are others there? I am not going in semi-naked in front of anyone." When they got there several local women were soaking in the spring with circles of steam hanging in the air above them.

"Come, try, put your feet in the water," Lacey pleaded. Doug was too embarrassed to tell her he had never learned to swim..

"I am going back. I'll see you before dinner when you're done." Doug retreated, heading back to their quarters in his slippers and robe.

Inside the hot spring Lacey took off her robe and slid into the water unnoticed. There were a number of others in the pool, several Japanese women and one foreigner.

"Enjoying the resort?" she said to the woman treading water in front of her.

"I'd enjoy it more if my husband weren't here."

"Oh, I am sorry. I didn't mean to intrude."

"That's okay. We're here because my husband wanted to try one last time to make it work. Bad idea. I am really done. Done."

"Again, I am sorry." Lacey felt herself sinking, wanted to go underwater, to hide from her own thoughts. When did you know you were DONE? But she didn't ask.

Lacey waved goodbye and backstroked to the other side of the pool. The soft lighting and warm water made her drowsy so it was time to get out.

When John reached the room, he kicked off the slippers he thought were way too flimsy and feminine and headed for the shower. The steamy water pelted his shoulders and he shook a little, knowing that he was actually seething with anger. At Lacey.

Who the hell is she, really? Flake or flighty?

He wished he could tell Lacey how he felt. He wished he had been honest. No, he couldn't swim, no, he couldn't play tennis, and no, he couldn't talk to a stranger the way she could. Damn, she could talk to a stone.

What did she think farmers did in their free time? Take tennis lessons? Growing up with the pigs and the hay was hard work. Not much room for fun when the day was done.

The water calmed him down. By the time he got out and wrapped a towel around himself, the anger was almost gone. But he felt a sadness creeping in.

"How'd you like the big bathtub?" Doug said as Lacey walked into the room, her towel and hair wet and gleaming, her face pink red from the pool heat.

"It was oishi, delicious. Too bad you couldn't enjoy it with me."

"I could have. I chose not to. There is a difference."

"Could have, would have. What's the difference? You choose not to enjoy many things these days. Especially me."

"Come on, Lacey, that's enough. You are still wet. Let's get ready for this shindig."

Paper lanterns greeted them as they entered the dining room through curtains parted by waiting attendants. Traditional Noren curtains and typical office party decorations lined the walls. They were designed with regard to the feng shui philosophy meant to bring luck and prosperity.

Lanterns hung from the ceilings, along the walls and above the dining table and could be seen glowing outdoors as snowflakes came down through trees swaying in the winter wind. The red and white lanterns were decorated with the Japanese symbols of "peace" and "prosperity."

They joined the others at the long tables, all dressed in matching blue and white kimonos, with tiny little blue birds on a white background, a thick black cotton sash wound twice around the waist and tied at the back. "If I didn't know better I'd say these threads look like prison uniforms," Doug observed.

"Shhush, Doug. You take offense at everything. I am here as a member of a corporate team. If you don't like it, fake it. This is my event. I tried to tell you to stay home."

"Just shut up, Doug whispered. You know I don't drink. And I am not going to change that for tonight. You might be wise to think about doing the same."

"Not right now. Don't be a bore. This is meant to be fun, remember. It's a night for forgetting and forgiving. So get busy," she snapped.

They stopped talking and stared at the feast in front of them. A huge boat of sashimi sat on the table looking like a miniature model of the U.S.S. Constitution, replete with sails made out of pieces of white fish and raw tuna. The boat was embedded in a block of ice representing the ocean. Scattered about on the ice ocean were pieces of cooked shrimp wrapped in seaweed strips called nori. Baskets of vegetable tempura lined the table on either side of the ship. There were bowls of miso soup for everyone and chopsticks at each place setting. Beside each soup bowl there was a bottle of Kirin beer to start the night off and a glass for the sake that would follow.

"Oh my god, it's beautiful," Lacey exclaimed, truly stunned by the sight of the culinary sculpture in front of them. "No forks in sight. Too bad for me. You are so much better at chopsticks than I, Doug. I may have to eat with my fingers or stab the fish with a stick." She said, trying to lighten Doug's mood.

The guests ate in silence, the only sounds the slurping of the soup, the sucking of sashimi with chopsticks clicking together and the puffs of breath taken to sip beer and sake. There were toasts to the emperor, the empress and the chief editor of the paper. There were smaller toasts between co-workers. And lastly, just as the night was ending, Lacey's editor raised his sake glass. From the other end of the table he said: "To our American friend, my friend, "Racey Bierce."

The night ended with a clear sign of Lacey's popularity that Doug now resented.

PART III: NEW YORK

He Said She Said

One night, as they were pulling out the tatami and getting ready for bed, they heard an announcement that changed everything: "The United States officially ended its military involvement in Vietnam today." The Stars and Stripes radio replay of a televised nightly news cast went on to say: "the war has divided the nation, defined a generation and changed how the U.S. military may operate in the future. In all, 58,000 American soldiers lost their lives and another 303,000 Americans were wounded. This is a sad day in our history."

Lacey was the first to say it. "It's time to go home, Doug. Now we can."

"I am not really ready. I don't feel I have done enough, or really anything to change attitudes here either among the soldiers or the Japanese. And if I go home, I will be a pariah in my own country. People don't know the difference between a deserter and a resister, between a conscientious objector and a coward."

"God Damn it, Doug. You are such a cynic. This is a good thing. The war is OVER, sweetheart. Be glad of it."

"I have been talking to my friend from the Southern Poverty Law Center here. He is thinking of going to Israel to work on a kibbutz for a couple of years. I think this could be a good experience for both of us. To live among a group of people dedicated to the collective."

Lacey's couldn't believe the words she was hearing for the first time. "How long have you been thinking about this? And why didn't you tell me?"

"I was going to get around to it, but now seems like the right time."

"I liked not researching Japan before we came, but I am not about to join a kibbutz as a cultural experiment. We should have lived alone together more to know each other before we came here. Instead we lived in another kibbutz, a commune, H.O.U.S.E. No way, I am not doing that again."

The distance between them had reached a pitch in Japan and they thought a long trip home from East to West might revive their frayed relationship. They left Tokyo in March and made their way back to the U.S via South East Asia, Russia and Europe before settling in New York City.

Arrival in New York brought new adventure and diverted attention from the fractures in Lacey and Doug's marriage. They found an apartment. Lacey took a job doing research for a professor and Doug found temporary work with Legal Services. They filled the two room apartment with "midnight furniture" they found walking around Greenwich Village. Things were on an even keel.

One night, Doug found a waterbed someone leaving the building had left behind in the hallway. Doug dragged it and the frame through the front door, laid the deflated mattress out on the floor, found the holes and patched it up like new.

The next night Lacey helped Doug fill the bed with water to put it in place on the frame they had placed in the bedroom. Lacey was very quiet throughout the exercise.

She filled her tenth gallon bucket of water, holding the bucket under the faucet in the tiny kitchen. Doug was standing behind her waiting to fill his. Without warning she said "you know, Doug, now that we have kind of settled in, what do you think about the idea of doing some therapy together?"

"You never brought that up in Japan, why now?"

"How many Japanese therapists do talk therapy in English? Sorry, that was a joke."

"Why do you want to do this?"

"Because I am bored and I think you're depressed. Like maybe you feel you failed in Japan. I don't know. I could be wrong."

"I'll be the judge of that. Why do have to dramatize everything?"

"That hurt. I'm just trying to find a way to get closer to you. Again. I feel we lost our way in Japan."

"You did. Not me."

"Ouch again."

"I am not sure I trust you. You went way out ahead of me in so many ways. I could never catch up."

"Why don't you just say Mr. ABC put a damper on our relationship? What didn't you say it then? I would have had more respect for you."

Lacey was mad now and lashed out: "What about me? How do you I feel? Guilty, maybe, but what about your responsibility for why I would stray, even just once?"

The sound of running water stopped and silence filled the air.

"I am going to get us help," Lacey said. Doug understood it was a command not a request.

Couples Therapy

One day, on her way back from the office of her new boss, Professor Rosenfeld, Lacey spotted a poster on the front door of a church on the Upper Eastside: "I'm Okay, You're Okay" it read after the pop psychology book of the same name promoting help for couples in crisis. The next day she called the church office and signed up for six sessions once a week on Thursday nights from seven to nine. Lacey wondered if "free" could really offer, but was willing to try.

Lacey and Doug arrived before the others for the first session. On one side of the church there was a small garden with a low iron grate fence and an iron-laced gate. They passed through the gate, walked down the path and entered the parish hall of the Episcopal Church. It was 70s hip: always Saint Mike's, never Saint Michael's.

Lacey noted the hall was huge, she thought about the size of a tennis court. High ceilings with enormous ceiling-to-floor windows stretched across the front wall that looked out into the garden covered in a blanket of clean white snow. It was early November.

There were cathedral-like arches at the top of the windows lending an added ecclesiastical feel to the room, a sense of calm and peace. Oriental carpets remnants donated from time to time by wealthy parishioners dotted the hardwood floor.

In the back of the hall was a kitchen equipped for Sunday coffee hours, church suppers and vestry meetings. A bin for "gently used clothing" sat outside the kitchen next to a pile of books for volunteers in the prison ministry project to take to inmates at the local jail.

In the middle of the hall were two long leather couches, one with its back to the windows, the other exactly opposite facing the dark outside. The sexton had been instructed to turn the lights down low before he left for the day to create a mood of calm for the upcoming meeting. In between the couches was a high-backed chair upholstered in green and red plaid. "The throne for the therapist," Doug said to Lacey in a sarcastic whisper.

It was still early. Lacey and Doug sat huddled in the middle of the couch facing the windows. She was wearing her one and only dress. It was pink linen with a blank border but casual. No pants for her. Doug had on his uniform: jeans, a beige corduroy jacket, the same one that lived through Japan, and brown cowboy boots.

"The church is quaint, don't you think?" Lacey said, offering a gesture of small talk.

"Probably built in the late 1880s or at the turn of the Century," said Doug joining in the effort to chat.

"I'm glad we're in this church. Reminds me home, of Sunday rituals, communion and safety."

"Speak for yourself. I don't care about the space. I bet it's not going to be safe for long once we get started," Doug said a bit ominously.

And then he was there. The man was at least six feet four, all bones and skinny with a goatee and a mustache. He wore a suede vest over a black turtleneck, black slacks and Wee Jun loafers with a copper penny in the toe of each shoe.

"Hi and welcome. I will be leading our group."

The man went off to the kitchen to get a glass of water to put on the table next to his chair just as another couple entered the parish hall. They came toward Lacey and Doug and sat down on the couch opposite them. Neither spoke. The silence was not unwelcome. Everyone was just waiting.

Lacey turned to Doug. "He said *leader* not *therapist*. He has a German accent. I hope we are not being psychoanalyzed by some Freudian. All I am looking for is a little talk therapy. And why is it free anyway?" Lacey was a bit worried she had led them into something too intense.

A third couple arrived and took their seats opposite each other, the man sitting next to Lacey and the woman on the other side next to the husband.

The man returned, all smiles, to start the initial meeting. "Hi, and welcome to all of you. My name is Reichert Kammermann, and, yes, I am German. But I went to Harvard Medical School and just finished my residency in Massachusetts. In this country most people just call me Rich. This course is free because I am excited to begin my practice here in the city and thought this would be a good way to begin."

At these words all three couples relaxed into their leather seats. Lacey took a moment to notice the three large, squishy, bean bags sitting on the floor near the couches. She smelled smoke in the air left over from last night's AA meeting in the same space. The strains of a choir were warming up in the main sanctuary.

"Well, that's my story. Who's going to follow me and tell us why you're here?" Kammermann turned his long legs, like arrows, toward the man who sat opposite his wife on the couch facing the back of the room.

The man began reluctantly. "My name is Sandy. I am here tonight with my wife because we are members of this church and because she had an affair with another member of this church that I am a part of and I don't know what to do."

He looked in his rumpled khaki pants and Bowdoin sweatshirt with the arms cut off.

The woman ware a dark, navy pants suit with a white buttoned down collar. Her hair was very short, very masculine. She wore no makeup. The man was bearded with wire rim glasses bridged over a large wide nose. He looked like he had been near sided at birth. His clothes didn't seem to matter as the pants were green, the jacket red and the sweater brown. Lacey thought maybe he was color blind as she had heard that was the case with those who couldn't tell colors apart.

"We are both professors at Hunter College." Lacey remembered seeing her in Dr. Rosenberg's office to talk about a course on Women in Literature. Right away she guessed they were two egghead intellectuals, neither knowing how to begin to talk about their feelings and their marriage. This made her feel safe at the start, though she knew she didn't have a clue where to begin either. Would Doug?

The leader turned to the third couple. "We have been living together for three years," the woman began, "and were thinking about tying the knot. My name is Bunny Beckham." This is Mark Barnes. He's at Columbia Law School after four years at Harvard. I am at Pratt studying fashion design."

Mark jumped in. "You're studying fashion design at Pratt because you got bored when you realized the study of feminism is a joke."

"No, it wasn't a joke. I wanted to go to law school to become a legal advocate for women. Lord knows, there aren't many. You made me feel there wasn't room for two in the profession without a competition so I chose fashion and followed you here."

"I didn't make you feel any such thing. That was in your head. Don't put the burden on me. You made your own choice."

"Now I am remembering those courses and wondering if I gave up too much of my identity to Mark's future legal career. Mark did not want to come here and thinks the whole exercise is a silly waste of his study time."

Kammerman had not interrupted anyone during these introductions that seemed to jump right into issues, but Lacey couldn't help herself.

"Why is she talking for him and talking all the time?"

"Please give them space, Lacey, these are just introductions," Kammerman said.

Bunny kept going. "Mark doesn't seem much interested in me. I can empathize with Elaine, although I would never do something about it by having an affair. I guess I could, though, since we aren't married. Sometimes I wonder if there's a difference between a committed relationship and a marriage. Gosh, I can't believe I just said that!" Mark sat on the couch, fuming, volunteering only silence.

Doug and Lacey were the last to speak. "I saw the sign and enrolled us," Lacey said, explaining nothing, just the fact that she was there.

"I dunno, I guess I am feeling distant from things around me and a little disoriented coming home," Doug said in a slow, measured way.

"You seem distant to me, too," Lacey said almost under her breath, though the group heard her.

"Lately, I relate to songs that are sad or speak of travel or flight," Lacey blurted without being prompted, trying to recover from the nothingness of her opening words.

"I'm sad, too", added Andy. "I don't really want to divorce Elaine but feel I have no choice now that I have been cuckolded.or whatever they call it these days. I call it cheating. How else can I save face? I don't even know if Elaine would ever want me again. Would you, honey?"

By this time Elaine was already bawling. Lacey was used to going into out- of- body travel when things got tough or complicated.

"I feel as if I am looking down at the situation from some place high up on the ceiling in this room. I don't feel sorry for Elaine or relate to her pain. But I am wondering if Elaine misses her husband or if he really wants to leave him."

"Lacey," Kammerman said, I think you would rather talk about anyone but yourself. You can't do that her."

Doug heard that. He, too, lacked a certain emotional involvement when he spoke.

"My words seem to float in the air above me with no real attachment in range of my heart or my ego."

Dr. Kammerman turned his knees toward Doug indicating he was about to ask him a question.

"Do you think you and Lacey communicate from the heart or the head?"

"I dunno," said Doug. "I just feel tired most of the time, maybe just not getting enough sleep," he suggested. "I feel bored every day."

Kammerman's knees moved slightly forward with his shoulders pushing into the next question. "When are the times you feel most bored?"

"Not sure," said Doug, hesitating as he spoke. "Maybe when I think about Vietnam and all that time I spent in Japan." Doug began a litany of the bases he visited on behalf of U.S. soldiers protesting the war from inside the military. Yokosuka, Atsugi, Iwakini, Itazuke and Sasebo and on and on, not saying anything, just naming the bases until Kammerman touched Doug's knee signaling him to end the list.

"That's just a list. That's what's in your head. What's in your heart about that time?" Kammerman persisted.

Slowly, briefly, Doug spoke with an earnestness that had not been there in him before. "Someone had to defend the defenseless," Doug blurted out.

"No kidding! THANK YOU for all you did to try to stop the war!" Sandy piped up to the whole group, while Doug continued to look down silently at his feet.

Lacey was getting impatient. Even though Doug was loathe to speak up in this group, Lacey had heard this lament many times before. She squirmed a little trying to assume on a look of sympathy which she did not feel because she was thinking about her own lack of emotion.

"I can't help but feel I came home to a country that was not ready to acknowledge for putting my life in harm's way to choose peace over war. When the war was over the guys who resisted by going to Canada found acceptance in a new country. The soldiers who came home were lauded. The resisters, like me, got no recognition and no thanks for our form of bravery."

Lacey could see the sympathy for Doug on the faces around her. She knew that they would be far less interested in her own story.

"I respect Doug's pacifism and choice to be a conscientious objector. I am far more self-centered, self-absorbed. I am far less heady than Doug and more emotional or so I thought. But I think I, too, am stuck in my head. Unable to talk about the lack of intimacy I feel in our lives I feel a great ennui. I don't know how to talk to Doug," She said not looking at him. Then she turned to Doug. "I guess I mean you."

Lacey started to cry. "I feel like a bunch of parts, all laid out on the ground, ready to be assembled by someone who hasn't read the instructions. I can't seem to put myself together."

"Lacey, was there ever a time when you did feel whole." Kammerman's knees were now pointed toward Lacey.

"No, not really. I've always been like a bunch of spare parts, like there aren't enough parts in me for someone to work with."

Kammerman surprised everyone suddenly by announcing "that's it for now. Good job for the first night. I suggest you each keep track of your thoughts on paper and save them for next time. See you in a week. Thank you and good night."

It was raining slightly outside as the group poked up their umbrellas and ventured out into mid- Manhattan in search of the nearest subway. Outside Doug and Lacey passed by "I'm Okay, you're Okay" encased in the glass box smeared raindrops and unreadable. And that's how they were feeling about their relationship: smeared in layers of unreadable misgivings.

Flying Solo

By the spring of 1974 Lacey was living alone in a one room flat on the Upper East Side of New York City. It was a whole new way of life, one she was not entirely prepared to live. In many ways Lacey found herself cut off from just about everyone and everything. She had alienated her friends who thought her marriage was a perfect union that she had no right to break up. There was no family there to console her: She and her stepmother back in Boston were at odds and her real mother, with whom she had not lived with since she was nine, was one of the thousands of vagrants wandering the streets right there in New York. The thought of running into her mother in the street scared her to death on most nights.

Then there was the mishap with Dr. Robert Rosenberg. Rosenberg was one those educators who wished he had graduated from Harvard instead of the University of Wisconsin. He was trying to make up for it by being the Svengali of a graduate program in communications and writing a book about the philosopher Hannah Arent for which Lacey was doing the research. On many occasions he invited her to babysit for his children or to have dinner with the whole family. He was always dieting, denying himself carbohydrates for weeks on end, paying homage to the great Dr. Atkins. He wanted desperately to be tall and thin and have a full head of hair.

One day Dr. Rosenberg invited Lacey to join him on a bench in Central Park across from the Stanhope Hotel on Fifth Avenue to review one of his recent excerpts. Anxious to please she agreed to meet saying "I'll bring us lunch, no carbs I promise. Meet you around 1:00 after class. Okay?" Okay.

Dr. Rosenberg had asked one of his classes to examine a quote by the great Irish statesman, Edmund Burke. For openers he read the quote aloud to Lacey as she unwrapped two hot dogs without the buns covered in mustard. "'All that is necessary for the triumph of evil is for good men to do nothing,'" Rosenberg intoned. "How do you think that fits in with Hannah Arendt's theory of political power? Do you think the two would have liked each other?"

"Are you kidding? That's a real stretch. How is anyone going to write about that?" Lacey said thinking that was an absurd assignment.

"Or maybe as much as you and I like each other?" Dr. Rosenberg abruptly posed, in a huge non-sequitur.

Lacey began to feel the need to get up and walk around a little, but she did not want to be rude, so she did not move.

"You know I have watched you over the last month or so. You make wonderful comments and I am beginning to think you have some talent as a writer. But there is something mysterious about you that makes me want to protect you, shelter you and learn about that mystery."

"I am out of here!" Lacey screamed inside herself but still did not move. Then she screwed up her courage. "What is this? You're talking to me like you're Arthur Miller and I am Marilyn Monroe. Sick."

Rosenberg didn't stop. "I mean what I would really like to do is have an affair with you and keep it quiet from all others if you feel the same way," he said low and softly as if he were afraid someone might hear him.

Her mind was clear. It made her mad that this meeting was not about her work, not even really about her. It was about what this little man wanted to do to build up his oversized ego. She realized that a relationship with this man had to be over for good, whether she ever completed the course or not.

"Surely, this is a big mistake" she choked a little on her words, trying to put them in the right order. "I am going to pretend this never happened. And so are you. Please excuse me. Lacey let her hot dog fall out of her hand onto the bench, quickly left the park, crossed Fifth Avenue to the Stanhope Hotel and ran home to her apartment.

When she got home she took a very long shower. She tried for several hours to feel sorry for Dr. Rosenberg rather than angry but couldn't. She wondered if this was what happened to girls who were suddenly single and alone in New York?

The following Monday she confronted Rosenberg in his office. "I can no longer work for you. I think we both know that. I am sorry because I like the writing and editing. I am not sorry that I can't work for a monster."

Lacey was pretty lonely without a job and now single and alone in New York. She spent days in her apartment and nights calling her old friend Sophie in Boston.

"That's too bad, Lacey. Why don't you come home for s visit? I have been dating again and we are moving along. Not sure what's next."

"I'll think about it, Sophie. Not ready to come quite yet." She did not tell Sophie she was thinking of divorce.

No Good Way to Say Goodbye

She did a double take. She had not seen Doug without a beard since the early days in Japan.

They had agreed to meet at a coffee shop on the Upper East Side. There was a counter with high top stools. Light streamed through the front window casting sun on Doug's face that gave his curly hair a glow. When Doug arrived Lacey was already sitting in one of the booths in the back.

"Hello. You look great," Lacey almost stammered. He had a look she could only have hoped for and now it was too late. She forced herself to remember the many real reasons they were no longer together.

"You never showed up for that last therapy session," Doug said by way of introduction. I continued on after that with the others. Kammermann has been very helpful these past few months."

"You wanted to see me, Lacey," Doug said not unkindly. He waved go the waitress for two cups of coffee. He shook his head no for sugar and cream he knew Lacey would not want.

"Yes, how are things with you? Lacey almost whispered.

"I like doing Legal Services in the Tombs. And I have met someone. She's a grad student in voice at Juilliard."

Lacey couldn't get over how clean cut Doug looked. He'd pass for a preppy anywhere. She felt a little wounded to think he had so quickly replaced her.

The coffee shop was full of graduate students from nearby Hunter College chatting happily and interrupting each other with verbal challenges about the authors they were studying.

"I was working for this professor, doing research for his book but something happened. I guess I was dumb to turn down that job with Parade Magazine just because the pay was so low. Giving blood once a month doesn't really pay the rent."

"I can help."

"No, you can't. You can't feel sorry for me." She wondered if she meant that.

Doug ringed his untouched coffee cup with his finger while Lacey played with a spoon. Minutes turned into forever. No one noticed Doug taking Lacey's hand in his, turning it over slowly, touching the smooth skin of her ringless left hand. Tears pushed up through his eyes and trickled slowly down his clean shaven cheeks.

"I am sorry, I am so sorry, Lacey." Tears filled Lacey's eyes, too. They held hands not tight but softly, gently turning the fingers over. They knew it was finally over.

A Southern Gentleman

Lacey joined a friend for a Christmas party in Harlem to benefit the poor kids in the neighborhood. On the way there she wondered vaguely how making Christmas cards for kids could improve the lives of needy children. While she was cutting a Maine potato into a Christmas cut out with little Joey, a low pitched, honey-smooth voice came said "Hi, there, that needs a little more help if it's going to be a bell rather than a blob!" Lacey smiled acknowledging her failed attempt to press the potato onto the paper card.

When the card making ended and the last cookie and Kool Aid had been devoured, Lacey had made a new friend, Trevor Martin. They rode the bus back into the city together.

"So, the obvious question, what are you doing in New York? I work with these kids as a social worker, but you seem different, kinda removed." Trevor ventured, almost answering his own question.

"I am kind of removed," Lacey began. "I just got 'removed' from seven years of marriage. Still not divorced. And I am looking for a job."

"I see," Trevor queried on, "is that a good thing or a bad thing? I mean the divorce?"

"I honestly don't know right now," her voice trailed off into the still cold spring air.

"We're almost here in my neighborhood. I get off at 78th Street." Then very quickly he said: we have an opening in our office for a public relations assistant. Would you like me to look into that?"

"I'd be very grateful. I live just a few blocks down on 73rd and third. It's just one room with very little in it." Lacey was sounding sorry for herself again, something she had been working hard to avoid.

"I'll be the judge of that. By the way, most people call me Trey. How would you like to come with me to the Sandbar Beach and Tennis Club winter party next week?" Trevor asked as if he had been thinking of the invite since the moment they met. Lacey did not have a clue that night that this would be the beginning of a tangled journey.

The night ended with a clear sign of Lacey's popularity that Doug now resented.

Lacey did not know what or where the Sand Bar Beach and Tennis Club was but she figured she had better find a good cocktail dress for the event. She found a thrift shop on Madison Ave. and bought a long dress, the top of which, was a chocolate colored knit jersey. The bottom half was a polyester skirt covered in little blue sail boats surrounded by white clouds. Lacey did not know yet that Trevor had an eye for fashion and for wealthy Southern girls. She also did not know much about Southern men. She had a theory though, that during the Civil War, many husbands died so the sons became tied to their mothers, turning them and the next generations into "mama's boys."

The party took place in a restaurant on the first floor of Rockefeller Center facing the skating rink. For the first time in a long while Lacey felt a painful pang inside as she saw her father alive in her memory in front of her on the ice teaching her to skate like a boy when she was barely four years old and still living in Greenwich Village before the divorce.

The real purpose of the party was to look over the pool of candidates applying for membership that year in the Sand Bar Beach and Tennis Club. Trey was already a member. He chatted easily with the young men and women, none of whom Lacey knew, but was sure she had seen at the Christmas party in Harlem. Some of the guys reminded her of the young lawyer in her therapy group, archly preppy and self-impressed. The women looked like the ones she had gotten to know at the Junior League back home in Boston before she joined the Peace Corps. Trey slid one arm around Lacey's waist and pulled her gracefully onto the dance floor. She thought, this guy really knows how to move. She was beginning to really like the self-confidence she saw in this guy that she had been missing in Doug.

The disco music switched from the Carpenter siblings' *Top of the World* to the slow, wistful theme song from the movie *The Way We Were*. *Memories* never failed to bring tears to Lacey's eyes. In the film Redford and Streisand came from such different backgrounds that in the end they couldn't live together. The first few bars of music in the final scene brought it all back: the failure that was Doug and Lacey's marriage.

She was glad Trevor was holding her too close to be able to see the tears on her cheeks as they danced a slow fox trot across the floor. By the time the song was over she had recovered herself and Trevor moved off to the side of the dance floor near the bar to bring her a glass of wine.

"Hello. What are you doing here? I haven't seen you at any of these shindigs this winter. Are you trying to get into the Beach and Tennis Club? Planning on being at Quogue this summer?" said the young man by way of no introduction.

Lacey turned to look at a handsome standout in a room full of attractive men. "My name is Jeffrey Bullet, they call me Jet, and I'd like to buy you a drink."

"Actually, I am here with someone who is getting me a drink right now, but thank you. What do you do?" she said trying to find the right opener for the stranger standing next to her.

"By day I work for an insurance company but what I like to do is play tennis," the stranger said enthusiastically. "Do you play tennis?"

"Believe it or not I played on the team in high school but I have been away from it for a long time. No one I have been around for the last seven years ever played tennis," She sensed Jet thought that was a quirky comment and didn't let it pass.

"Well, who have you been around?" he continued.

"I mean I was married and he didn't play tennis. Now I am not and I would like to pick it up again," the words slipping out of her mouth.

"Deal. When would you like to play?" The pleasant man concluded suggesting a time to play the following week at a bubble on 28th Street. "See you there," Jet waved goodbye just as Trey returned with Lacey's drink.

"Who was that? I haven't seen him before at these ice breakers," said Trey who seemed not to want anyone to intrude upon his date that night. "He probably won't get in if he doesn't know anyone," Trey said somewhat curtly.

But I know him, she thought, and I would like to get to know him better. She felt that same electricity that was there with Doug in the beginning. Lacey was clearly smitten by the curly dark haired tennis player with the black wire rimmed glasses in the herring bone jacket and rep tie. The appeal was strong and clear and mutual and had nothing to do with manifestos or political missions or the Vietnam War. How refreshing! How dangerous.

Trey and Lacey took a cab to her apartment when the mixer was over that night. Lacey opened the door only slightly as she did not want Trey to see how bare it was. He held up her chin to the light in the hallway and turned it toward his face. "You are a very attractive woman, Lacey. Too bad you are so screwed up," he said as simply as if he were commenting on the weather. He kissed her gently on the lips parting with "and that dress will have to go. Those sailboats are ugly. Good night," were Trevor's final words. Or so Lacey thought.

At the bottom of the stairs he shouted up "Next we go to Bendel's to buy you some decent clothes!" Professor Higgins had just discovered his own personal Eliza Doolittle.

The Trouble with Love All

After a lapse of more than a decade Lacey was nervous about playing tennis. But she had fallen in love with what she called her "life sport" long ago and was going to make the best of this date. The tennis bubble on 28th Street Lacey was mostly empty early on Saturday morning. Lacey anticipated the day with pure joy to have someone to play with. It didn't hurt that Jeff was tall, dark, handsome and obviously an athlete and sports lover. Although Doug had played football in college, he was not really an athlete, hampered by a stigmatism in both eyes. Lacey didn't know much about Trey's past except that she knew he played the piano for many years, was artistic and loved to be on the dance floor at a moment's notice.

Lacey walked to her side of the net. In high school she had played only doubles. Singles was new to her. She felt instant relief when she struck the ball and impressed Jeff with her first hit. The two did not talk much. There was no need to. They were having a perfectly wonderful time in sync without words, just hitting back and forth, moving side to side in the cold bubble court as their bodies began to sweat and their movements continued in a kind of dance almost like a ballet.

"Man, that was groovy!" Jeff burst out about twenty minutes into the hitting routine. Lacey took that to mean he was having as much fun as she was.

"D'ya think you'll join the Sand Bar Club this summer and maybe share in a house in Quogue right next to the Club?" Jet queried as she remembered Trey's certainty that this man would probably not get into the Club.

"Oh, I don't know, I have to get a job first," she answered simply, afraid to say, yes, if I get to see more of you!

They hit for the full hour, practicing forehands, backhands, overheads and serves, laughing easily when one or the other missed the ball. It occurred to her he might be a good dancer because of the way he moved to the ball from his hips. Most of all from across the net she wanted to put her hands through his dark curly hair and get very close to him off the court. Too bad the hour was over and it was time to get off the court.

Meanwhile it was getting old giving blood once a month just to have enough cash to add to unemployment. Lacey was very grateful when Trey convinced his boss to hire her as the public relations director for the social agency where he worked as a program director. Trey was nothing if not a persuasive Southern gentleman.

It was early spring when she started her job at the agency. There were long days when she had to interview the parents of children with retardation. She had to admit, pretty early on, she was the wrong person for the job. Meetings with helpless parents were tedious and boring. She was too impatient and too lacking in the empathy needed to advocate for these special people. She was sorry she hadn't taken the job at Parade Magazine just because the salary was so low. At least there she could write, interview interesting people. She was not a care giver. She needed too much care herself.

In some ways living with Doug had rubbed off on her and was now a part of blood. On days when she became disheartened at work, she would recall the march on Washington, trying to change the country's mind about war and days of draft counselling in Doug's home office. She was now more interested in the big social and political issues at the national level than in helping individuals with disabilities.

One day, after learning that Barbara Walters had a retarded sister, Lacey got the idea to invite Barbara to do a commercial about awareness and advances for people with mental retardation."

"What makes you think you can pull that off, Lacey? You don' know Barbara or anyone who knows her. You have to have connections, you know." Trey was quick to say.

Lacey was not discouraged. "It's about the mission. I think she might just do it if she sees how sincere we are and urgent to improve the lives of people like her sister. I have to try."

In Lacey's mind the ad would be shot on a school bus with Barbara talking to a bunch of elementary school children.

"I see two children with retardation on the bus headed for school. Two other kids on the bus are talking with the retarded kids. Barbara gets on the bus at Madison and Fifth. She talks with the kids about her sister. Then she talks to the camera and asks for support for the New York ARC. Cut."

Lacey enlisted Trey's help to write to Barbara Walters. "Come for supper at my apartment to look over my first draft. You make edits or changes or scrap the whole thing if necessary."

Trey climbed the stairs to Lacey's second floor. "Wow, with what little you have, you have made some improvements here. Nice work," Trey approved Lacey's humble digs with a somewhat critical eye. She thought he was just being nice, but she didn't care, she was after just editorial guidance.

They worked late into the night redrafting the original invitation to Barbara Walters to include the benefits to her of doing such a public service ad: visibility in the non-profit world, increased visibility as a caring sister celebrity.

After what seemed like only an hour the final draft was finally completed. Lacey thought she and Trey were a pretty good working team. Trey's thoughts were on a completely different path.

"Did you get all your stuff from the old apartment yet? Your things might really cheer up this place. Have you started seeing anyone else yet?"

"It's not that easy or simple. Doug has kept a lot of the stuff we brought back on our trip home from Japan. It took us nine months to bring home those goblets from India, a Faberge egg from Russia and some other things. But most of all he wants to keep the pictures of us from our wedding and other times. Not sure why," Lacey's voice trailed off quietly.

They were sitting on Lacey's double box spring mattress leaning over Lacey's legal pad with the Barbara Walters draft on yellow paper marked all over with number two pencil.

Trey was no longer listening. He leaned toward Lacey and kissed her gently, his soft blonde mustache grazing her lips then nestling her neck. Lacey was not thinking about making love. She was still not whole, half woman, half she was not sure what. She didn't want the responsibility of being present for this man or any other, but she was also afraid to be alone. So she leaned in at first, succumbing to Trey's kisses, little by little opening up to accept his warm body, like tasting a little bit of salt and then wanting more after you have sworn off sodium for a long time. Gradually Lacey craved more until they both were unclothed in the small space of Lacey's bed, making love, exploring each other's bodies.

It was new for Lacey to be with a man not much taller than herself, easy to reach for kissing and rubbing feet together, staying intimate in slow conversation after the final release.

"I love your body, so smooth, your skin. I like your hips, too, so cuddle-able, If that's a word," Trey said, stroking her hair and kissing her back all over.

Lacey, self-conscious about the fat teenager that lived inside her, was surprised Trey found her body attractive. Doug had never used words like that. She had always felt that Doug made love like a caretaker not a lover. She felt guilty she had been the one most often to initiate sex in their marriage. As she lay with this new man she wondered if she had been too aggressive for Doug. But certainly not for this guy.

She smiled to herself. It was way past midnight and she and Trey had not moved from the mattress in the last two hours. She got up, went to the space that was barely a railroad kitchen, opened the empty refrigerator and poured chardonnay from the half empty bottle. She turned on the radio and came back to the bed where Trey lay under the covers. She guessed he was spending the night. As she moved to lie down next to Trey she heard the words now daily in her head coming from the song on the radio: "I haven't got time for the pain, I haven't got time for the pain." She had forgotten the last line in the song "not since I found you." I haven't got time for the pain, no not since I found you.

Trey opened the covers for Lacey. "Not since I met you," Lacey sang out the Carly Simon and smiled down at Trey, who clearly got the message.

Playing Singles

"Hi, remember me? Tennis? The 28th Street bubble? It looks like we will be sharing the house," Jet mused. As soon as she heard his voice she sensed the excitement in his. She could feel the blush rising in her cheeks.

"I'll be there because of, I mean, I will be with Trevor Martin this summer," Lacey said softly.

"That doesn't mean we can't play tennis, does it?" Jet put forth eagerly.

"Trey isn't really a tennis player."

Singles! Lacey wished she really were single at that moment. She could feel her heart leaping through her throat right then and there. She felt an almost animal urge to be with this man with the dark curly hair, the wire rim glasses and the lanky long legged, rippled body. There was nothing cerebral about the way she was feeling.

"How about we play over the Fourth of July weekend? I am tied up in the city until then."

They agreed to wait until the house members had settled in and summer tennis had begun. Jet didn't seem to care, or maybe he didn't know, just how deeply Lacey had become involved with Miles.

"See you then. Are you sure I can't see you now?" Jet gently pushed. Lacey hung up smiling. Lacey both dreaded and longed for the day to come.

The Pygmalion Effect

Lacey did not like being told by Trey that she needed to dress better for work and play. He informed her they were making a trip to Henri Bendel's.

"You know, Henry Willis Bendel was the first person to bring the fashions of Coco Chanel and others to America. He set up shop on Fifth Avenue."

"That's interesting. I have always been a Coco Chanel fan," Lacey said, trying to get into the mood to shop against her will.

She didn't say much as they approached the big glass window cases with mannequins dressed for every occasion. For a moment she flashed on an old boyfriend in Boston who once told her, "you're a pretty girl, it's just that you have no style." That still hurt, but she put it out of her mind as Trey pulled her toward the evening dress department.

"Why do I need to be here?" Lacey asked.

"Because you'll be coming with me to evenings at the Sand Bar Beach and Tennis Club of which you are now a member."

"Thanks, but I can't afford that and I don't even know if I would like the people" she sulked.

"You will," he assured her with self-confidence and a sense that he knew more about these social things than she did.

"I want to remind you that you have never been to Boston where real social standing is different, not the kind you have in Georgia." She could play the snob card, though she didn't really like to play that game.

Trey knew nothing about the Boston coming out parties or that her name appeared with others on the coveted Byrd's List of the 100 most outstanding debutantes. She remembered the feel of her father's arm through hers as they moved together on the grand ballroom floor. She could still see the long white gloves that covered her arms and how long it took to do up all those buttons on each glove. She had curtsied low as her father, dressed in his coat and tails, presented her to the Cotillion Committee of 1962.

"How about this?" Trey pointed to a tight, gold, lame gown with an empire waist-very simple but very fancy. She loved the dress instantly. She began to think this might be fun and ceased her pouty objections.

"Like Professor Higgins, I feel like am leading a major revolution to overhaul your style, young lady," Trey said. Lacey went to the fitting room and came back in the dress.

"Looks great. I am buying it. Let's move on to the makeup counter."

"You know, there was no need for lipstick or mascara in the Peace Corps and really no need for makeup, in fact, anywhere in my life until now. Now that you say so."

In a moment of panic she flashed on something her father said many years ago. "You know, Lace, that mustache over your lip is really very dark. Kind of like an Italian widow." She was mortified and embarrassed. Saving a month of babysitting money, she sought out the nearest electrolysis to remove the hair as well as the dark line that ran between her eyebrows.

Now at the makeup counter, looking in the hand mirror, she was glad she had taken her father's advice long ago. Dad had been very much a man's man, all about sports and raking leaves and pitchers full of martinis. She wondered if he would like this eager young man who seemed to know so much about fashion and feminine ways.

⸻ ✦ ⸻

"You all are so sweet to take me out on my birthday," Trey drawled over lunch week at the deli across the street from work. Lacey sat quietly while the office secretaries gushed over Trey's celebration of his successful completion of three decades.

"Where will I ever find the perfect girl to marry?" He asked to the adoring assistants sitting around him. They ordered Ruben sandwiches all around.

"I love sauerkraut and pastrami almost as much as I love New York itself. So thank you all very much!"

"But where am I going to find the girl of my dreams? She has to be someone who looks as good in the morning without makeup as she did the night before."

"You must be kidding. That's unreal."

"I always wanted to marry someone from Boston, a pretty classy town."

"Give me a break, Trey" Lacey said, only half joking. "Who ever really gets to pick the town their future spouse comes from?"

Later that day Lacey wanted to treat Trey to a birthday celebration of her own. They found an empty table at G.G Melon's in a quiet corner where they could hear each other in birthday conversation. "This was a great idea, Lacey.

They ordered bourbon on the rocks. As they sat talking, Dustan Hoffman got up from the bar and left. Lacey was thinking about the man sitting across from her. *What a celebrity voyeur he is. He'd probably chase down Greta Garbo in the rain if he thought he could get a glimpse of her.*

"How long are you going to live in that tiny one room walk-up you call an apartment?" He lifted a second bourbon to his lips and nodded a toast to Lacey.

"Not sure. Doug leased it for me as a parting gift. The six months lease will be up soon."

"How about you move in with me? I have enough room in my apartment with two floors and an outside garden. You could save on rent and food. It would be perfect for us and it's near the subway for work."

Trey began humming the theme from Casablanca, then launched into the words softly. "You must remember this, a kiss is just a kiss, a sigh is just a sigh. The world will always welcome lovers...pause, pause as time goes by." He went silent waiting for her to respond, predicting assent.

"Are you for real? I just got divorced." But she did not say no.

The Warm Up

Memorial Day weekend marked the start of the season in Quogue. Lacey and Trey took the train to Long Island on Friday afternoon, rented a car or rode out with one of their housemates, a much older friend of Trey's named Marlin Rutherford. He had worked for many years for Conde Nast, the publisher, and had recently been let go. He was suing for age discrimination and, while he waited around for his suit to come to trial, he joined Trey for some summer fun in the Hamptons playing bridge.

That first weekend Lacey saw some similarities between H.O.U.S.E. in Des Moines and her new summer digs. The cottage was full of like-minded souls who agreed to share food and rent and to abide by house rules. They were mostly single, working stiffs committed to their jobs in the city and dedicated to having fun whenever possible. And they were socially committed-albeit to a social class, not a cause.

This time, however, her roommates weren't hippies, they were yuppies and the house had a lot better perks and definitely better looking guys. The only beard on site was Trey's, everyone else was clean shaven and baby-faced with sideburns. No activists were present, only young, aspiring socialites. Lacey wondered whether to share with anyone that she was the ex-wife of a conscientious objector who barely escaped prison. The group called their weekend retreat "the preppy palace in the ruff."

Trey was too Southern to be a real preppy but he was the one who found the house and paid the rent up front. "I like the idea of taking care of business and then collecting from everyone on the back end. Keeps me connected with everyone. I like being indispensable."

"I'm surprised. I kind of like everyone. Most of the house mates are longtime city dwellers. The kind of New Yorkers who think the city is the center of the earth and maybe the planet," Lacey observed to Trey. "I like that. Very cocky. I hope it rubs off on me. I could use some of that."

Lacey met most of them that first weekend. There was Walter Turner who worked for City Bank as a broker who preferred playing poker, while on business doing bank loans with hotels in Las Vegas. Walter had gone to Dartmouth on a scholarship from back woods Maine.

Lacey never knew Ranga's last name. He had come from Jaipur as an exchange student to a New England prep school and went on to play squash at Harvard. He had chosen to stay in America and was determined to marry an American heiress.

Meredith Buckley was one of the first women ever to become a senior vice president in any bank in New York. She was talented, had an MBA from Wharton and at thirty-three was absolutely trying to find a husband. She was a former girlfriend, now friend, of Trey's. More than anything she wanted to have a child and talked about going it alone if no one turned up to be the father. She joked that if necessary she might partnered with one of the house members.

Lenore Weatherfield worked for Newsweek in the advertising Department. She was tall and willowy and never far from a cigarette or a glass of wine. She had a Philadelphia accent was unmistakable. She liked to plan the Quogue dinners and keep track of them in a menu scrap book from which she would recount dinners to house members with comments about the evening gatherings.

And then there was Jet whom Lacey already knew. Jet was from Hartsdale, New York and went home to visit his parents frequently. He graduated from Colorado College and from law school, though he never said from where. While waiting to pass the New York bar he was working for an insurance company. His looks were straight out of a Brooks Brothers catalogue and he had a smile that could melt chocolate. At twenty-five, he was younger than most of the house members. His roommate, Tim Curtain, had been Jet's roommate at Colorado. He was Jet's frequent tennis partner, built like a fire plug with a square jaw and sandy hair constantly in his eyes with the airplane shades he never took off, even at dinner. Jet called him "net man." sk

The cottage turned out to be the perfect place to entertain and relax. The stark white wooden shingled two story box had once been a fisherman's shack. The cottage had two stories. The first floor was one large room with a small kitchen at the back and a toilet next to the kitchen. Every inch of the first floor was painted white like the cover of a Beatles album: white wooden dining table with white wicker chairs for eight, white wooden rocking chairs with off-white cushions that sat next to the open windows surrounding the front of the cottage. On the front porch roomies shared cocktails before lavish dinners on Saturday nights. There was an outdoor shower out back to be used after a swim or in the early morning for those who went jogging on the beach.

Upstairs were four bedrooms and a bathroom, again all white wood. Weekenders doubled up in the bedrooms as necessary or slept in sleeping bags on the floor in the main room below. At night one could see through slits in the woodwork to the stars outside and hear the wind howling or the waves lapping the shore at high tide.

Behind the cottage was a backyard of weeds and sea grass that stretched down to the beach considered to be the site one of the world's most beautiful coast lines. Quogue mates gathered on the beach at low tide in late afternoons to pitch horse shoes and drink mint Juleps made by the ever resourceful Southern gentleman, Trey.

To the left of the cottage facing the ocean was a huge open deck rising from a block of cement planted firmly in the sand. The Sand Bar Beach and Tennis Club was the hub of entertainment for the weekenders next door.

The Fourth of July weekend was going to be a big deal at the house in Quogue. Almost everyone was importing a date for the weekend. Trey left work early on Thursday without Lacey and drove out to Quogue early with Marlin. He planned to set things up for the Friday night dinner and the Saturday night dance at the Sand Bar Beach and Tennis Club. He'd hired the DJ and organized a raffle with door prizes.

The Game Heats Up

"Lacey Pierce here. How can I help?," her standard response when the phone rang because it was almost always a desperate mom on the other end of the line calling to ask for help or making a plea to a Congressman for more funding for the mentally handicapped.

"I hope so," came the low the voice on the other end. Lacey didn't recognize it, couldn't quite place it.

"Remember me? The bubble on 28th Street? Tennis on the Fourth of July?" I found your number in the new Club directory. I thought you might like a ride to the beach house.

She had thought of Jet often, wondered what he was doing at the insurance company, whom he dated and played tennis with, but had stopped now that she was living with Trey.

"Yes, yes, I would like that," Lacey said.

"Where can I pick you up? Your apartment or your office?"

"I'm in the Flatiron Building. I'll come downstairs and meet you at 5:30," she said, trying not to sound overjoyed by Jet's call. See you then."

Lacey hugged herself and jumped up from her desk, practically doing cartwheels into the next office, which was Trey's, only he wasn't there and she suddenly realized how glad she was that he wasn't.

Lacey left work ten minutes early and went downstairs just outside to the front door. It was a hot and humid Friday afternoon. It looked like it might rain but the clouds were not making that clear.

She wanted to see him coming, wanted to see him before he saw her to see if he looked as excited as she was to get together again. She worried she wasn't good looking enough for this dreamboat of a guy. She squeezed the worry out of her brain and straightened her skirt and hair while she waited.

And suddenly there he was in a red Corvette convertible with the top down and very inviting beige leather seats. Barbara Streisand was crooning Memories from *The Way We Were* as Lacey looked into Jet's dimpled smiling face with the sexy wire rimmed glasses and the dark curly hair flying everywhere in the wind. He opened the car door for her and she slid into a whole new world.

"Had you been to the Hamptons much before your joined Sand Bar?" He said.

"I have only been out there for two weekends," Lacey replied.

"It'll take a while to get through traffic and bottlenecks," Jet said. She didn't care how long it would take to get anywhere as long as Jet Bullett was there beside her.

"If you want to see the rich and the famous, you head to West Hampton which is about 100 miles from Manhattan. If you want loads of art galleries and shops you head for South Hampton about six miles further out. East Hampton is the furthest out.

"Say I have great idea. Let's stop for dinner somewhere and let the traffic clear out before we head to Quogue. We'll get there late but we will get there a lot faster."

"Look, I have got to tell you something. You met Trey, I mean Miles Martin, at the mixer last winter before we all joined Sand Bar. I have to tell you I moved in with him. I'm sorry. I should have told you sooner." There, she had finally said it. "And no, I don't want go to dinner."

"Don't you think I know that?" Jet said without skipping a beat. "I really don't care. I knew the minute I met you I wanted to get to know you. I sensed you're a complicated person underneath that cheery smile. Then when I played tennis with you I saw your lovely spirit all over the court."

Lacey sat on her hands dumbfounded at what she had just heard. Jet felt the way she felt. She could feel the undertow in her body and the longing to pull over to the side of the road to let Jet smother her with kisses and all matter of affection. She imagined making love to this new stranger in some parking lot with the engine running while Paul Simon sang *Fifty Ways to Leave Your Lover*. "*Just slip out the back, Jack and set yourself free.*"

She had tried desperately to make life with Trey work but now in this time and place this guy was messing up her plan.

"I am looking forward to playing tennis again with you." She wanted to say "make love to you" but held her tongue.

When they arrived at the house in Quogue members were straggling in and luckily Trey was next door at the club making arrangements for the next night. Lacey thanked Jet for the ride and went up to the room she shared with Trey to unpack her stuff.

"Hey, Lace, glad you could get a ride with Jet. I had to put up all those decorations and get the wine delivered." As Trey reached to kiss her ear, Lacey pulled away.

"Yes, it was nice of him. Look, I am kind of tired from the week. I think I'll turn in early."

"P-A-R-T-Y pooper! Never mind, I'll go down and have a drink with Betsy. Unlike you she's a night owl and can drink me under the table."

The next day the village of Quogue was an explosion of sun and warmth. There was no excuse not to play tennis because of the weather. While Lacey was still in bed, Trey left early to pick up groceries for the long weekend.

Lacey lay in bed for a long time. She recalled how in Iowa in the commune Lacey had been the one in charge of collecting rent, food shopping and morale building. There they jokingly called her "earth mother." Here, in what she referred to as the East Coast Commune, she was considered more of a silent partner to Trey who took care of everything. She wasn't sure she was going to like this new role.

Lacey got out of bed, dressed quickly and grabbed some coffee just as she heard the rumble of Trey's VW coming up the dirt driveway. She came out to help him unload. The words fell out of her mouth. "Jet asked me play tennis with him today."

Trey didn't smile but he didn't say anything either. He reached into the back seat of the car to pull out the bag of marshmallows for the "s'mores" he was planning for a group roast on the beach. He moved quickly past her and slammed the screen door on his way into the kitchen. Lacey slinked off quietly to find her tennis duds in her duffle bag up in the bedroom.

Jet drove up just in time to greet Lacey in front of the house. With the top down in his red corvette and the wind blowing gently across his tanned, smiling face, he was beautiful to look at. For an instant she felt a tinge inadequate about her own looks. She quickly shifted her thoughts to the game ahead. "Hop in on the right side and let's get out of here."

"We're in luck. The have extended membership to the Quogue house for a reduced rate for the summer. There are sixteen outdoor clay courts, as well as a pool and a lunch and bar deck. What a deal for us! We'll get to play lots and Tim can join us."

They found a free court right next to the parking lot. Just as Lacey was worrying that her white skirt and top were not very attractive, Jet rescued her. "Nice outfit," he said.

They started to volley, slowly. The rhythm of the balls hitting the clay and the warmth of the day were making her lightheaded. Volley, hit, hit, hit, no bounce, move to the net. Jet called out "good job!"

They played for their allotted hour and the time flew. They would have stayed longer had not the next people scheduled for the court shown up right on the dot.

"That was fantastic! Let's get some lunch on the deck and stay for a while and talk."

Torn between guilt and a desire to know a lot more about this graceful, gorgeous man four years her junior, she simply nodded yes. Lacey had absolutely no appetite for eating. Her hunger was beyond burgers and beer.

The deck was covered in sun tanned couples eating lobster rolls and hot dogs. They found an outdoor table where a couple was just leaving. Lacey neatly placed a white cloth napkin over her white tennis skirt to calm herself and sat opposite Jet.

"Where were you before you came to New York? I have a feeling there's a lot more to you than summer in the Hamptons."

Lacey moved the napkin around in her lap. Should she tell him everything or nothing? "I was working for a professor, editing his book, when an unfortunate incident occurred causing me to quit the job."

"Did he make a pass at you?"

"Something like that? So now I am broke and living with Trey."

"I get that. Or, really, I don't get that. You don't seem like his type."

"Not only is he my roommate but also my boss. At that moment she remembered the Trey called his mother to tell her about his new girlfriend. He failed to say that Lacey had been married. Was that a black mark against her she should not share with Jet?

She waited for Jet to open up.

"Law school was tough for me after college in Colorado. I've actually missed passing the bar exam the first time and am wondering if I'll ever get there or if I should even be a lawyer."

"I could never admit something like that," Lacey said, impressed by his openness.

The waitress came and went several times but they ignored her. They hadn't even opened the menu. "This is the third try. You'd better order now, kids, since there are others in waiting in line over there," said the middle aged waitress with no smile, fat legs and bad teeth. "You kids in love think you can take all day and just sit here."

"Lacey, what would you like to have? Maybe we should split something. Your choice."

"I like the idea of sharing." *I want to share everything* she said silently.

You know, we have to do this again. In fact, the U.S. Open is coming up in the end of August. You want to go with me? That is, unless your roommate has plans in store for you.

I *would go anywhere with you.* "Well we'll have to see. I am not sure what Trey has planned. He seems to plan everything. I hope we can do this again."

The late afternoon sun was going down as Lacey and Jet flopped down in the car dumping their racquets in the way back. Before returning to the house they sat for a while, not bothering to start the engine, just looking into each other's eyes and holding hands. Danger ahead.

Rage at the Restaurant

One tennis game was not enough. They could not resist seeking each other out. Tennis was just a way to make their relationship seem casual, innocent even nonchalant.

"Okay, let's just start out hitting in close," Jet began, taking charge of starting the game.

She wanted to be close to him on the court, and off, but kept her cool and tossed him a smile as she handed him a ball from the can she had just opened.

They each took a step back from the nest and began to hit with short, then longer and longer shots until they reached the back of the court.

Then they started a set. By the third game Lacey was down 0-3 but she didn't care. "Nice shot. You flipped it right back at me. I like that." Jet was full of compliments, his wavy curls blowing in the wind. "Are you sure you're not just trying to lose to turn me on?" Jet shouted across the net. "You had me in the first game, but not because of the score."

Lacey laughed tossing her serve in the air with a graceful arc and landing just inside the service line. Jet returned a drop shout that Lacey managed to reach and to put the ball passed Jet out of his reach."

That's one for you. Come here. Lacey ran to the net to retrieve two balls. Jet flung his arms around her before she could bend down to reach a ball and held her face in his hands, kissing her hard, opening her mouth and laughing and kissing all at the same time. Í adore you. I can't let Trey have you all to himself." Lacey hung on to Jet for what seemed a long time but was only seconds. "I feel the same way, but I don't know what to do about it."

"I'll tell you what we'll do about it. Let's have dinner before we head back to Quogue." Lacey kissed him again and walked to the back of the court. They played a few more games. And then it was over. Their time was up. Jet paid the $50 bucks for the hour. They changed out of their tennis clothes. Jet was already in the car when Lacey got there.

"Well, I really shouldn't, you know, Trey will be expecting me back at the house," she said.

"What's the big deal? You're not married to the guy. There's more to you than I know and I'd like to get to know you better."

They chose a tiny restaurant on the beach close enough to Quogue to get home before dark. They sat outdoors at a small square table covered in a plastic checkered table cloth made to catch the butter spills from steamed lobster and the juice of squeezed clams. Other couples, who looked married, sat at the few tables nearby. The June night air was cool and dry and they were both feeling relaxed after their exercise on the court.

This time Jet sat down beside Lacey and put his sear sucker jacket around her shoulders.

The raw oysters came first. Jet squeezed the lemon onto his first choice and slurped the juice into his mouth. The sucking sound stirred something deep inside Lacey, down below, and she could feel the sweatiness between her legs rising inside her. Jet's sandals were touching her legs. She hoped that she had shaved her legs recently enough that if Jet touched them they would be soft.

The waiter came with the clams. She sucked each one slowly from its shell, sometimes using a little fork that came with them and sometimes just with her tongue. She dipped the first little neck in the melted butter and pressed it between her lips before sucking it slowly into her mouth.

Jet slurped and sucked, too and pretty soon Jet and Lacey were slurping and kissing each other, leaving the oysters in their shells in front of them.

"I want you right here, right now," Jet said. "Can't we just spend tonight together? I want all the time in the world with you."

"I don't know what to say. I want to be with you. But I am not free. Not right now. I knew I was making a mistake to move in with Trey. But I was too weak to say no.

Suddenly there was the loud sound of a car coming to a halt in the sand that passed for a parking lot at the edge of the restaurant.

The car might as well have been at the table, it was so close to Lacey and Jet seated facing the parking lot. Dusk had fallen, and the restaurant owner had just turned on the Chinese lanterns that hung from a string above the terrace.

Trey pressed down hard on the horn as he sat staring at the couple no more than ten feet away from him. Jet and Lacey quickly moved away from each other, but stayed seated at the table.

He was laughing wildly. It was hard to tell whether he was angry or laughing at catching Jet and Lacey together. He kept his hand on the horn.

The restaurant owner came out in his food spattered apron. "Get your hands off that horn, mister, this is my restaurant!" He shook a fork at Trey to stop the noise. Trey ignored the warning. "You yuppies from the city cause so much trouble out here!"

Trey did not get out of the car. He relished watching the two squirm in their seats, leaving the mussels and oysters uneaten.

"You can take it from here, Lacey, I am not playing this game," Jet bolted from the table, leaving Lacey furious at Trey not wanting Jet to leave.,

"I'll see you in the city," Jet said, tossing a $100 bill on the table.

"Get in the car!" Trey shrieked.

"How could you? You live with me. I saw the way you looked at him. I could see it in your eyes.

"God damn it! I haven't done anything wrong," she began. "I've told you before I was married for seven years. I have never had the chance to really live alone or figure out who I am now, now that I am single. I'm a different person now. I don't know how I feel or what I am committed to. New York is very different from Iowa, Tunisia or Japan. Can't you just leave me alone for a while instead of sneaking up on me? I don't need this."

They rode home in silence. When they got back to the house in Quogue dinner was in progress. Meredith, one of Trey's former girlfriends, a bank vice president, now his confidant, was the chef for the night. She was preparing the marinade for the lamb shish kebabs for the grille being readied outside by her date for the weekend. The kitchen window was open. The sea wind was blowing the white lace curtains in Betty's face as she stood at the kitchen counter.

"Can you close the window, Lacey, so I can finish this without getting sand in my eyes?" Meredith spoke almost casually, then quickly turned to Trey. "What's going on here? Jet just blew through here, grabbed his duffle and took off in his car. And Trey, you look white as a sheet. What's happened?"

"Why don't you ask Lacey," Trey suggested. "Maybe she has a different version than I do."

She wandered off discreetly to the room she shared with Trey, hoping he would stay away, watching the mounting moon alone as long as possible.

They passed the rest of the weekend in frozen silence. Trey stayed up as long as possible that night before climbing into the hammock on the porch. He found solace in telling Meredith all that Lacey had done to break the trust in their relationship.

✳

Lacey was up before daylight on Sunday. She slid out the back door and hitchhiked a ride into town with the milk delivery man. She waited on a bench outside the Mug and Muffin until it opened, read the New York Times for hours and caught a train in time to reach the apartment by in the late afternoon. She did not have a plan. Maybe she would stay with Sarah for a few days until things blew over.

As she crossed Third Avenue to the apartment at the corner of 78th Street she could see people standing in the street just outside the flat that she and Trey shared. They were looking up at Trey in a window on the second floor hurling things out onto the street below.

"What are you doing? That's my sewing machine, the one Doug's grandmother gave me!" Lacey was shrieking now at the top of her lungs.

"I don't care who gave you what, I don't want to have anything more to do with your things. Or you. As far as I am concerned you are as crazy as your mother."

Lacey picked up the machine that lay smashed on the street among some of her papers Trey had tossed out along with a purple bathrobe. The top cover had split into two pieces right where the "Sin" and "ger" were originally joined in pale blue plastic on one side.

"You deserve to be thrown out on your ear," Trey snapped as the passersby continue to gawk at the spectacle.

Clothes tumbled out of the window as someone quickly grabbed a sweater, another a tennis skirt and a teenage girl caught a pair of red platform shoes.

Lacey was so shocked that at first she just stood there in the crowd on the sidewalk in stunned silence. She felt like Bubalina in Zorba the Greek when the village women rushed in to steal all her possessions, leaving the house bare and her dead body alone lying on the only thing left-her bed.

Then, picking up nothing, she just walked away. Jet lived at the other end of town near Saint Mark's Place which could be dangerous at night. She didn't care. She would find him and spend the night there.

She walked from 78th down to J.G. Melon's at 73rd to use a phone.

"Hi, Jet, I made it back on the train today but I am afraid I can't go back to my apartment tonight. Can you come meet me at Melon's?"

"I was just leaving with Tim to watch the U.S. Tennis Open in another bar. But I can ditch him and join you uptown. Are you all right? Trey seemed out of his gourd yesterday."

Upper East Side elites had been gathering at Melon's since 1932. As Lacey slipped into the landmark bar she adjusted her eyes to the dim yellow lighting and the ruddy-cheeked preppies drinking martinis next to casually dressed older couples sipping sherry and munching on in wooden bowls. She moved to the back where there were a few empty seats. She looked vaguely at the menu painted onto the wooden boards that offered famously thick, juicy hamburgers, the house's signature dish.

Even though he looked every inch the preppy in those glasses, Jet was pretty near-sighted and to feel his way to Lacey who was perched on a stool at a high table in the far corner.

"God, it's so dark in here I had to crawl like a blind man to find you? Lacey said nothing. Vince Scully and Pat Summerall were replaying segments of the day's matches. Lacey had gone to the tournament with her dad a number of times and every year at this time she thought of him. Not much could distract her from tennis. She wanted to go to all the Grand Slams around the world. She did not want to go back to Trey's apartment.

"Lacey, what the Hell are you up to? Dinner with me. Then no dinner. Then Trey. Now you are here alone? What do you expect from me?"

"Jet, never mind about me, come watch this for a while. Can you believe Manuel Orontes beat Connors 6-4, 6-3, 6-4? Out of nowhere. I'll bet that's the only major he'll ever pull off.

"For Christ's sake, Lacey, is that all you care about right? I am thinking about us. Can we go home now? I kicked Tim out who's probably watching the game at Nancy's. We can see the rest at the apartment. Besides, it's

Sunday night and we both have to work tomorrow," He urged, sounding a little whiny and not much up for fun.

Back in Jet's apartment they watched more tennis while Jet cooked a steak and Lacey sipped wine and took off her only remaining dress and underwear and put on Jet's bathrobe.

"I'm glad Tim isn't here. It was awful. I got back to the apartment and Trey was hurling my stuff out of a second story window yelling that I didn't deserve to keep my things. He was the same kind of wild he had been at the restaurant. I'm scared. I don't where I am going to be able to live"

"Hey, sweetheart, it's okay. You are here with me now. Tomorrow will be soon enough to fix it." He was content to let her spin her wheels while he took a back seat making dinner. He didn't seem interested in helping her. Maybe because they were still, in some way, strangers. Hadn't even made love yet.

Sitting in front of the TV in Jet's Brooks Brothers navy blue, velvet, robe with the white piping and initials on the pocket she occasionally glanced at him cooking the steak on the porch grille just outside the kitchen and wondered where she would go if the evening ended with dinner.

Jet produced a great steak with much fanfare and pored them both some Cabernet. He was trying to do his part, be cheerful in spite of her consternation. They ate pretty much in tired silence but rubbed their feet together under the table for what Lacey hoped was coming next.

The kisses started tentatively, then grew delicious and wet with open slobbery French licks and caressing each other's ear. But as time went on, Jet seemed to lose interest in love making or to lose anything other than in pleasuring himself. He came quickly, too soon for Lacey to really turn on and lose herself to him. He fell asleep soon after, leaving her wide awake and unsatisfied in the dark, hot unfamiliar surroundings.

She got up from the bed and went into the living room where the second-hand gray leather couch sat beneath the open window, showing stars that signaled the coming of cooler air. She had mounted the romantic occasion with longing and great anticipation only to be dropped off a cliff never reaching the top of the love mountain. She realized that as much as she was attracted to Jet, she was disappointed in him sexually. Jet was a less experienced lover than Trey. She wondered if good or bad sex was indicative of the length of a relationship. She went back to Jet's bed and tried not to think about the consequences coming her way the next morning.

A Mountain from Molehill

Lacey and Trey worked on different floors in the Flat Iron Building in New York. That was a very good thing when Lacey came to work the next morning at 175 Fifth Avenue.

She wondered if people in her office noticed she had on the same dress as last Friday. She didn't care. She was worried about the moment she would see Trey. *What had made her take on two men in such a seemingly manipulative way without regard to their feelings?* She was always painfully sorry after she made a mistake. That's why people forgave her. Up to a point. She hoped that would be the case today.

When she got to her desk there was note on it written in longhand on yellow legal sized paper. It was folded, addressed to LACEY ROGERS in bold capital letters.

At that moment she wanted to be out of that office, that floor, that building, that job. She felt as childish as the time she quit that job as a nurse's aide when she was barely nineteen. She had been on the hospital floor barely three weeks when one of the nurses handed her a bed pan and led her to the room of a very constipated elderly man who had not had an "epiphany" in the two weeks since his surgery. Lacey entered the room brightly, said hello and asked if he was ready to move his bowels. He said he wasn't sure but would try. No sooner than a minute after Lacey slid the porcelain pan under the man's bum, a loud eruption began, like lava spewing from a volcano. Feces went everywhere in the bed, down over the mountain of sheets to the floor. Lacey rang the bell for help with the clean-up but no one came.

Before the start of her shift the next afternoon she carefully covered her face in white talcum powder that she had seen her mother use on her own face. Mixing a touch of mascara into a little of the powder she created a feint shade of grey under her eyes. Looking like death's door, she marched into the HR office. The head of the office was an elderly nurse who hadn't seen a bed pan in twenty years. Miss Whatley had a pasty face and two much eye makeup.

"Can I help you? Do you need something?" she barked.

"I am sorry, Miss Whatley, but I cannot do my job any longer," Lacey began, her head down and her voice low, "apparently I have mononucleosis and am not allowed near patients. Starting immediately."

That was easy then. Not this time. She picked up the yellow packet, opened its neatly folded pages and read the brief note:

Where did that happy, wonderful, peaceful girl with a bright future go? She was not the girl I saw at the restaurant. Is she gone forever? You can be the most wonderful girl I have ever known and also the biggest bitch.. Who knows how to deal with you?

That's the way I see it. You are asking me to accept less of you than I had before and still hang on. No thanks.

Trey

Lacey refolded the three pages. She looked up at the window opposite her desk. Outside the sky was a blank canvass, not even a cloud to distract her. She shredded the words into little pieces and dropped them in the waste basket

Had he really said "loved" in the past tense, not "love", as in now? Was he gone? She felt crushed and torn, like the slips of paper she had just discarded.

At lunch in the deli across from the office, Lacey ran into Trey's assistant, Monica.

"Hi, Monica, how's it going? I heard you got engaged to your sweetheart from Queens recently. Congrats! When's the big wedding?"

"I think we'll wait a year or so. I just want to be sure before I do something I hope never to have to undo."

"Smart girl. Wish I had thought of that the first time."

"Oh, you were married before? I didn't know. Trey never mentioned that. Guess you won't be marrying him."

"Maybe not. What do you mean?"

"He didn't tell you? You weren't at the staff meeting this morning. The boss announced he's taken a job in D.C. Effective immediately."

Game, Set, Match

In spite of Trey's ultimatum and departure, their relationship had not yet run its course. She went to D.C. to visit Trey over New Year's to try to sort out the tensions that kept pulling her back to him. Over the holiday, more than once Trey alluded to the similarities between Lacey and her mother who was mentally ill and had been institutionalized many times.

They were sitting in a café near Trey's apartment on New Year's Day. "Here's to a new start in a new year," Lacey said, offering peace between them at least for now, though she was uncertain about Trey on many levels.

"You know, you are a beautiful girl, like the pictures I have seen of your mother, but like her, if you continue on the path you're on, one day, you will end up crazy like her,"

"Are you trying to scare me?" Lacey said, half scared, half repulsed by his accusation. She was glad she was taking the train that afternoon.

⸻ ✦ ⸻

"Hi, Jet, can you come get me? I'm at the train station. Just got in from D.C."

"Look, Lacey, I'm tired of these games, you want to see me, you get yourself here to my apartment."

"I couldn't wait to see you. I have missed you so much," Jet whispered, licking Lacey's ear and caressing her mouth gently.

"I missed your charcoal eyes and those glasses. She opened her mouth wide and welcomed his tongue against her teeth. Lacey felt the growing heat at the center of her body and swayed dreamily underneath Jet's lithe and light body. He was tall, even in bed, and his dark curly hair fell lightly across Lacey's face. So different from Trey, she thought, who was short, blond and very hairy both front and back and down below. *Maybe this time things will be different, better, intimate.*

She pulled off Jet's glasses to kiss his cheeks, his nose and to nuzzle the black curls that hung in his eyes. No matter what Trey said she didn't think she was pretty enough to match Jet's playboy looks. Wasn't that proof enough that she could never keep him? She knew, at least, Trey did not have an eye for other women, only for Lacey, even though she had been a big disappointment to him.

While she was contemplating this, Jet all too quickly entered her and with a few heaves and sighs came hard and very fast, leaving Lacey in a dead heat with her own thoughts. He had come fast in their first love making but this seemed like a speed race. She could tell he really didn't know much about how to arouse a woman or, maybe even more to the point, had no interest in doing so. As she lay beside him she recalled the time he had said he thought all a guy had to do was C-O-M-E to make a woman happy.

Lacey needed a break from both men. She tried to concentrate on work, but even the happy mongoloid kids who came to the office with their mothers annoyed her. She contemplated how to quit her job gracefully. This time the face powder and mono trick would not work. On the day she was planning to write her resignation, Monica came to her office and handed her a note that had been dropped off at the reception desk. "Looks like you get more mail around here than the rest of us," she said. "By the way, I decided not to wait a year. We're getting married in September. Hope you'll be there to cheer us on."

"Thanks, Monica. Right now I am not sure where I'll be or where I'll want to be."

Like the one from Trey, it too was on yellow legal pad folded up tightly. Lacey sensed the anger before she read the first page.

Dear L:

I've postponed writing to you until the dust has settled so that I could reflect upon our relationship without the bitterness I felt in early January.

Yes, Trey has you now. Evidently he is content with having half or three fourths of you, but you know in your heart he cannot have all of you.

Your life has been one of taking, of control. You cannot have it any other way. You have hurt, you have lied, and you have deceived. You want someone totally for yourself, and when you get to that point, you lay elaborate plans to slowly emasculate that individual to the point you lose respect for him. I do believe you are afraid of a relationship where you cannot have total control over your partner.

I thought I would win you because I thought Trey was less of a man. We talked about the search for the father figure. I thought I was it. I was wrong and wronged.

Jet

Deju vu. She read the letter once. Once was enough to get the full brunt of Jet's condemnation. It was not so different from the accusations Trey had hurled at her. Maybe she deserved their collective wrath, but, hell, she was only barely out of marriage and deserving of some confusion. It was time to break free. These guys wanted someone she was not, but she did not know who that was. She must try to find out. She very much wanted to go home.

Familiar Voices

The sights and the sounds of Yankee accents, the noisy hum of train tracks, were all signs Lacey was sure, meant to welcome her home. Sitting by the window next to strangers made the ride pleasant. She remembered riding in an Afghani train out of Kabul with that same feeling, how foreigners on a train could feel strangely familiar. Everyone coming from someplace formed a kind of common bond in transit.

The week before Memorial Day she'd made the decision to go home early for the holiday to Boston to for an old friend's wedding. Forget the job, the men and the mayhem. She wasn't ready to commit to anyone or anything for a long time. She kept seeing the smashed sewing machine in the street in New York, an omen her life was becoming a bunch of discarded bits and pieces. She felt like an unwanted gadget, a spare part ready to be tossed out and picked up in the trash.

The sound of the porter's broad "A," "all a-boahhd" welcomed Lacey to South Station. She was glad her brothers had scattered for the weekend so she wouldn't have to explain not visiting family. Her stepmother had married her fifth husband and moved to New Jersey.

"What incredibly good timing, Mo. I am so glad to see you! It's been a hell of a year. Work's been hard. New York has been hard. I am glad for the excuse to get away for a wedding. And, of course, to see you. It's been seven years since you were my maid of honor in Iowa."

"And six years since you ever bothered to write me back. All those Red Sox scores I sent you in Japan and not a word from you."

"Sorry. I guess for someone who wants to be a writer I haven't been putting pen to paper for quite some time. I am sorry I never wrote back." Lacey wondered when would be the right time to tell her about Doug.

"Sophie is finally getting married again. You always said that first guy was a rat-mean as hell."

"Yeah, well, I haven't always been the best judge of men either. I am looking forward to seeing the church again. I haven't been in ages. Not since we graduated from the Academy."

"Well you'll love this. Dad's playing for the wedding and the choir will sing during the ceremony."

"C'mon let's get into the green monster. I'm parked just outside on a meter. It's been with us all the time you've been gone. They hugged once more on the platform before hopping into the Bradleys' green Chevy wagon with the familiar erzatz wooden panels.

As they drove into town Lacey noticed that Middleford hadn't changed much since she left after high school. It wasn't just the Brasseaux's car. The same trees still lined the same pot-holed streets that the town did not repair seemingly to discourage outsiders from moving in. In many ways Middleford looked much like the opening scene of Back to the Future when Michael J. Fox returns to a town stuck in the life of the 1950's.

And yet some things were gone now. When she was young there were two distinct villages in the town. Middleford village had been the home of her family's businesses. Her uncle owned Prescott's, a grocery store renowned for its butcher shop and the store butcher, Frank, the "Hatchet Man" who could carve a great roast beef or lamb for Sunday as well as any surgeon. The Women's Exchange, owned by her aunt Grace, sold gifts and knick-knacks and had a lending library to entice women to take out the latest novels. People would stop by to purchase last minute gifts for Christmas or birthdays and pick up a copy of the latest novels, like Peyton Place.

The other village was Central Village, home of a dry cleaners, a drug store, a Chinese laundry and most importantly, Harry's Ice Cream Parlor. On Fridays, when there were no afternoon classes at the Academy, Lacey and her friend, Sophie, walked there in search of tuna fish sandwiches and butterscotch Sundays topped with marshmallow fluff and walnuts. Some of Lacey's happiest memories were buried in the walls of that emporium now abandoned and boarded up.

"Do you think he could possibly care for me? I'm snowed already!" Sophie asked Lacey as the seniors crossed Central Avenue late one Friday afternoon.

"That creep? What do you see in him? Or I should say WHY do you care? He's mean, and besides, he doesn't treat you well. He talks down to you,"

"But he is so good looking, and honestly he tries to be sweet to me. I understand he may have some problems but I know I can help. And he needs me," Sophie said. Five years later, at age twenty-three, Sophie married her high school sweetheart.

"I'm glad Sophie has found happiness," Lacey said. She wondered about the ill-conceived choices in her own past and whether she would make the same mistakes in the future.

The Bradley's house was close to the street in the main section of the school campus. Mr. Bradley was the head of the Middleford music department and the glee club. Mrs. B. was a willing partner and often the host of campus receptions or the many teas that welcomed sports teams, parents and faculty after weekly matches with other prep schools. They were the ultimate power couple on the campus.

Their house was a white colonial with an ample back yard that looked on fields that were filled in good weather with girls' field hockey and lacrosse players. There were books everywhere in the house, a Steinway in the main living room. There was Mr. Bradley's study to the right, just inside the front door filled with musical transcriptions and scores and score of Gilbert and Sullivan lyrics and copies of the New World Symphony. Upstairs Mrs. B. had her own sewing room filled with strips of fabric, a sewing machine and bright colors of wool for knitting ski sweater. The kitchen was small but airy.

Lacey loved the light that filled it each morning when Lacey would arrive from her house down the street to wake Molly up and have breakfast with the family before she and Molly walked to school. She loved being at the Bradleys.

Lacey carried her bag up to the spare room on the second floor of the house that was so familiar. The flowered wall paper with the green back ground welcomed her. There was the canopy over Molly's bed with the white lace and the big pink puff below over the summer blankets. Molly had made up the bed for her and would be sleeping in her sister's room who was now married and living in Westchester, New York. Molly's husband was at home in Hartford at his teaching post in a middle school where Molly also worked as a music teacher.

"So glad to see you, Lacey. It's been way too long," Mrs. B said folding her ample girth around Lacey in a big hug. I can't believe how I have missed you for the last how many years? Fifteen? Now I can't believe you're home!"

She looked at her friend's mother. She had adored her from the first time they met when she was in sixth grade, the first time Molly invited her over to her house. There was something about her straightforward intelligence and unforced humor that let Lacey know she had a grounded sense of right and wrong. Now she was afraid of Mrs. B.'s impending judgment of her.

She finished her coffee slowly. "You know how I've missed your prunes and the breakfasts we shared in the morning before school in the old days? I've missed you, too, not just the prunes. And I haven't been very good about staying in touch. A lot has happened since Molly used to send me Red Sox scores in Tokyo in newspaper clips."

"I can't believe I haven't seen you since the wedding years ago," said Molly, acknowledging the lost time between them. You've been everywhere while I have just been in Providence teaching in boarding school the whole time."

"You were there for my wedding. I hope you'll be there for me now." She waited a few seconds. "I am getting divorced."

Molly and her mom let the silence linger. Then they spoke as one. "Of course, dear, we are here for you, dear. We love you, not the state of your marriage or your divorce. Come now, you don't think we would ever stop caring about you, do you?"

They had lunch on the patio out back and later that night Mrs. B turned a wealth or refrigerator leftovers into a marvelous dinner cold sliced lamb, minted carrots, and green beans with almonds.

The next morning Mrs. B surprised Lacey in the kitchen. "You've come to the right place this morning. Prunes with tea, ta dah!"

"You're the best. I wasn't kidding when I said I have really missed your cooking. I even once tried to make your Indian pudding in Iowa but without success." They laughed and joked around the small kitchen table in the late morning. Then they drove to the church in pleasant silence.

Outside Grace Episcopal Church there were cars and people everywhere lining both sides of the street. The sun was high in the sky close to 11:00 o'clock. It was not too warm. The weather was smiling on the event.

The church doors had been polished and the heavy oak shined proudly as the guests arrived. Mr. B., Molly's dad, was playing the organ. The choir was still warming up with "Loves divine, all loves excelling, joy from heaven to earth come down." Lacey hummed the hymn and sang the words she knew softly to herself as they waited in line to go in. How I have missed this place, she thought. The communion, the community, the comfort of it all, being at one with others. She hadn't felt that way in a long time.

She walked between Molly and her mother up the two sets of stone steps through the arched doors. She passed by the long rope hanging down from the bell that would soon herald the start of the wedding march. She stood in the back of the church for a moment waiting to be seated her after Molly and Mrs. B were escorted to the front of the church.

Until she heard the choir sing that day she hadn't realized how much she missed harmonizing and being with people who liked to sing. Singers were mostly interesting, quirky people who made time to be with other singers and had stories to tell. She'd heard the saying many times, "whoever sings, prays twice." That worked for her, especially since she didn't believe in prayer. When she knelt at the altar to receive the body and the blood, she barely sipped the wine and put the wafer in her shoe. Community was her God, not the three in one spirits.

Jeb, Sophie's younger brother, a late teen with a shock of red hair and a Brooks Brothers double breasted navy jacket with gold buttons took Lacey's arm. He whispered: "I remember you. I was ten and you and Sophie were seniors. You didn't like Sophie's boyfriend either. I always remembered that when she married that jerk. But this time it's different. I am glad you're here."

"Me, too. I've been away so long. Can't believe you're all grown up. Makes me feel old? Can you keep a secret?"

"Secret." He crossed his heart with his left hand while still holding on to Lacey with his right.

"I 'm getting divorced too, but not from such a bad guy."

Lacey took her place on the hardwood seat in the pew and Jeb went back to usher in another guest. She kneeled on a cushion named for some parish donor, bowed her head, and tried to pray. No supplication came to mind.

Instead she lifted her eyes to take in the whole scene. She waited several minutes just to breathe in the place, the familiarity of it and the distance she had travelled, Iowa, Africa, Japan and New York. She looked up high above the altar and felt she was seeing those saints in the stained glass window for the first time. She flashed on all those arcane facts she had to learn in Confirmation class.

There was Saint Michael, carved in colored glass, weighing the souls about to enter heaven; and Saint Elizabeth in her purple robe with the crown and roses, the widowed princess who gave time and money to the poor hundreds of years ago; and John, the Apostle, in his red robe with book and pen about to spread the Gospel. People need saints to keep them on the straight and narrow, she reflected, and how splendid the church founders thought to put them in front of us. They reminded her how much she had once loved ritual and tradition, even when she liked to poke fun at one or the other.

Lacey recalled the prank she used to play in the back of the church on Christmas Eve. Huddled in the pew with her cousins during the late night service, they would start singing the hymn one or two measures late, throwing the entire congregation off within seconds of the first notes of "Oh, come all ye faithful...." It was tremendous fun to ruin Reverend Goring's processional and recessional hymns once a year. Lacey and many parishioners referred to the minister as "Boring Goring" for his lackluster sermons and clammy, welcome handshake in the receiving line at the end of the service.

Looking at the choir now, she thought the members were like the ancient trees lining the streets outside, still standing in their places after decades, predictable and firm on Sunday mornings for the ten o'clock service through rain and sleet and snow and the hurricanes of late summer. It gave her comfort to think that they were still here every week even though she was not.

Strains of the Pachelbel Canon floated over the congregation, signaling the guests to rise in anticipation of the bride's walk down the aisle. By the third measure all eyes were on Sophie Costas walking arm in arm with her younger brother. Like Lacey, she had lost her father in her early twenties. Sophie stopped at the footsteps to the altar, let go of her brother's arm and turned to face Edgar who had come forward with an eager and confident step. He had been married before.

"Dearly beloved, we have come together today in the presence of God to witness and bless the joining together of this man and woman in Holy Matrimony."

Lacey wasn't listening. She felt a pang of anguish over the reminder of her own broken bonds. She looked beyond the couple and over the head of the very tall minister to Saint Michael. The stained glass saint depicted as Michael was the likeness of a parishioner who designed the window in his image when the church was built in 1895. Some egotist, she thought. But was the man in the glass window judging her now?

"The union of husband and wife in heart, body and mind is intended by God for their mutual joy; for the help and comfort given one another in prosperity and adversity…."

Lacey had once thought so, too. One thing she was certain about was that Sophie had made a good choice this time. Six years older than Sophie, Edgar had gone to Middleford Academy ahead of Sophie, who was in the sixth grade when he graduated then headed to Harvard. They had bonded early, although Edgar's mother disapproved of Sophie because her family was Greek. They parted ways in college and then got back together. By the time Edgar got through the Business School at Harvard and Sophie was divorced, he was bold enough to tell his mother that if she objected to their marriage he would move to Texas and dig oil. In the compromise, he got Sophie to agree to marry in the Episcopal Church. Now he was designing and patenting those large computers used by most every major corporation and the government. He had more than made enough to take care of Sophie for the rest of her life.

Lacey wondered how she could have been so right about the first man her friend married, and yet so wrong about the choices of the men in her own life. Would there ever be an Edgar for her?

The newlyweds kissed, turned in a single together step and walked slowly back down the red carpet greeting every guest with a wave and a smile as they walked out of the church into the welcoming sunlight.

As Lacey joined the crowd of well-wishers outside, she heard choir singing the recessional hymn, Love Divine All Loves Excelling. On the descending notes "joy from heaven to earth come down." Tears of joy for her friend and for herself filled her eyes. The familiar melody let her know she still belonged here. In her own way she was faithful to God through this community

Sophie tossed the bouquet from the church steps right at Lacey who caught it rather unwillingly. Guests went to their cars to go to the reception at the nearby country club. Lacey wasn't sure that she wanted to go and see all those people who would ask her about Doug.

"Oh, come on, Lacey, you have to come. So many people will want to see you."

Mrs. B. said encouraging Lacey to connect with old friends.

Lacey knew Molly's mom could read her thoughts. "You'll have to tell them sometime."

"You're right. And not just the people here in Middleford. Yes, I can finally say, I am single, if not yet divorced." A small piece of her soul was returning. The spare parts were coming together.

Memories All At Once

One place that had not changed in Middleford, and perhaps in every town, was the cemetery. She had passed it coming and going to school. It comforted her to know it had been there for hundreds of years with curving little roads and pathways that ran between graves and family plots like the one owned by her family. Even Howard Johnson, the famed restauranteur, chose to be buried there because he thought Middleford a more socially prominent place to be interred than his hometown next door.

She had never really taken time to pay homage to her father in person. The day of the funeral she flew back to Tunisia without accompanying the family to the gravesite. It had been too painful. George Pierce had died more than twenty years before, but now that she was back in her childhood home, she must go see him.

It was almost summer in the warm early morning before the sun would be up. As she lay in her bed at the Bradleys,' she dreamed of a tomb from which her father rose into the sky, looking down on her, saying "Hey, Lace, put a smile on your face. I can't stand it when you don't smile." It was the same dream every time.

Though she wasn't ready for the cemetery, Lacey did want to visit her old school. The twenty-six acres of green grass and white fences looked the same as she remembered. The girls' gym was gone and in place of it was a new building with squash courts inside and clay tennis courts that stretched across an area the size of a football field. Gone was the single court where once Lacey and her dad had practiced.

The smells and sights on campus assaulted her with painful, yet positive memories. "O God our help in ages past, our hope for years to come," the Episcopal hymn rang in her ears as she recalled Thursday mornings in chapel and the strains of that hymn at her fathers' funeral in the church of her childhood.

She could smell the dirty sneakers in the girls' gym, the Friday lunches of fish and English graham crackers with cream cheese and raspberry jam. She was back at the ninth grade sock hop dancing in her socks to the sounds of Dream Lover on the record player. And there was the girls' rest hour. She and another girl on an army blanket every day for an hour after lunch in the Goodwin room. It was a pleasant blur.

"How are you Miss Jackson," she said, addressing her former head mistress formally. She felt foolish tying to sound cheery in front of the woman who was not a fan of hers during high school. She felt like a hypocrite but smiled into the conversation.

"Come have a cup of tea with me and give me news of your life. We've missed you. You haven't attended any reunions." Lacey doubted anyone missed her.

"You know when you left here, you weren't known for your grades but you seemed to have survived."

"Thanks, as you remember, you weren't exactly ready to endorse me for college."

"I think you just weren't ready yet. But I applaud you for joining the Peace Corps."

Lacey remembered the rumors about Miss Jackson. After graduating from Radcliffe and a failed romance that ended her engagement to Harvard man, she was appointed to take succeed the venerable Miss Faulkner as Headmistress of the Girls' Upper School at Middleford. With no experience. She recalled the slings and arrows she and other classmates suffered from the verbal arrows of Miss Jackson.

They had a polite cup of tea while Miss J. told shared current news about her Middleford classmates. Lacey was glad the woman was all about pleasantries and didn't ask her about her life in New York. *Stay on the surface whenever you can.*

"Great to spend time with you. I promise to make it to the next reunion. Can't believe it will be our fifteenth in 1977!"

On Hallowed Ground

The next day was Memorial Day, the last day of her visit home. She decided to visit the aunt and uncle she knew were always home. Uncle Ward was married to her father's sister, Marta, who never liked to leave her house and spent her days caring for a small dog with a large gaping wound in its side that never healed. Uncle Ward was the family doctor for her and her many her cousins growing up in the town.

"How are you doing Uncle Ward? It seems like just yesterday that you wrapped my sprained ankle and helped me escape having an x-ray. You always kept us out of doctors' offices. I don't think I ever really thanked you."

"That's okay, Lacey. It was my privilege to take care of all of you. Besides, I loved your dad. He was the only one who would listen to my war stories because we were both in the Navy during the last conflict."

"What was he like when he was in the Navy, before my mom married him. You must have known him when they were dating."

"Well, I wasn't like your dad. I was working my way through Tufts Med School while he was tripping the light fantastic at Harvard. He was on every team. Football, hockey, baseball. He even won a tennis tournament his senior year. And he was in that fancy club, the A.D. He had it all, really, until he met Markie. His mother tried to stop him. But he was determined to marry her, all beauty and aloof as she was."

"Why would granny try to stop him if he loved her?"

"Because she knew of Markie's past history. How she had landed in a mental during the spring break of her senior year at Miss Hall's School. No one knew but granny learned from some close friend."

"So what was he like as an officer? He sure looks good in the photos in his white uniform."

"Your dad was handsome. But kind as they come and a damned good Lieutenant Commander out there in the Far East. After the war he went to work in New York for an insurance company. His troubles didn't start until after you came along."

"Whose fault was that?"

"Certainly not yours. Childbirth and maybe her past came back to haunt Markie with the birth of each child. I am told today she wanders the streets of New York most days."

Lacey wanted to change the subject. She felt guilty about being afraid to contact when she lived in the same city.

"By the way," Ward began, "I have long been unable to bring myself to share something with you but I think now is the time, now that you are older."

Lacey waited. It took a long time for Ward to speak.

"Your dad knew he was sick before the real cancer came and he was diagnosed."

Uncle Ward's words hit like a brick out of nowhere.

"Does that mean Dad was ill and never said so when he said goodbye to me that day I got on the bus to go to Tunisia?"

"I can't say for certain because I don't remember when we had that conversation, but that is very possible. Let me see. Just a minute. "

"When did you leave?" Uncle Ward asked, flipping the pages of his medical journal. alth   "February 5, 1967, the day bus left for Logan and we flew to New York, Rome and on to Tunisia."

"Yes, here it is. We spoke just after Christmas when we had all been together for the holidays. George came to see me in early January."

Lacey felt sick to her stomach. She didn't know if she was going to explode or throw up first. "Uncle Ward, I am sorry. I have to get out of here. Now."

Lacey left Uncle Ward in the parlor and scrambled out the door to the car she had borrowed for the day from Molly. The tears trickled down her cheeks, at first slowly, then came in a torrent of sobs. She sat there for a long time and cried until the well inside her was dried up and she sat there limp and spent.

Finally Aunt Marta came out to the car. "Are you okay, Lacey? Ward wanted me to check on you."

"Just having trouble starting the car," Lacey said, turning to the side so Marta couldn't see her wiping her nose and face. Lacey waved her off signaling she was okay. Her arms and whole body went numb as she fumbled to put the key in the ignition.

She entered slowly, parking her car just inside the cemetery entrance where forsythia clumps bloomed and the sun shone through the huge overhanging oak trees. She picked up the bouquet of white daises she had brought and started walking. It was Memorial Day and a sea of little American flags dotted the 100 acres placed on graves by surviving family members and volunteer Vets.

Stately pines and hemlocks towered above the many plots. It was late afternoon and blotches of sun shone through the branches above like the ones in a Cezanne scene only there was no hillside, just flat ground and thousands of graves and family plots. Azalea bushes led the way to the Pierce Family spot. As she got closer, she could see the names of her departed relatives, weathered and faded. She came to her father's resting place. Someone had planted a small flag in the ground in front of the grave. The words carved in stone forever pierced her heart: George B. Pierce, January 3, 1916 to December 25, 1967.

She knelt down, kissing the ground where her father lay beneath, weeping quietly as she placed the bouquet on the ground in front of the granite grave. *He died on Christmas, and deserved the best holly then. But it's summer now and the pastel flowers are out of place, just a lame memorial. No flowers can bring him back.* She picked up the bouquet, ripping to bits first the chrysanthemums, then the daisies and finally the few roses and greenery and threw them on the ground, watered by her tears.

Lacey sat down on the ground, her back to the stone, closing her eyes against the sun. She sat a long time with her father, wishing he were there to help her now. "Put a smile on your face" came back to her. Not today, Lacey thought, not today.

The Accidental Messenger

The twenty-minute ride to the train was filled with rain but few regrets. She had said good-bye and see-you-soon to the Bradley's. She paid the cab driver and got out at 128 Station.

She had been home for less than a week. As the train pulled out of the station she could feel bad memories slipping away like dead skin, leaving room for new growth healing a bad wound. She was rolling away from the past, ready for a new journey.

Lacey felt strange, almost light headed, a little giddy. A great weight was gone.

"You headed to D.C.?" The woman in the seat beside her asked, more looking to pass the time than for a real answer.

"No, just to New York. In many ways I've been travelling a lot," Lacey said.   The woman heard Lacey's muffled words and surprisingly shot back "I know what you mean. I've just travelled through a divorce. She put her hands up to indicate the quotation marks.

"Really? How long were you married? Do you mind my asking?" She was hesitant, but what the hell, it was just a short ride so why not humor the woman?

"Not at all. Glad to have someone to talk to. I sense maybe you're dealing with some big things, too." She popped open a can of diet soda and eased her back into the stiff seat. Lacey sat up straight, wrestling with whether or not to listen.

"I should have done so earlier instead keeping all the blame to myself. I didn't realize how much women need other women to validate them, but now I'm open to all of my female soulmates." "Validate" was not a familiar term to Lacey who didn't consider this woman a "soul mate."

"How long were you together?" The train had just halted for its first stop.

"Prov-i-dence!" Five minutes went. Lacey and the woman said nothing, waiting for the noise of the exiting passengers to subside.

The train began to rumble again and slowly move out of the station. The attendant came rambling through from the next car carrying a large case of sandwiches, little cartons of milk, bags of nuts and several Cokes in bottles. Lacey reached for a ham sandwich, gave the man two dollars and began to eat in silence. No sooner did she take a bite, than the woman bolted into conversation.

"The trip lasted twenty years," she chuckled. 'A bad journey. I am headed to New Haven to see an old college roommate who was a bridesmaid in our wedding. I have to let her in on the news." Lacey offered the woman half of her sandwich but she waved Lacey away.

"That twenty years seemed like forever. If he said "white," I said "black." If I wanted to see a movie, he wanted to see another. We could never agree. And when it came to raising children we were polar opposites. He would rage. We were never on the same path after the beginning. At first it was all flowers and candles and kisses and love-making. Soon after the wedding the control freak in him took over. I am telling you, it was a nightmare."

"I can't imagine twenty years with anyone." Finishing the last word, Lacey instantly regretted her comment.

"That's okay, honey, guess I couldn't either," the woman admitted.

Lacey hated being called "honey" and wanted to stop right there. But something made her continue. She flashed on the day she left Doug, the apartment scene with Trey as they hauled away the Japanese chest. There was nothing final, no angry words, no real closure, just a kind of fading into distance. "What was it like for you, I mean the last part, the leaving, not the marriage?"

"All I can say is that the biggest reason people get divorced is that guys want wives to stay the same as when they met them. You know, big boobs, long hair hanging and a figure like a toothpick. Women want guys to change the way women have to, to adapt when they have children, juggle jobs or seek self-expression. Isn't that what we do? You know what I mean?"

"I dunno. You may be right. I'm getting divorced. But I don't really know why. I don't hate him. We didn't have children. He didn't want any. I did. He said I wouldn't love him as much if we had kids. I didn't really think so. Kind of selfish of him, don't you think?"

The woman gave no response. They rode in silence for what seemed like a very long time. The silence was almost comfortable, each woman lost in thought as the train clicked its rhythm on the tracks. They still had not spoken when the porter came through the car to pick up their tickets which were tucked in little slots at the top of their seats. "Hahtfud! Hahtfud! Don't fuh-get your belongings. N-ooo Haven is next!"

"He took up all of my time. He was an architect who needed me to be his office manager, bill payer and chief bottle washer. I guess that's why we had only one child. I got tired of being the caregiver and showed my angst, not by telling him, but by having an affair with his business partner. I really blew it. What can I tell you? I guess I was really looking for an out that would make an impact -right?"

"Did you feel guilty about the affair? Have regrets about leaving him?"

"At first. He was angry, but incapable of showing it, then in denial and finally just sad. We were both sad at the end. A couple, really two immature people, who couldn't make it together."

"Why?" Lacey almost shouted. Startled by her own shrill voice, she pulled back, moving away from the woman in order not to seem anxious for an explanation.

"Whoa! Sounds like you have your own story, girl."

"All I can tell you is that I acted out of sheer boredom with my husband," the woman said. "Ennui can be a real killer. I unwittingly acted out my frustration by having an affair. It was really nothing. I slept with John a few times and we agreed pretty quickly that we were better friends than lovers. When I told my husband he had so little to say. I wanted him to get angry, proclaim his love, and beg me to come back. He was a great big nothing. I just kind of gave up."

Lacey felt the chill of memory run down her spine spreading through her whole body. A certain deja vu tugged at her insides. She saw the American reporter's apartment all over again, the photographs of his family and Vietnam and the wave of passion she escaped, feeling scared yet attracted to him as she left. She had raced home naively thinking Doug would reassure her of his love with passion and wild abandonment. In retrospect, listening to the other woman she felt ashamed at her obvious misguided expectation.

"I'm still not very clear about all of that," the woman said, the last part of her sentence inaudible as the words trailed off into the air. For the first time Lacey saw that the car of the train was filled with cigarette smoke. She hadn't noticed it at all. She thought their conversation was like the smoke:

floating in the air, clouding one's thoughts, a bad and negative habit no one really wants but can't stop. She turned to the woman.

"Me either." Lacey sagged. They road in silence through Hartford. When the porter called out "N-00 Haven" the woman pulled her travel bag out from under her seat, put on her coat, slung her purse over her shoulder, and was ready to go.

"Good luck to you, honey. I know we will never meet again. But I'm telling you, there's a lot of freedom to be had out here on your own if you take advantage of it. They don't say carpe diem for nothing. You go seize the day! Stop feeling sorry for yourself and get on with life. I'm going to. After I see my old roommate, look out, D.C. here I come!"

The overhead sign came in view as the train stopped in New Haven. Passengers moved in a line to get to the exit. The woman who called her honey, whose name Lacey never knew, slipped away. She was gone and it was too late to thank her for her unsolicited advice.

The rhythm of the train tracks was making Lacey sleepy. Through the window she saw flashes of trees whipping the patches of green, sticks poking up everywhere against the steely slate sky in the late summer morning. She fought off the drowsiness by repeating over and over the list of all the stops on the Northeast corridor. Boston, Providence, Hartford, Stamford, Philadelphia and n to New York…. She prepared herself for her next round of inquiry with Dr. Kammermann in New York.

Unfinished Business

"Man, Sometimes it takes a long time to sound like yourself."

--Miles Davis

The divorce was finally legal and Lacey began slowly to find renewed energy in the fall of 1975. She was beginning to feel like the poinsettia in her apartment she had bought to perk up a lonely Christmas. It was the wrong the plant now for this season, still holiday red, but it needing little sun and water all these months and was still thriving in the last days of summer. In many ways she felt like that sturdy plant: surviving but out of season.

Luckily, Doug had been kind enough to continue to pay her rent even before she was out of work and right to now.

On the first day of October she strode through the front door carrying a new leather briefcase. "Welcome to Parade, Miss Pierce," the receptionist chirped as she showed Lacey to a desk out on the floor with other writers, editors and proofers. She felt alive for the first time in a long while. She didn't care that the salary was only $9,000, three thousand dollars less than in her last job. She had made that mistake in not coming to Parade the first time. There was no Trey there any longer to confuse her choices.

"Hello, Lacey. My name is Jason." The smile made Lacey instantly put her at ease. The gray flannels, the buttoned down, blue, broad cloth shirt and the bow tie were all familiar signs of home for Lacey. In a Brooks Brothers blazer, with his blond hair neither long nor short, the side burns carefully crafted, Lacey guessed they were a signature stamp of his casual, informal style in all things that mattered to him.

"We're so glad you reapplied and that we were able to find an appropriate role for you here. Looking forward to working with you." With you! She had pretty much been alone since going home in the summer and had been looking for a job steadily for almost two months. The money Doug had given her wasn't quite enough to get by. She had given blood again twice but wasn't going to do that again for fear of becoming anemic.

"I'm the editor here. I went to Williams but being in the boonies in Massachusetts was four years too long for me! As luck would have it I got a job on a paper in Kansas City before coming here and in my spare time I'm writing a novel. Just call me Jason Hemingway. Actually, it's Hemmings, but you get the idea!"

Although they were roughly the same age, she felt older. He seemed so full of bouncy youthfulness, so completely unjaded by life. She hoped a little of Jason's zest would raise her spirits.

"I never made it to Kansas City. I am originally from Boston, but spent a few years in the Midwest" she said.

"Once you get settled at your desk, I'll show you around. Some of the staff are going to a Harry Chapin concert later this week. Maybe you'll join us."

Lacey sat down at her desk and took in the feel and sense of her new surroundings. She liked being in the open with others. She was pumped to do whatever it took to do the job here, even if all she did was proof read all day. She hummed quietly to herself *slow down you move too fast. You got to make the morning last.*…Simon and Garfunkel were her silent partners.

In the beginning she kept to herself, learned the ropes and proofed or edited copy for Jason and other staff. She was content to go home at night to the one room flat she has been able to hold onto in her old neighborhood because Doug had continued to pay the rent.

One night on her way home after work she passed by the church where she and Doug had gone to therapy. She felt guilty that she had quit. She had dropped out right when it might have helped her. She saw that the "I 'm Okay, You're Okay" poster on the front door was gone. Free sessions were no longer offered. She guessed Kammerman had finally started his private practice with a few clients from their old group. She wondered if Doug was one of them.

Work was going well, she had made friends and was going to political rallies instead of to the Hamptons. But she knew she had unfinished business waiting for her.

She found his phone number and address now on Lexington Avenue uptown.

"Hello, Dr. Kammerman, this is Lacey Pierce. I was in your group a while back."

"Well, hello, Lacey, I would know that voice anywhere! How've you been?"

"I was wondering…that is if you are seeing new patients. I guess I mean old patients. I mean former patients. I am one of those."

"Yes, fine. I am. If you wish to come, I am free at 6:00 on Thursdays. Next week?. I have a private office now at 63rd and Lexington."

"Good for you. I mean, yes, I can be there. One last thing. Is Doug still seeing you?"

"Ah, Lacey, my dear, I cannot say. Patient Confidentiality. You know."

"Right. See you Thursday."

After a brief welcome, he let Lacey know that Doug had moved on and was doing well.

"Actually he has started a new relationship and is moving to the Ozarks."

"Damn, good for him, a total revenge for the way I acted. Touché. Is she moving with him?"

"No further questions allowed."

They talked about the men who had entered and left Lacey's life. He was on one side of the court punching questions at her with Lacey on the other side playing defense but never quite making a counter punch. There was no need to review all that had gone before.

Then he veered into new territory on the court. "Tell me about your parents, Lacey. We never really talked about them, only you and Doug." The inquiry came casually as if the question had just popped into his head spontaneously. She didn't want to get into any real issues with him. But he had other plans.

"My mother is somewhere here in the city. I know how to find her. I just don't. She frequents my grandmother's apartment but spends most of her time wandering the streets of the city carrying all of her belongs in a single leather bag."

"How about your dad?" the doctor proceeded.

"He died a few years ago while I was in the Peace Corps. On Christmas."

"That must have been hard. Were you able to attend his funeral?"

"I flew home in time for the funeral but went right back to Tunisia."

"Do you miss your dad often?"

"I try not to. I keep busy. I went to a lot of schools as a child. With each change I tried not to miss the kids I had known before."

"That's not the same thing as a father. "Do you miss your dad now?"

"Of course, what a dumb question," Lacey said.

"Why so testy, Lacey? Sounds like you miss him a lot. You may be reluctant but let's try a role play involving a dream."

"I don't want to play your stupid mind games."

"Just be quiet and try. I promise this will not hurt."

Kammerman directed Lacey to close her eyes repeating softly "go back, go way back, have a dream and have a conversation with each of the players in it. Within minutes Lacey was in a trance

"I am on the back lawn of Granny's house just below the kitchen porch. Dad and I are coming back from errands and a long drive in Granny's 1949 black Plymouth. The car is shiny black. Dad loved that car all polished with its white-wall tires. He was so proud of keeping it spit polished and looking like new in 1958. We are laughing, joking, bumping into each other on purpose. He takes my arm in his when suddenly I see my stepmother Jane, coming down from the porch and stepping right between us. She's glaring at me, her eyes throwing daggers at my heart when suddenly….I wake up."

Kammermann persisted. "Go back to your dream and continue," he soothed.

Lacey closed her eyes again sliding back into to her fourteenth year. "Dad, I love you. You are the kindest, gentlest, most fun father anyone could have. Why did you have to go so soon? Why didn't you tell me you were ill that day you waved me good bye to Tunisia. I would have stayed to be with you. Do you know that?"

Then she turned in her chair to address her stepmother. "Jane, can't you understand Dad can love you and love me too, because there are different kinds of love? I don't want to take him away from you, but give me my thing with him, too. Don't give me the silent treatment. Let me know your feelings, even anger. I don't want to be confused!" At the last she was shouting, her eyes still firmly shut. Tears were fighting their way out of her until she let go.

She began to tremble, then shake, and then weep uncontrollably. She was keening like the women in North Africa, who wept for days for their dead husbands. She moaned. "I miss you, I miss you, I miss you so!" When she finally got control of herself, she was still fourteen and still in the trance but suddenly self- conscious and embarrassed by the emotion that she had just let out. For a moment she thought there might have been someone else inside her speaking.

Kammerman was silent for what seemed like a long time. Then he spoke slowly in a low, clear voice: "I am your father and always will be. But I must leave you now. Can you let me go?" Slowly Lacey opened her eyes and she heard from deep inside her…... "Yes."

As soon as she opened her eyes she knew something had changed, but she didn't know what. Had Kammerman hypnotized her? Had she put herself in a trance? She felt a sense of serenity, an unfamiliar lightness of being in her body.

Lacey was content to let silence envelop her. A few more moments passed. Kammerman broke the silence. "Do you remember a while back when we talked about vulnerability? About love and vulnerability? We talked about how to truly love another, one must be vulnerable, allow oneself to be open to commitment. Up to now you haven't been able to do that. Too scared, clinging to uncertainty and a lost past you built a wall against relationship and marriage. And you refused the loss of your father. I cannot speak about Doug, of course, but I can say it takes two people to create an insurmountable wall in a marriage. You have been through a lot tonight but you have accomplished much. Time's up."

She left the doctor's office and headed into the November air. She could swear it felt like spring because she so warm, light, as she headed home. It was still fairly early and she was happy to walk to her apartment. Though she didn't yet fully understand, she knew she was feeling alive and that somehow the full meaning of that night would come to her in time. She was done with therapy. She didn't need to go back.

When she got home the flat looked different to her. The gray walls no longer a symbol of a drab life. She felt more expectant and less uncertain. She saw the flowered covers of her journal sitting on the bare desk next to the second hand typewriter she had bought and left untouched.

She reached for a pen and opened the journal she had not touched in months.

She printed the words FINAL JUDGMENT. She wrote the date November 13, 1975 and began *Doug and I were two young people who brought insecurity and a fear of real commitment to our marriage.* And a few minutes later she added: *Tonight I let my father go.*

Lacey finished the second entry, put down the journal and moved to the typewriter. She started to type, to hunt and peck with four finger the way she had back on the desk at Tokyo paper. "There's a saying in the carnival that once you taste it, it stays in your blood. But few people would want to own the whole mirage, the trickery, the tents, the rides, the games, and the whole gaping morality play whose history stretches from holiness to hucksterism. But Johnny Pino did."

She did not type well or fast but she knew now she would never stop. She was free and whole and on her way.